Relativity
First Contact
BOOK I

ARCHER A. GRANT

Cover by Chris Era

ISBN: 979-8-9912908-1-4

DISCLAIMER

Because of my roles working for the United States Government and security clearances I hold; this manuscript is subject to a thorough security review by the Defense Office of Prepublication and Security Review. It has passed all reviews and any requested changes have been made.

I am required to add the following disclaimer: "The views expressed in this publication are those of the author and do not necessarily reflect the official policy or position of the Department of Defense or the U.S. government. The public release clearance of this publication by the Department of Defense does not imply Department of Defense endorsement or factual accuracy of the material."

DEDICATION

This book is dedicated to my loving wife and intrigued children. They spent countless hours listening to me talk about my ideas and even suggested some of their own. This wouldn't have been possible without their patience and encouragement.

For a more in-depth look and visualizations of the characters, ships, and worlds, visit my website at:

www.archergrantbooks.com

For a glossary of terms, visit the website or jump to the end of the book. Be sure not to spoil the ending!

If you would like additional information about upcoming books, such as Relativity: Returning Home, and The Breaker Series, visit the website and join the mailing list. I'd love to go on this journey with you.

ACKNOWLEDGMENTS

I would first like to thank my wife again. The support and encouragement has meant the world to see all of this get off the ground. She listened to my ideas about characters and their story, the art involved, and bringing my story to life. Even though she was likely just humoring me some of the times when I really nerded out, she was genuinely interested and always there. No matter what, she always gave honest feedback and I trust her opinion over all others.

In addition to my wife, there is a great friend who, one of the busiest people I know, did an early and thorough read-through and provided great, handwritten notes that looked like they were typed, as only he could. You know who you are, and I thank you.

This project first started back in 2009, when a college professor encouraged me to write more. I had ideas in my head, but never in a million years thought I could be an author of anything more than an operational order, test plan, or technical manual (those are not overly interesting to most people). But those interactions sparked an idea that I would later seriously pursue on and off over the next 15 years. So, thank you, professor!

I'd also like to thank my kids. They had more input than they even realize. Much of the book was outlined on my phone while I rocked them to sleep. I would get up well before the family and type out the chapter that I outlined the night before. I can't wait for them to read it.

Many of those early mornings and late nights, I was joined by one of my dogs lying next to me or one of my wife's cats in my lap. Apparently I make a good couch.

I would like to thank the professional team that provided my first copy edit. Their suggestions, ideas, and improvements in style and story made a real impact on everything going forward.

To the graphic designer, who took the ideas and some cave man drawings and turned them into the vision I had in my head to help everyone see what I saw. Thank you.

There are many on YouTube and bloggers whom I watched and read endlessly to help learn about the process, get through certain steps, and just find motivation to continue. Thank you.

One more thank you to the reader. Whether it's one (just myself) or many, thank all of you. For anyone that is considering writing something themselves, the hardest part is starting. Please start.

FORWARD

This book was a challenge to myself and to my capabilities. I enjoyed the process, including the frustrating parts, and learned far more than I thought I would about a number of things. This is my first attempt at any type of writing outside of the engineering academic setting. It's possible I bit off more than I could chew, but I'm taking the chance, anyway. Because I am who I am and my brain works the way it does, the hardest part is worrying about whether it's good enough or if anyone else will like it. That held me back from making progress many times. I finally decided that this book was for me, and if others enjoy it, that would be great. If someone doesn't like it, that will be great too. That way I'll get feedback on which I can improve. I'll never know unless I try. So I encourage you to read this with an open mind and travel through the pages with me. When you're done, let me know what you think and what I could do better through reviews or through my website. I will end this with a preview written by a friend.

"This story is riveting and paced with excitement, wonder, and a cast of humble characters that resemble the familiar emotions, strengths, and plights of the human race and military construct. I appreciated the clear melding of fascination with flying, space, and exploration with your background expertise in matters of engineering and research and development. It's a nice blend of that which inspires you, with the technical expertise of your own professional experience, in order to lend details to the writing. And that includes the accuracy of both the altruistic and asinine natures displayed in the military which is validated from your real-life experiences. This novel is an easy read for all ages and meets your intent of a sci-fi space story that is both fun and believable and lends itself well to a series. As a fan of reading and fictional novels, and a former Air Force Combat Pilot, thanks for the fun story!"

Without further delay, welcome to Relativity!

PROLOGUE

Leader Danuibi–Center Staat Capitol Building–Razuud

Leader Danuibi sat idly in thought, contemplating the day's tasks. As the others around him stared cautiously at one another and back at their view screens, waiting for him to begin, the gaze of his dark brown eyes softened as they overlooked the long table, his mind wandering from topic to topic. Before the meeting began, he enjoyed the sliver of time he had to think about anything. Or to think of nothing if he wished. He felt the dry air on his face. The small, wiry hairs covering his body disguised the stiff, rugged skin underneath. This reminded him of a time long ago in his childhood when he roamed the open dusty plains of his people's land, usually against his parents' wishes.

A slight shiver made its way over his body as he remembered how simple his days used to be before war and politics ruled his life. He slowly clasped his arms across each other involuntarily. As he did so, he brushed over a faint scar he got on one of those outings with his closest friend. They were inseparable. The thought of Artur and those times warmed his soul. He hadn't spoken to him in some time. His arms were much smaller than they used to be, but as with most Razuuds, his legs still held tremendous power and it showed.

The door slammed open to his side, startling him back to the present. He did not look because he knew who had entered. Averting his gaze so as not to give any extra attention to the intruders. He continued his stare across the table. A few of the more enthusiastic members of the council came scurrying in next, visibly relieved that the meeting hadn't yet begun. Leader Danuibi would begin on his accord, though, not theirs. He wanted just a few more moments to himself. As he glanced around the table, his eyes wandered to the windows. The windows currently displayed a massive underground city. He had selected that image intentionally as a reminder to him and the other delegates the reason for this meeting. Their home, their way of life. War threatened to take it all away, but also distracted them from a more prosperous future. On top of that, these underground cities were becoming overpopulated and the workers who built them were getting upset about the living conditions. The time came when something had to be done before the inevitable revolt would have to be squashed.

He walked the all too familiar tightrope. Appeasing the workers while keeping the leaders fat and happy, himself included. All the while fending off an invasion from the stars.

Leader Danuibi tapped a few selections on his personal device and the windows gradually became transparent. The table sat longways in the room, parallel to the long wall of windows. He stood slowly, feeling the injuries of past fighting in his legs and body. As he did, he had to turn left to face the window. He walked with intent over to the closest window, bouncing ever so slightly with each step. A limp, perceptible only to those who knew him reflected only a small portion of the pain he felt. Something he couldn't afford to show in his position as the leader of the capital city Rutaun. His city. His world.

Razuud anatomy used the advantage of multiple joints on the legs that allowed them to stand tall with less traction or to have a much stronger base when they lowered down and had more of their feet contact the ground. They could walk upright in either position but typically walked in the lowered position, as it required less energy.

He arrived at the window after a few strides. As he gazed over the cascading metal skyscrapers out in front of him and even further into the swirls of dust all the way to the edge of the horizon, he felt overwhelmed. Or maybe exhaustion set in early today?

He could no longer remember the reason he walked to the window. He thought of his house among the labyrinth of caves and dwellings underground on the outskirts of Rutaun. These buildings on the surface of the planet felt unnatural and he didn't think he could ever get used to it. His eyes couldn't adjust to the light or grasp the expanse of the exposed land. That was the problem of his people to overcome, not him. He looked forward to return to his home underground as quickly as possible.

The thought of his home calmed him momentarily. Enough that he remembered why he went to the window in the first place and turned them transparent. He purposefully turned his voice amplifier all the way down before he started speaking. His voice, like all of his kind, carried a soft tone that barely made it to the end of the room. This was out of necessity in the early days of his species; loud voices carried too far in caves and would alert danger. Loud Razuuds didn't have long lives.

"Water." Leader Danuibi finally began speaking. He

paused to make sure everyone began paying attention to him, causing confused looks. They all had to strain to hear his words. Confusion palpable in the large room.

He didn't let the silence last long. "Water is at the center of everything we have built. Our most precious resource. It is what etched out our way of life underground, as if by design. The bedrock for our beautiful sprawling cities." He slowly turned the volume up as he spoke. The slight cracks in his voice showed his age. The cadence showed his wisdom.

He straightened his traditional blue vest, outlined with gold trim. He had matching pants that terminated high above his upper ankle so that he could fully plant his bare clawed feet if needed, without getting the pants dirty. The formal garments signified a special occasion for him.

There were few areas with visible water on the surface. Nearly all Razuuds preferred living underground within their comfort zone. "We have long since reached our limit. The expansion to the surface in cities like this, our beloved Rutaun, is just a symbol of things to come." He could feel some of the disdain in the looks of the council members at that statement. None of them really wanted to be there, above ground, high in a swaying building. The most unnatural feeling overcame him. Leader Danuibi required the council to at least meet in the Center Staat building occasionally, high above the ground in the middle of the city. "Our people need to see that it isn't so bad up here and what better way than to show them? Once they accept that they have no choice but to be up here, then we can continue with work back in our homes."

Most of the other leaders didn't really want to voice their opinions and challenge Leader Danuibi. He had gotten them this far. He made room in the caves by beginning the above-ground expansions on their world and transplanting the workers. That, along with his storied career, had earned him the position he now controlled.

Above ground, the view from the Center Staat building in the capital city of Rutaun looked like an artist's rendering. Looking out, all the buildings were the same, only smaller in scale the further from the center they got. A sense that all buildings and therefore all creatures were looking up to the command in the center, their ultimate leaders. Maintaining the feeling of dominance over the people and land. This underscored the practicality and necessity of this shape because the ground underneath could not support the weight of any larger buildings further out. All the major leaders from around Razuud designated the Center Staat building as the primary meeting location for any above ground dealings. Rutaun maintained its status as the largest of the few above-ground cities on the planet. The people of Razuud preferred the view of various stalactites and stalagmites in the underground cities over the barren landscape of the outside world. The city leaders tolerated this for a short while, thanks to the ability to program the windows of their buildings to show whatever view they desired. Being high above the ground in the Center Staat building afforded them the benefit of realizing the sense of scale at what they controlled. An impossible feat while underground.

Leader Danuibi occupied the position of leader of Rutaun, the capital city of the planet. As such, that made him the ruler of all Razuud. As he sat observing his council members and pondered his position and what role he played in the future of his people, he reached up to his chin and petted what little hair he had. A common action for the Razuuds and a sign of deep contemplation about their next choice of words or actions. He could feel the smooth wrinkles on his face that were showing his age and the years he had poured into Razuud. As he moved his hand over the soft leathery texture of his skin, he could sense a change in the atmosphere.

A chemical cue, not an auditory one, that he sensed through his body and skin notified Leader Danuibi that a hostile threat lurked within the group. This registered almost as a smell, but with a more animalistic twist to it. He could taste and feel it within his body. His youthful self would have attacked. His current self could differentiate between a real and harmless threat. This was a harmless threat as he knew where it emanated, Leader Darnwich.

Leader Darnwich did not fear Leader Danuibi or the position he occupied nearly as much as he should. Partially because of his young age, he did not fully understand everything that went into Leader Danuibi's role. That and because of his ruthless reputation and lack of fear with authority. Leader Darnwich recently joined the ranks of the leaders. Until Leader Darnwich came along, there were only two ways to get onto the council. A leader could earn his place by hard work and a devotion to their city, an exceedingly rare approach. Or the second way, by being born into this life and having the funds to bribe themselves into the position. The more common method. Leader Danuibi heard rumors from trusted sources that Leader Darnwich had discovered a third way. Leader Danuibi suspected several murders were linked to his clever treachery, either committed personally, by proxy, or both. Leader Danuibi still couldn't figure out exactly how he got this position. The fact remained that even if someone could prove it now, once a citizen rose to the rank of leader, they would become virtually untouchable. Leader Darnwich's city was the last underground city to be constructed, located on the other side of the world from Rutaun.

After a few moments of the other leaders bickering amongst themselves, Leader Danuibi suspected Leader Darnwich would take that opportunity to interject himself.

Sure enough, Leader Darnwich held up a hand to silence everyone.

"Leaders, Leaders." Leader Darnwich bellowed as loud as his throat would allow. Leader Danuibi noticed him fumbling with the volume on his projection device. Trying, but failing, to perform the same trick Leader Danuibi had.

"We all know why you are unhappy with these new plans to speed up the expansion of the above-ground cities. It costs too much and gives too much comfort to the workers." As Leader Darnwich paused, Leader Danuibi looked around casually, gauging his fellow councilmen's reaction. He noticed Leader Danuibi staring back at him, seemingly unconcerned with who he may or may not be convincing. If he could help it, he would speak to each of them privately to make sure they continued to support him.

When Leader Darnwich continued, Leader Danuibi noticed he struggled to carry a softer tone. The young leader quickly lost that struggle as he continued his speech, shouting this time, or the closest thing to a shout he could manage. "Plans like these are becoming more common with you, Leader Danuibi. The other cities can no longer sustain this amount of development. You care too much for the workers, especially after the recent revolts they have conducted. The workers' actions should not be rewarded with better living conditions but with swift force putting them back into their place as workers." He said, conveniently neglecting the history and progress of his people, directing all his anger towards Leader Danuibi, who he held as responsible for their current predicament.

Leader Danuibi remained calm and slowly but proudly walked back towards his seat. His shoulders were back and chin held high. He sat, portraying as much confidence as he could. A confidence that he did not entirely feel. It wasn't the current meeting about expanding the living areas or even the open aggression by Leader Darnwich that caused him concern. The other leaders had been breathing down his neck about funds and overflowing cities long enough for him to get used to it. His biggest concern remained the ongoing war that took place in orbit around their planet and how that impacted his people. He wanted to resolve this swiftly and move on to matters of higher importance.

The leaders had gotten so complacent and used to the war that they wanted to argue about building new cities. This bothered Leader Danuibi. He felt concern and genuine fear for his people if this continued to be the focus. "Are you finished, Leader Darnwich? I am fully aware of the situation. The workers will continue to be unhappy if the circumstances do not change. All cities are overflowing. We all must contribute to the new city to ease relations with the workers." He didn't need to lobby for approving the city. He already had most leaders on his side to begin construction. "And what about the fighters? You must not forget that this benefits them as well." Leader Danuibi continued. "You of all Razuuds should accept this, especially because it is they who have allowed you to be here. You must not become like the Tartins." Leader Danuibi let his insult sink in for a moment. He noticed a slight twinge in Leader Darnwich's face.

Leader Darnwich finally interjected. "The fighters stand by my side. They know that with me, things won't continue the way they are. You want to give the workers a new city, I say we kick them out to figure it out on their own. Your weakness will allow the common workers the same benefits as Leaders. Maybe the Tartins have the right idea."

Leader Darnwich had turned the awkward pause into a violent threat. The room erupted with angry chatter and threats. Leader Danuibi and all the older leaders were ingrained with the knowledge that the old ways were filled with civil war and death. It far surpassed what they were seeing now. They could not go back to those ways and they certainly could not become like the Tartins. Leader Danuibi knew the danger in that. He stood quickly, raising himself to the tips of his toes, which elevated his stature considerably. His teeth were glaring.

Amid the deep commotion, Leader Danuibi heard a chime echo through the room that emanated through his and everyone's view screen and devices. People typically silenced these automatically during meeting times. Sure, sometimes someone forgot, but not everyone. Leader Danuibi noticed everyone ignored the monotonous tone, it mixed with the chorus of carried on arguments. He almost did the same, but decided against it. He pulled open the screen. Realization fluttered across his face as he read the message.

'EMERGENCY ALERT. INCOMING UNKNOWN HIGH-SPEED OBJECT. IMPACT WITH RUTAUN EXPECTED IN...'

He didn't have time to finish reading. He glimpsed something bright out of the corner of his eye. That drew his attention towards the windows. Just when his gaze landed on the landscape beyond, a bright flash of pure white light pierced the sky like a perfectly straight lightning bolt. The light reflected off of everything in the room. The once raucous room fell instantly silent. They all turned to look out the window. The windows automatically dimmed from the dangerous light, protecting the occupants inside. A streak of smoke remained in the sky as the ionized air lingered and conformed to the air currents of the planet.

An overpowering shockwave of dust and debris ripped through the city, rapidly expanding in all directions from the center of impact. By the time the shockwave made it to the

Center Staat building, it had ballooned to a height well above the top floor, where the leaders sat stunned. Several of the leaders groaned in what could only be terror and turned away as the shockwave smashed into the side of the building. The windows rattled, and several broke or cracked as the intense pressure of the air rushed by.

They could all feel the building swaying and shaking violently under their nubby feet. The intense shaking forced anyone not already on the ground from fear to be thrown violently to the ground by force against their will. Leader Danuibi's reflexes and experience from war had urged him to the ground just before others fell. Shards of glass from the broken windows flung throughout the room, not stopping until they embedded themselves into something soft, often a Razuud. Leader Danuibi got struck on the outside of his upper leg while in a ball on the floor protecting his head. He saw the piece of glass sticking out. He thought to himself that he added another war injury. This thought startled him. How could he be so calm at a time like this to think of something like that?

First, the shaking stopped. The swaying waned shortly after. Dust from the outside landscape now filled the room, making it difficult to see. The near constant wind on the surface of the planet quickly pushed the cloud of dust past the city to cover some other part of the planet as it dispersed. Leader Danuibi slowly got up. He gazed out over the city of Rutaun with his mouth hanging open. He had to squint to make out the horrific events unfolding before his eyes.

Starting from the far edge of the city, he could barely see the impact location and subsequent explosion. No, that wasn't quite right. There was no explosion, not what he typically saw during war. Something was different about it. The purely kinetic impact created a void which imploded around whatever had streaked through the sky. Rutaun began to cave in and collapse on itself. The newly formed canyons were snaking their way to the center of the city, effortlessly crumbling everything in their path. Something had struck the ground beyond the edge of the city. The collapse followed the path of the shockwave, slowly expanding as it made its way towards the Center Staat building.

Whatever had caused this had been moving extremely fast and impacted the planet with such force that nothing could withstand it. The expanding wave of destruction slowed as it reached the much stronger inner half of the city. By this point, much damage had been done. An arc of collapsed city encompassed a large swath of living spaces.

The view shocked Leader Danuibi back to the ground, where he sat dumbfounded as his mind raced to figure out what had happened, and more importantly, what to do about it. In the background, alarms rang in the building and Leader Danuibi could hear even more distant sounds of crumbling buildings far below, over the hiss of the rushing wind. His fear shifted to anger. The only logical conclusion he drew pinned the blame squarely on the Tartins. What else could it be?

They had never tried an attack like this from space before. After all, they wanted the planet for themselves. They needed the resources. Maybe they gave up on that effort? Either way, he would make them pay for this.

CHAPTER 1

Ramat–Advanced Individual Maneuvering Shuttle–Earth Lagrange Point Four

Lieutenant Colonel Ramat 'Trap' D'Pol sat suspended in his cockpit's seat trapped in a composite bubble, weightless. An electromagnetic gel filled the gap between the bubble and the outer hull of the ship. Much had changed since his time in the North American Navy. There, he used to be an atmosphere-based fighter pilot stationed on an aircraft carrier. Now he commanded the Seven Hundred and Seventy-Seventh Space Test Squadron–an incredibly unique position. The only space fighter test squadron currently in existence. It also happened to be one of only a handful of space fighter squadrons around the world.

But here he sat, ready to complete the first formation faster-than-light check ride. Captain Maggie 'Face' Lorrent also sat in her own fighter. They were so close that he could almost reach out and touch her craft. If it weren't for the layers of gel and exotic material between them, not to mention the vacuum of space, he would have tried.

One thought went through Ramat's mind right then. 'Holy Shit'. He knew the significance of what they were about to do or thought he did.

During the infancy of faster-than-light testing, large, unmanned drones were the primary guinea pigs. After that, the technology still took up large amounts of space, and running the systems took large crews. Eventually, the size and complexity got to where they could build a one-person ship around it. That one person didn't have to know anything about how the system worked, the ship's computer took care of the complicated parts. They conducted this test using an autopilot function programmed into the computer. The manned fighter spacecraft required a person, despite the significant capabilities of the emergent artificial intelligence autopilot. The ultimate lethal combination and the tip of the kill chain spear. They were going to conduct the first transition through the Light Gate, return, and have the rest of his squadron do the same, pair by pair.

Ramat looked at his communications panel to make sure he had an open line with Maggie. As soon as he saw the light turn green, he began talking to her. "This test is really going to open a whole new tactical advantage for us, Face. I trust your skills and experience – you're perfect for this flight."

"Thank you, sir." Maggie's auto-tuned sounding reply buzzed in his cockpit. The comms systems had a tendency to take the human sound out of the voices.

She earned the role and he wanted to remind her of that.

They had discussed similar topics on previous performance reviews and debriefings, but Ramat always thought it important to let his people know they got to where they are now for a reason and to trust that.

Maggie continued. "Before you know it, we'll be taking all of the Lucky's through together. One big happy family."

She always had a knack for the big picture. Another thing Ramat liked about her.

Space near Earth became far too crowded over the years to risk a battle there, so countries began making what started out as research outposts farther out into space. Those quickly turned into strongholds. Being able to stop a threat deep in space by having your entire fleet show up out of nowhere would be a key advantage over a single ship at a time, completely uncoordinated.

After a brief pause, the business of the day recaptured their attention. Maggie went through the pre-test checklist with Ramat. Any number of things could go wrong and one or both of them would be lost forever. Ramat took a couple of deep breaths to get his heart rate under control. The fear of death or the unknown didn't cause him anxiety. Those were things he accepted long ago in his line of work. He mostly had concern for his squadron and what could happen to them. Presently, what could happen to Maggie? He knew they all felt the same way about this as he did, but ultimately they followed orders he gave. They trusted him. He didn't want to let them down. He pushed that thought to the back of his mind when he heard Maggie over the comm link.

"I have completed all steps on the pre-test checklist; we're ready to begin." Maggie said.

"Copy, Lucky two." Ramat responded, using the ship's number now that the test was officially underway. "We are ready to proceed."

Ramat lined up with the Earth Light Gate using small thrusters and accelerated using his main electromagnetic pulse engine. Maggie matched his every move. Their relatively small ship looked like a grain of sand on the beach in comparison and easily fit within the circumference of the Earth Light Gate. While checking the computer screens to ensure the vessels were aligned, Ramat paid homage to his Naval heritage and gazed at the outside view of the gate itself, making sure he was on the ball, just as Ramat liked to think. The daunting size made it difficult to comprehend what he saw as reality. It made a large arcing circle. When he thought about it, it almost resembled a football stadium turned on its side. It had a similar shape but much larger. As the activation sequence completed preparing for their journey, a slight purple blue haze filled the space where the green grass of a field would have been. Blinking red hazard lights lined the structure all the way around. He wasn't sure how someone could miss seeing this monstrosity, but flying had a tendency to trick your brain. He thought it to be an appropriate precaution.

He needed to be at a certain speed while passing through the light gate in order for the transition to be optimal. "Control tower, Lucky's one and two are lined up and ready for approach. Requesting permission for formation transition."

"Lucky one, this is Earth Light Gate Control, you are cleared for transition. Safe flight and Godspeed." the Earth Light Gate traffic controller responded. They saw little traffic because of the cost of traveling through it. This being the first time two human ships went through in formation the formalities had stepped up a couple of notches.

Now that they had approval, they accelerated to the appropriate speed and headed towards the gate.

As he approached the gate, before the transition process began, he took a final deep breath and waited.

He couldn't feel the transition. He couldn't feel anything for the briefest of moments. In actuality, he didn't exist for that time. As his body and craft were deconstructed at a sub-atomic level, light photons temporarily bonded to them and reconstructed them instantaneously. Once the ship is completely within the light gate, the transition takes place instantly in an anticlimactic flash of dull light. Within a microsecond, the space the ship once occupied becomes free and clear, void of any trace.

With no notice or visual cues, the light gate began the recharge sequence and prepared for the next transition with no thought to the object it just threw at near the speed of light.

In between blinks of an eye, Ramat went from traveling at a relatively low velocity to traveling near the speed of light.

"Lucky two, Lucky one, how do you copy, over?" Ramat spoke right away to confirm the radio links were reestablished.

"Lucky two, I read you five by five. Links look strong. My computer is finishing up the post-transition checks, but everything looks nominal. Current speed is 0.97 LS."

"Nice work, Face. This transition process is something else. I can't even comprehend how much energy it took to get us going this fast." Ramat contemplated out loud. They had little to do while waiting for the computer to confirm they could make the next transition, so they talked.

"I have a degree in it and still don't understand it." Maggie responded. "In order for the light particles not to get destroyed in the process or fail to attach, they have to keep pumping energy into it. That's the majority of the rings, power storage. The computers and hardware are pretty small."

No one had yet developed engines and power systems that could accelerate a ship anywhere close to the speed of light. Most thought it impossible, and so far, that still held true. This process, in a way, skipped the acceleration piece. In a single transition, a particle could be accelerated to between ninety-five to ninety-eight percent of the speed of light. The power available at the transition site determines the exact percentage that something would be accelerated to. Because everything broke down to the molecular level, ships of different sizes could theoretically travel through the light gate together and reemerge at the same relative speed and separation from each other as when they began. That way, multiple ships of various sizes, even an entire battle fleet, could pack into a single large transition point and unleash the entire might of that force simultaneously. More practical purposes also include transporting large numbers of people or supplies to explore and research places never thought possible to go. The other less talked about perk of accelerating in this way meant that the human wouldn't get killed by the acceleration forces.

They both heard a low ding coming from their cockpits. This signaled that the ship's computer had finished its post-transition checks. The lack of an alarm signaled a nominal transition. They could continue the test.

"Pre-transition check complete – ships are synced and ready for transition two." Maggie reported. "We don't want to take too long, don't need rescue coming after us on a false search because we were sightseeing."

"Agreed, ready when you are." Ramat responded and simultaneously hit the command for the autopilots to take control and start the transition. As soon as Maggie did the same thing, the ships would fully sync up. The precision had to be incredibly precise, so a computer had to conduct this next part.

With their hands resting on the controls, the ships began a methodical ballet of movements, rearranging themselves to the proper configuration.

"Deploying fighter light gate." He said as he watched a pair of hoops expand out in front of his ship and separate until they created a cylinder that fully enveloped his ship. "Transitioning in three, two, one." Ramat counted down and again took another deep breath before the transition. Ramat repeated the process, but this time using a disposable light gate just larger than the ship itself and relative to his new speed.

When he finished the second transition, he would go another percentage faster than before. With another blink of an eye, they reconstructed themselves but were traveling even faster.

"Lucky two, Lucky one, how do you read me, over?" Ramat repeated the process to establish comms.

"Lucky two, I read you four by four, a little fuzzy, we'll let the ships work that out." Maggie replied. Referring to an age-old scale of how well two people on radios can hear each other. A five by five represented loud and clear. Slight interferences could reduce the clarity like they were currently experiencing. "Post-transition checks are still running. Current speed is 1.92 LS. Looks like our smaller light gates were on the lower end of efficiency." Nobody had come up with a cool name for it yet, like Mach speed when traveling through the atmosphere, so LS or light speed would have to work for now.

He continued scanning his screens and surroundings, looking for any error messages, any sign that they were in trouble that needed action. He released a breath that he hadn't realized he had been holding. After a few moments, he began working on his test observation checklist along with Maggie.

"All systems are green, no warnings, the computer is running through internal and external scans. External shift view is as expected." Ramat reported. The screens showing the external view didn't register light in the same way as when their speeds were below light speed. A mysterious world lay in wait, filled with discoveries of particles and maybe even objects that lived at such great speeds. The shift view allowed Ramat and Maggie to get a glimpse of their new surroundings. Looking at a night sky filled with stars, he found the glows and streaks to be familiar. The difference being each star appeared as a different color, and none of them were holding still. Also, none of them were as far away as a star. Many were just outside his ship, zipping by and dancing around, some even making contact and bouncing off harmlessly.

They both heard the low ding again from the computer. They were on track. As they went through the checklist, they wanted to be methodical and catch any slight discrepancy between what they expected and what they actually saw. His number one priority continued to be his people. He wanted to make sure there were no surprises for his people. Their lives were ultimately his responsibility, and he looked after them as if he were their own parent. Well, a parent who would give permission for their kids to fly a prototype spaceship and engage in unprecedented activities.

Maggie had finished her checklist and report. She noted a few anomalies with the audio and the external shift view. The flight controls were operating as expected. "It feels like we're back home at L4, she handles like a dream even at these speeds." Maggie referenced the Earth Lagrange Point Four, or L4, a point along earth's orbit around the sun. This unique balance point of gravitational forces allowed an object to remain in front of earth far enough to not interfere with earth activities but close enough that they could reach earth rather quickly if they needed to. Their new engines reduced that time and cost even further.

"Just like the day I got her." Ramat thought back to the first time he flew this new generation ship at the beginning of his tour as the Lucky's Commander. He looked at his monitors and saw that Maggie had completed all checklists and signed them off. He had done the same. The time to prepare for arguably the most dangerous part of the mission had come.

The complication of the return trip lay in the lack of an Earth Light gate. They relied solely on their disposable fighter light gates from here on out. First, they had to cancel their forward speed by utilizing two more disposable light gates, pointing the opposite direction.

The first transition went off seamlessly, as did the second. This brought the pair back to about the same speed they were going when they first set off on their groundbreaking test. The only difference now being they were about fifteen light minutes away from their starting location. That may not seem like a lot, but that distance would take months or years to reach with current engine technology. They did it in a matter of minutes. That only scratched the surface of their capabilities.

If something happened now, it would take some time for those back on earth to figure out exactly where they were and to figure out how to get them back. He would soon find out if that was going to be necessary.

He had little time to stay floating out that far because of the protocol set up for rescuing them. If he didn't return by a certain time, there would be an all-out search. As they did maneuvers, now at more normal speeds, the outer shell of their teardrop-shaped fighter spun around, the engines rotating independently of the body of the ship. The thrusters fired and the reaction wheels spun up and down to impart spin and cancel it out when they reached the desired direction and speed.

"As much as I don't want this fun to end, it looks like our time out here is running short. Let's get headed back towards earth. We don't want them worrying about us too much." Ramat joked. An indication on his screen flashed. The time came to wrap everything up and begin the return checklists.

"Copy. All checklists complete, ready when you are, sir." Maggie responded. From here, the ships would do a majority of the rest of the work.

Because of some of the unknowns of the pointing accuracy of the disposable light gates, they currently did not return through the Earth Light Gate. If they were off by a fraction of a degree from those distances, it could do untold damage to the light gate, earth, or travel on forever until the pilot died, likely due to boredom. For that reason, they would have to use another disposable light gate. Due to how many disposable light gates he could carry in one trip, he would not be achieving speeds above light speed on the return trip, so it would take a little longer. Roughly twice as long, in this case. After utilizing one light gate to accelerate towards Earth and another to decelerate to normal speed at the right moment, they were nearly finished with the test.

"All systems check out – we are within our location margins and in normal space. We should be able to hear Control within a couple of minutes." Ramat heard Maggie say over the radio. He had the same information. But he always taught her to over-communicate when time allowed. She would never know when someone might overlook or miss information.

They entered normal space less than a light minute from the Earth Light Gate that they left from. It would take some time for the control tower to detect they had returned and some more for their response to reach their flight. They didn't want to get too close to the gate because a slight error could send them right into the gate with no way of adjusting course before slamming into it or other support ships.

With most of the stress of the test behind him, Ramat felt he could relax. After all, he was a fighter pilot in a fighter ship, and might as well get some practice in. Ramat made his first sharp banking turn, lining up behind Maggie's ship. He easily noticed the acceleration compared to the unnoticeable but extreme increase of speed when going through the light gates. The suspension fluid in his suit squeezed, released, and stimulated certain well-calculated areas that worked to keep Ramat from blacking out. The fluid in the spaces between the ship's hull and cockpit did the same thing. But as he turned, the inner cockpit could rotate independently to maximize how long the pilot could stay awake. No physical window led to the outside world; only the gentle glow of the screens that gave him that perception. Because of this, the direction he faced didn't much matter. His inner ear had something to say about that, but he got used to it. This briefly brought him back to initial flight training and the overwhelming sickening feeling that the mismatch of information gave him.

Ramat snapped back and highlighted Maggie's ship with a targeting computer.

Ramat knew at this point Maggie's ship looked like a Christmas tree lighting up with warnings. He activated his comm channel and spoke. "Space BFM, what do you do when…" He couldn't finish the sentence or lesson on Basic Fighter Maneuvering when Maggie abruptly changed directions. Her ship accelerated, smoothly at first, but as she gained more speed, the Slow Oscillating Pulse, or SOP, engines kicked in, causing the ship to alternate between surging for several seconds and a more steady but slower acceleration. The rapid pace of her improvements impressed him. He had to use almost all of his experience to keep pace and keep a lock on. Almost all of his skill being the key word. While she made significant improvements and remained amongst the best, she still had a lot to learn, he mused.

The biggest problem he saw in the current fighter training revolved around not enough real-world experience. The balance of not enough real-world training because of the lack of a real-world conflict troubled him. On one hand, he fought so future generations didn't have to. On the other hand, future generations lacked the experience to be effective in combat. Not enough experience meant no space war. But as tension continued to rise among their adversaries and even some of their friends, no experience if a war broke out meant more deaths. He pondered how he could create more effective training scenarios to better simulate what they thought a combat situation would look like.

With a couple of BFM lessons out of the way, they now returned to Space Platform Kennedy, or The Spin, the large rotating orbital platform they called home for this deployment. The next pair in the squadron lined up to repeat the flight. Two by two, each member of the squadron conducted the test; all made it back without issue, as he hoped for. Some of the squadron members got the feeling they were guinea pigs for the scientists and super nerds. As long as they got to keep flying these ships, they were OK with that.

The Lucky's were the only squadron actively stationed on an operational orbiting platform, the Space Force Platform Kennedy, known as 'The Spin'. They called it The Spin because it was the first military platform with rotating modules that provided a small portion of gravity, allowing for longer stays. Other squadrons would stay there for short periods. This would be for a specific test event, returning to earth once the job was complete. The ships would stay to get maintenance in a station keeping orbit until the next event. Because of the rapid test schedule, the fighter squadron and crew stayed at The Spin for extended periods.

The rising tensions with the Southern Hemisphere United Republic also made having an active fighter squadron on The Spin a sound tactical deterrent. Cracks within the Northern Hemisphere Nations shown through as normally friendly countries differentiated their approach to handling the SHUR. Ramat could feel a sense of urgency over preparing the station. He also saw briefings about the acceleration of creating new stations and increasing fleet sizes to meet this new threat.

He knew that their next test could prove transformational for what appeared to be a looming war.

Once all members were successfully back at The Spin, they made their way to the debriefing room. The debriefings were important to collect all the lessons learned from the mission and pool them together for the squadron to benefit from. Ramat also used this time to relay to them what they could expect out of the next set of test missions. "Everybody settle down." Ramat wore a proud grin on his face. He could see the faces of his team reflected on his own. He didn't want to temper the mood.

Major Charlie 'Wisp' Broadway bellowed in his place. "Everybody, listen to the boss, we have important shit to talk about." As Ramat's deputy, it often rested with him to lay down the law and command order through a healthy dose of fear and being strict. A common relationship between a commander and his deputy. Charlie nailed the role.

"Thank you, Wisp." Ramat continued; everyone became silent at the first word from Charlie. "Let's not forget why we are here. It appears our rivals are making progress on their faster-than-light travel. They aren't up to us yet, but it will only be a matter of time. Our job is to make sure they always stay behind us. Our next test, as many of you should have guessed, is to repeat what we just did but with the whole squadron." Everyone expected this to be the next test, but now he said out loud, it became real. "If successful, which I believe we will be, this will provide an unmatched tactical advantage." He paused one more time to scan the room. The future sat before him. He could see himself in their shoes a long time ago. So much to learn and so much left to do. "Enjoy your success, you earned it. I'm authorizing a 48-hour ship leave, bar tabs on me for the first 24. But be ready when you return. There is a lot of work to do."

CHAPTER 2

Riley–Space Institute of Advanced Studies–Earth

Riley McCovee sat in his cramped dorm room, most of his belongings already packed away and loaded up into his car. One last memento remained on his desk. A picture of him being held by his grandfather as a child. He claimed to remember that day, although he's not sure if it's because he actually remembered it or because he heard his parents tell it so many times.

Thinking of that story always grounded him and made him smile, no matter what was going on around him. He didn't remember the end, returning home after dark on a day that started early in the morning. His little eyes couldn't stay open and his parents told him they were getting worried until his grandfather pulled into the driveway. Riley's grandfather, the beginning of the Riley name, had snuck him out of pre-school to go hiking in the woods around his town. Riley's parents weren't told much about where they were going or what they were doing. As Grandpa Riley walked from the driveway to the house holding a sleeping toddler, Riley, his parents were happy to have him back home, and his dad took that picture. It was a grand adventure for the small boy and he remembered the feeling more than anything. They had a deep bond. Riley's grandpa retired right around the time Riley was born. He lived close and would often watch Riley when his parents went away on business.

Riley closed his eyes and wondered what it would be like without him around. He quickly pushed that thought aside, his thoughts returning to the present. The thought of it made him sick, knowing it would be like losing a parent. He had this fear more often now that his grandfather had moved in with his parents over the last year, unable to fully care for himself.

Contemplating the time that had passed, he considered how long it had been since he last saw his family. The final year of his schooling required him to stay on campus to help simulate what it would be like to be separated from family and the outside world. He didn't like the feeling but knew he would have to get at least partially used to it. He kept that picture as a reminder of all the sacrifices that brought him to this point and why his future role was crucial, even if he didn't yet know how.

At least, that's what his grandfather always told him. Riley's father and mother were away from home more than his friend's parents, and when they were home, they talked little about what they did. Ever since a young age they always told him not to mix work and family time. They said he always needed to focus on the present and give that attention. While that may be partially true, as he got older, he suspected there were other reasons they didn't talk about work.

His grandfather would talk to him about all sorts of topics when his parents were away. They all had a central theme, a moral, when he thought back to them. Mostly centered on doing the right thing, being the bigger person, although some were just goofy and he didn't always understand. Whenever the stories veered towards his work, being a soldier, Riley noticed the vague language he used. Riley's parents always told him not to pry into that part of his life and that if his grandpa wanted to talk about it, he would.

So, Riley left it alone but always wondered what his grandpa had done during his time fighting. The little he knew revolved around counterterrorism and later a key role during the Claim War. He knew a little more about his role during the Claim War that followed shortly after that. They were dangerous times for most of the world.

No one wanted to call it World War III. It wasn't as costly in terms of death, nor could it have been called an outright war in the traditional sense. But the consequences of escalation would have made it the worst war in all history. The Claim War was the most publicized war in history. The fighters in it gained more recognition than had ever been seen before. For better or worse. That resulted in Riley knowing a great deal about what his grandfather had done in that war. His grandfather was a national hero in the news. He had no clue what his parents did, so it was easier to bond with and relate to his grandfather when he told him things about the wars.

With a deep breath, he stood up, grabbed the picture and his diploma and walked into the hall, closing the light aluminum door behind him. The soft clank echoing in the once full rooms. The dorms at his college were designed to familiarize the cadets with the lifestyle of a career on a space station. The section of dorms that housed the military students mimicked more of a Carrier-class space station. Not unlike an aircraft carrier of the past that operated on Earth's oceans, a Carrier-class space station was home to all classes of spaceships.

There was currently only one operational, with another

completing construction. Riley knew he would soon be on one of those ships in orbit. He had visited it a couple summers ago as a cadet, a rare but valuable opportunity. This would be different. He would actually work on one. The thought made his heart race. He'd been dreaming of this day for a long time. He would soon be on his way to Advanced Space Maneuvering School, ASMS, or colloquially called A-sims. Since he already passed basic shuttle school, which is the precursor pilot training for all pilots, they selected him for ASMS. They reserved this school for the best pilots in pilot training.

Here, pilots would learn to fly the next-generation fighter ships. Even though it had all the characteristics of a fighter, the politically correct name for it was Advanced Individual Maneuvering Shuttle or AIMS. Optics were important because aggressions were still frowned upon in space, so having a ship with its sole purpose of being aggressive, at least in its name, wouldn't do.

With graduation and commissioning into the North American Space Force behind him, he had time to make one last stop before heading to the shuttle pad on his way to his first duty assignment at the Space Force Guard Ship Minotaur, The Minnow for short. He hopped in his car and headed home. Although he wanted to see his parents as well, his grandpa was staying there until his health improved enough to move back to his house on his own. He would have seen his grandfather first had he not been with his parents. His grandfather was stubborn and independent. Riley knew he was hanging on to that independence as long as he could, even though in reality, he would never live alone again. Riley would have felt the same way. The desire to be free, and ensure others shared that same opportunity, drove his family into the work they did. It's what defined them. His grandfather may not be there much longer. He couldn't bear to think of a time when his grandfather wouldn't be there anymore. With his upcoming assignment at the Minnow, there was no telling when or if he would see them again.

As he turned off the highway into his town, he attempted to turn the autopilot off. He heard an auditory beeping and a warning from the vehicle. "Autopilot is mandatory on this route. Autopilot engaged." The monotone voice echoed through the car. The car increased the volume to ensure it could be heard over any other distractions.

"What the hell?" Riley murmured to himself, a little disappointed. He looked at the road, and that's when he noticed that there had been an update. He remembered reading a new law passed recently that said any new road developments were required to accommodate mandatory autopilot sensors. The comparatively light tint of gray to the material gave it away. Although the sensors were buried well underneath, he couldn't see them, but he could identify the use of the new material based on its comparatively light tint of gray. As he continued driving, he could tell that it was smoother, too.

"Forget this, I don't like this new feeling road, it's too smooth. Time to turn the autopilot off." He continued talking to himself as if the car was his passenger. With a couple of taps on his phone, he interacted with the car's computer and disabled the autopilot. He wrote the program himself during one of his computer science courses. He got bored with the regular curriculum and branched out on his own. Riley wanted to drive, actually drive himself. His skills complemented his confidence, allowing him to get away with it. There were sensors all along the roads and in all the other vehicles that could detect if most drivers had manually taken control of a vehicle in a restricted area and would report the incident. He could lose his license with a severe enough infraction. That would mean he would have to ride shotgun in the passenger seat, even if it meant leaving the driver's seat unoccupied. The risk did not outweigh the reward, in Riley's opinion, therefor he continued his self-driving. He hadn't been caught yet and his young mind, like most young minds, convinced him he was invincible. Because most of the autopilots are linked, sometimes the car's movements would be unexpected or seem ridiculous, but if he drove himself, he wouldn't know these changes were coming. That's why the only time he would not get out of autopilot occurred when other cars were near him and linked at very high speeds. That could be dangerous for him, but he was more concerned about injuring someone else needlessly.

As he approached the house, the light on the front porch flickered, mimicking an old flame lantern, casting shadows in a seemingly random pattern. His grandpa and dad sat out on two old handmade wood rockers. As he pulled in, Riley's dad stood and walked down the porch steps towards the car.

"Driving manual again, I see." Riley's father said, grinning widely. "I wouldn't expect anything less from you, Riley."

"How could you tell, pops?" Riley responded.

"Ever since they put the new road in, I can't stand using it. I want the freedom of driving myself, at the very least when nobody is around." Riley's dad retorted.

"It's safer that way, we don't need you hitting the neighbor's mailbox again." Riley quipped. Hearing the story a thousand times from his childhood, he knew how his dad was going to respond.

"It wasn't my fault – I swear they moved it overnight. Bursting into laughter, they both enthusiastically stated in unison.

They made their way up to the porch where Riley's grandpa

now stood. They embraced each other. "Looking good, Grandpa." Riley complimented. Riley almost had a tear in his eye. Not seeing him for so long and all the change coming to his life seemed to stack up and hit him all at once.

"Oh, you know, put on a few more pounds. All of this home cooking from your mom." his grandpa responded. They all shared another laugh and made their way inside the house.

As Riley grabbed the doorknob and pushed open the oversized white door, he could hear his mom. "Dinner is ready. Is that Riley I heard?" She half yelled from the kitchen.

"Here, mom." Riley responded and went into the kitchen to give his mother a hug, their normal greeting. The McCovees were not as shy as some families when it came to affection and, to some extent, feelings. They rarely spoke of their past. The stories were too difficult to tell, or they weren't allowed to. Both of Riley's parents worked for different government agencies growing up and were secretive about what they actually did. Riley's grandfather served in some other special unit he could never really talk about in the military for some time before the Claim War. His grandfather had a borderline legendary reputation among the infantry military units while serving in a Special Forces unit. He never really understood why, but whenever he interacted with any land-based ground forces in his various training, they all seemed to recognize his name and tell him how cool it must be to have the legendary Ripchord as his grandfather.

Riley rarely tried to pry information from his grandfather. On the couple of occasions he did, he was given no information. Riley assumed that much of that information was protected and classified. Riley never talked to his family much about what they did. He knew his grandpa had lost a lot of friends during his career and always seemed to avoid talking about those years. So Riley resorted to getting all of his information from any news source or talking with any soldier that asked him.

After a rosemary baked chicken dinner with roasted vegetables from the garden, Riley's mom and dad worked together cleaning up the kitchen and doing dishes. They made this a nightly tradition anytime they were both home together. Riley went outside to find his grandfather. When he got out onto the newly updated but rustic-looking porch, his grandpa pushed himself up out of the chair.

"Hey, Riley, I was just coming to get you for a nighttime stroll." Grandpa Riley said, preempting Riley's question.

As they began walking, Riley's grandfather spoke, softly at first, but Riley could tell it was something he had been eager to speak with him about, but also dreading. Something about the hesitation in his grandfather's voice made him feel like this talk would be different. "I wish we could see you more often, but what you are doing is important. You'll see. The world will never stop having a crisis, and it seems that a McCovee is always smack in the middle of it. So far, we have come out on top. I don't expect that to change with you. Just don't forget to pause every once in a while. Family is the most important thing I have done. They will always be with you, the service will not." He rarely opened up about his service. When he did, he always made it clear that he always preferred to be with his family. But when a person has a calling, it is important to attend to that as well, and often it takes priority.

"Thanks, grandpa." Riley drew a blank on a more impactful response. Something that said he genuinely appreciated it. So he left it with a simple thanks. "Grandpa, I've heard people calling you Rip from time to time. Where'd you get that nickname?" Riley asked. He had always wondered and hoped it wasn't too intrusive of a question, although he knew it related to the early years with his Special Forces unit.

"Ah, it's tough to talk about. Chalk it up to a skydiving accident. I'll just say, I had to pull mine and my entire team's ripcords before it was too late. They were all unconscious, see? So, I had to go around to each of them and pull it for them. Luckily, they were all alive and came to pretty quick when I pulled their masks off. We were not in a very friendly place if you catch my drift." He paused, thinking about a time long ago. "The team was told it was contaminated oxygen bottles, everyone but mine." Riley's grandfather paused for a second. His face scrunched a bit, relaxed, then did it again. An internal struggle evident on his face. Riley got the sensation that he had told no one this story before. Riley could see the troubling moment's flash behind his eyes. Sadness overcame his expression. Grandpa sighed before continuing. "You know, I lost a good friend that day. I made it to my entire team, except one. I couldn't get to him in time and had to make the choice. Die trying to get to him or live. I don't regret my decision, but I do hold the weight of that decision every day." Riley could see some tears welling up and his grandpa abruptly turned away. He wiped the tears before they could roll down his cheek. His grandpa let out a quick but low laugh, a coping mechanism Riley had learned over time. He had a similar strategy. "Listen, you may come to a point in your career where you need to make a similar choice. Don't make it lightly. But after you do, face it and move on because I know you'll have made the right one. Just be sure to live and tell someone about it. Don't hold onto it."

Riley's grandfather stopped looking at Riley and looked back up the road. Seeing how far they had gone, they both turned around and headed back towards the house.

As they turned, Riley's grandfather turned to him. "You wanna catch a ball game tomorrow? The Orioles are in town this week, looking for a sweep."

"That would be great." He loved baseball, but the extra time with his family would be nice. As he was growing up, the three generations of Riley McCovees went to many games together. He knew it could be the last time they all got a chance to go and wouldn't miss it for the world.

CHAPTER 3

Ramat–Space Force Platform Kennedy–Earth Orbit

Ramat stood off to the side in front of the mission room, where Major Charlie 'Wisp' Broadway was wrapping up the debrief of the last simulator mission on board the SFP Kennedy. Charlie had shut down the video wall, showing the detailed playback of the scenario they had just executed.

"Does anybody have any go-backs?" Charlie asked, making sure everyone had said all they wanted to. Prior to conducting the actual full formation faster than light test, this was the last simulator mission for the squadron. This simulator run executed under all ideal conditions: no input errors, no outside issues, exactly the way the team wanted it to go. This helped build confidence with everything going perfectly, but also helped the team key in on anything out of place when the actual test occurs.

Ramat knew there would be at least one question. One that weighed on all of their minds. Their superiors had ordered all of them to carry multiple missile-sized nukes on board their ships. He had been over it with them, but seeing as this was the last training mission before the actual test, he assumed it would come up again.

Lieutenant Michael Xavier spoke up. "Uh, yeah, what about those giant freaking nukes in my missile slots that I have no control over!?"

Charlie spoke, but Ramat jumped in to handle the question. Charlie was a great Operations Officer, and as such, he was a lot more direct. Ramat worried he might say something like, 'Suck it up and follow your orders'. The precise response Charlie gave the first time this issue was brought up. Ramat had a little more tact than his Operations Officer, Charlie, and at this point, the subject needed to be addressed carefully. Lieutenant Xavier was talking about the solution that his leadership came up with to ensure their highly classified ships and pilots could not fall into the wrong hands, specifically the portable light gate system. If there was any hint of trouble, such as someone being suspected of turning their ship over to a rival country or another country attempting to capture one, their leadership devised a solution. This solution included triggering a large devastating chain reaction that would leave nothing left to analyze. To that point, his squadron did not like that it could happen seemingly without warning or any say on their part.

"We're working on that. But as you've been briefed, the threat of capture is real. The Kennedy's ops squadrons are going to do their best to protect us. I don't like this way any more than the next Lucky. If we are able to pull this off, it could virtually eliminate the idea of space combat for the foreseeable future. No other country would want to fight out here if they knew we could show up whenever and wherever we wanted, hit them, and leave without them getting a shot off. We can't let our adversaries get their hands on this technology, under any circumstances. Brass decided this was the best way to do that." He let the severity of the situation sink in. He didn't want his squad to know that he also was uncomfortable with the idea of sitting on a nuclear bomb that he did not have direct control over.

After many battles with his leadership on the subject, followed by threats of being removed as the commander, if he didn't comply, he gave up on addressing the matter through official channels. There were always unofficial channels, though.

Ramat continued. "It is a dangerous test flight, but it will likely be the greatest single event since, well, ever." He paused again before continuing. "Nobody, and I mean nobody," he looked around the room once more to make sure no one had an ill-timed remark. The room was somber and uncharacteristically quiet. "will hold it against you if you do not wish to participate in this flight."

The simple nature of the people in the squadron told the story. None of them were backing down. The room remained silent. After a few seconds, sensing nobody had any more questions or remarks, Charlie spoke up. "Alright, go get some chow and rest, back here at 0530 tomorrow ship time for the mission brief and pre-flights. Dismissed."

Ramat spoke up as the squadron began walking out of the room. "Wisp and P, please stay behind for a minute." The rest of the squadron wouldn't think twice about this. It was fairly normal for the boss to keep Charlie and someone else behind. Usually, it was to discuss in a more personal setting how they screwed up that mission, and how they can do better next time. However, this time, he kept them behind for a different purpose.

With the door shut and locked and only the three of them in the room, Ramat sat back down, turned to P and asked, "P, how's the progress of taking control of the nukes?"

"They're mine boss. It took a little bit, but when you give the word, they become inert flying nukes or whatever else, you name it. I can have them make you coffee if you want." P responded. P was Captain James "P" Parrant. He came across as a farmer boy from the heartland of the United States of America. He had the southern charm and even a little bit of a drawl, but his parents emigrated there from the outskirts of Paris, France. With the divide of the Northern and Southern Hemispheres coming to a hostile standstill around those times, it was safer to be in the Americas than almost anywhere else. They moved to the outskirts of Chicago, Illinois. James never farmed in his life, but when he was told he could be and do anything he wanted to in America, he took that to heart and took on the persona of a southern boy. He perfected it while growing up when he found people accepted him more that way, as someone who wasn't quite from there.

"And you can take care of it mid-flight, and reverse it if we don't need it? I don't want any alarms going off before we leave."

"Yes, sir." James shot back. Ramat was making sure that everything was taken care of. He caught a hint from the shift in James's body language and the way he snipped back that James was getting a little annoyed. 'Understandable, given the circumstances', Ramat thought to himself, 'he doesn't want me up in his business'. Even though James was one of the newer and younger members of the squadron, he had earned enough trust to not be questioned as much. The gravity of the situation required just a little more oversight than normal.

James was here for a reason, and that reason revolved around him being exceptionally good and thorough with computer-related issues. James, being one of the youngest graduates of the Space Test School said a lot on its own. The fighters they were flying these days required a renewed level of tech savviness. Touchscreens and visual selections almost entirely replaced switches and knobs, and there were even some functions that the pilots could control with thought, although the broader use of that technology was still in development. Pilots would need to go deep into programs and dialogues to find what they were looking for or even update software scripts on the fly. Having someone like James who helped write some of the software code had many benefits for the team. This also allowed him to quickly resolve issues by taking over other crew members' ships if they needed help.

Ramat insisted, almost to the point of ordering James, that he, the commander, held responsibility if anything went wrong. But James had the upper hand, since he would actually do the work, and stated that he wouldn't do it unless Ramat was kept mostly in the dark. Ramat could tell that James didn't want him to take the fall if he screwed something up and got caught. But that wasn't Ramat's style. If something went wrong, he would take full blame.

The details were not that complicated, at least not to James. "Boss, The Anti-Spoofing AI was only integrated into the heart of the Kennedy, that software doesn't exist on the fighters yet. Ours only keeps intruders out of the hen house, it can't do anything once something is inside."

"So, we don't have to worry about it tripping that portion?" Charlie responded.

"No, where we will be in space, it will think everything is hunky-dory. I created a hidden tasking file for weapons planning, just like any other one. It will override the existing tasking file sent by higher-ups and I can modify it like any other payloads."

"They didn't put any type of security on it?" Ramat asked.

"They did, but I've been breaking that type of security since grade school. The tricky part was getting past the restrictions of convincing the nuke that it had engines and that it was allowed to be in space. And also, to make it a dud. There are a lot of safeties put in place to make sure we abide by the anti-nuke treaty. I don't need to tell you how bad it could be if these hit the wrong thing."

Even if everything went right and someone found out that they were defused, there would be some upset people at some extremely high levels. What the squadron had going for them was the fact that no one at a higher level could openly reprimand them for it because they weren't supposed to have them on board. They were a back-up in the event an adversary attempted to gain control of a ship and all other safety factors failed. The North American Space Force was light-years ahead of the competition in this particular field and would do anything in its power to keep it that way.

"Alright P, you got it." Ramat said back after thinking hard for a moment. "Go get some chow and sleep with the rest of the crew. See you tomorrow."

James turned to walk out the door. Ramat turned to Charlie when the door shut behind James. "You think this is the right call?" Ramat asked, almost as if he directed the question to himself too.

"Yeah, Boss. There's no telling if they had some sort of remote trigger they could detonate if they got uneasy. Let's just hope we don't need them, and if we do, we make the call." Charlie responded.

What wasn't said between the two was that either of them would detonate their fighters without hesitation if it meant the rest of the squadron could escape whatever looming threat. In their squadron, only a few of the pilots had flown atmospheric fighters and also seen combat in them. They knew and even had to make some of the tough decisions during combat that put their people and themselves at risk.

Exiting the briefing room, they gave each other a slow nod of understanding. They knew what needed to be done.

CHAPTER 4

Mark–World Council Delegation Room–Earth

Mark DeCanus sat relaxed on the bench outside the side entrance to the newly minted World Council Delegation Room, a slight slouch noticeable. The main entrance was a little too grand for him, like something out of an ancient Greek architect's wildest dream. Even the side entrance was overdone with its massive, real oak double doors. They had an eerie creak when they opened and then closing with a thud, making it impossible for him to slip in or out unnoticed. It was either there on purpose so that nobody could enter or exit silently, or the maintenance crew didn't feel like fixing it.

He reviewed some proposals that his assistant collected. They were a mix of paper packets and some sent to his tablet. As he flipped through, a few caught his eye: "Expanding Trade Rights with SHUR" and "Co-Leaders of the World." They gave him reason to dig a little deeper into them. He recognized the authors for each. 'They can be a little nuts.' he thought to himself. They could be nuts along with their ideas, lending credence to the reason that many of their proposals didn't make it through the aides' review. But Mark had specifically asked for the crazy ideas, the ones that nobody else would look at to see if they had merit.

He called his assistant. After not even one whole ring, his assistant picked it up. "What can I do for you, Mr. DeCanus?"

"Yes, can you set up a meeting with the authors of 'Expanding Trade Rights with the SHUR' and 'Co-Leaders of the World'? I like their tone. On their surface, they aren't attacking the SHUR but putting them on a level playing field. That's a start." Mark responded sharply. The hearings were about to start, so he needed to cut to the chase.

Mark wanted the fighting with the SHUR to stop. He wanted everyone to work together. He thought it so strange that the northern half of the world was on the brink of war with the southern half of the world simply because of an imaginary line between them. It reminded him that even if some things change, others don't. Mark spent most of his time looking for a way, one piece at a time, to get all sides to work as one.

When Mark got off the phone, he glanced up at a screen hanging on the opposite wall in the hallway. A screen played one of the popular news stations. He couldn't quite see which one. It was a long way away; he strained to see what it said even with his glasses on. Scrolling across the bottom of the screen read *Celebrating 50 years of Discovery*. Ah, yes, Mark remembered. The days were merging with how busy he was lately. Today marked the 50th anniversary of one of the greatest rare earth metal deposits discovered, with many more following shortly after. They all were in the southern hemisphere of the earth. He saw people dancing in the streets as the camera panned over the crowd at a parade. They looked happy. He wanted that for everyone.

These discoveries also massively disrupted the existing

world order, as Mark recalled. At first, people thought it would be for the better. Wealth, jobs, hunger should no longer be an issue. He remembered meeting with delegates from Africa and Argentina. This occurred during his time in service. They had a confidence to them that, at the time, he mistook for learning to use their new ego. Later, it became clear that their confidence stemmed from the way they had been treated the whole time leading up to this point.

Along with the creation of several additional space launch sites and manufacturing compounds there, the pace of change accelerated. Their 'ego,' as Mark once thought of it, was actually the knowledge that they were going to be the top dog, and nobody could stop them. That didn't sit well with the established United Nations. Any country associated with those new resources broke free of the UN, fracturing the remaining members and leaving them struggling to keep up the appearances that they were still maintaining what they stood for. Each remaining country continuously disagreed on the best way to handle the rapidly evolving situation.

Mark could hear murmurs around the room. "Can you believe they are playing this in here?" and "What a bunch of crap, they got lucky and are rubbing it in our faces." This went on for a few moments until someone finally changed the channel to a more appealing and self-serving network.

What began as a good thing from many standpoints quickly turned sour. Many third-world countries shot right to the top over the last fifty years. With their newly discovered wealth and power, they sought to challenge the established world leaders and actually beat them in creating a unified southern hemisphere coalition. This turned into the Southern Hemisphere United Republic, also known as the SHUR. Instead of being seen as the unifying event it was, leaders in the north took it as a threat. People not part of it usually said it as a joke, 'Sure', you guys are great. While those that lived there pronounced it as 'Shore' to signify their strength and endless land from one shore to the next. The Northern Hemisphere nations were caught off guard and, individually, couldn't do anything about it.

About twenty years after the discovery, Mark came into the fray as a civilian. He was a fresh new North American representative at the United Nations, which by this point in time had digressed from its former mission, as people were realizing. It had finally stabilized at the point where the citizens of the nations in the UN thought of it as a formality, a shadow of its former self. Soon, they selected Mark to lead the effort of unifying all of the remaining nations, not just as an alliance but as one, like the SHUR. He needed to get it back but stronger and better than before. He had gotten his start after retiring from his final tour in the Army as a foreign liaison officer. This smoothed his entrance into the political land. He overcame what seemed insurmountable odds to get to this point and it only cost him the first half of his political career. But his main dream was much bigger; he was bent on the unification of the world and saw it as the only goal worth achieving.

He saw uniting the northern hemisphere as something that should have happened automatically, and the only obstacle was the ego of the different territories, who were afraid they would lose their power. They all failed to understand the reasoning of what collective power could bring. He had little time to see his plans through by the end of his career without something speeding up the process.

There were some, however, one in particular, that was at complete odds with his fundamental ideals. This was true for all political and social arenas. Opposition lurked in every corner.

Rictor Inagru strolled on the dark marble tile floors up to Mark with a seemingly intentionally loud thud with each step. He had a swagger to his step that Mark could only describe as overcompensating for lack of spine. The walk told Mark that Rictor thought whatever he was about to say would blow him away and get him to see the merits from his point of view. Unlike many in the UN and almost all the smaller political players, Mark saw right through his tactics, and even though he never forcefully displayed his true motives to the larger political community, despite being arrogant, Rictor was quite clever and made his plans clear to Mark.

Rictor held the position of Vice-Chair for the Outreach committee, tasked with helping to bring other countries back to the UN and, more importantly, get financial support. While he technically worked for Mark on this committee, he was also one of several Vice-Chairs on the UN as well. No longer a representative of the old United States, this gave Rictor even more power and autonomy.

Rictor stopped right in front of the screen as Mark watched, blocking his view. Either Rictor didn't bother to check if he was interrupting him, or he deliberately did this. Rictor's raspy voice, an octave higher than Mark expected the first time he heard him speak, formed words. "Did you see the report on the new military movements those dirty SHUR are carrying out?" Rictor more stated than asked. He didn't give enough pause to allow for a response, even if Mark wanted to respond. "Who do they think they are? And to think we used to call some of them our allies. Disgraceful!"

Mark had connections. Friendships that he had made over the years, to include one in particular at the Army Warfare School. This friend now led the Battle and Tactics branch of the Northern Hemisphere Nations, or NHN. These were formed relatively recently as a push to show the benefits of breaking up the old ways of thinking about small states and countries. It was a start, at least.

One piece of information Mark received from his friend resulted from wargames conducted by the NHN. They had conducted this exact wargame to see what would happen if the NHN enacted stricter trade routes and blocking trade of certain necessary items to the SHUR. What happened was exactly what was expected. The SHUR countered by repositioning their military forces to show that they were unhappy with the new restrictions and would retaliate and escalate if things didn't change. Until this point, the wargame had been fairly accurate. The movement by the SHUR was in response to a bill that Rictor passed; he managed to convince enough people to buy off on the trade restrictions. Mark saw the actions by the NHN as unprovoked and the response by the SHUR justified.

Mark had to wonder, what had Rictor offered those who sided with him? If Rictor was anything, he had an uncanny ability to get people to change their long-standing beliefs, and at least for short periods of time, align their goals with his. Mark was no stranger to this game; it was just at a higher level of playing with Rictor.

Standing, Mark looked distractedly at Rictor and spoke. "Is this the response you were hoping for, Rictor? You know you're putting people's lives on the line. I bet you have some great response, some way to spin this to your advantage."

"As a matter of fact, I do have the perfect response. It's all about the bigger picture, Mark." Rictor quipped back.

"I can't wait to hear it." Mark said, trailing off, with obvious disinterest in the actual idea.

"You know, I'm not such a bad guy if you get to know me." Rictor continued with a smirk. Either acting like he didn't notice that Mark wasn't into this conversation, or he was trying to bait him into saying something that he could use later. "You could learn a lot from me. You have a great deal of potential. I wouldn't want you to waste it on a false sense of morals."

"Don't talk to me about morals!" Mark responded with a bite. Now he had his attention. He would not stand by and listen to someone like Rictor, with his history, talk to him about morals. "I know just where I stand. Putting innocent people's lives at risk for your big scheme doesn't pass my test. I know what you are. Your big picture has only you in it, at the top, while the rest of us are left figuring out what happened."

"You're right. You won't know what happened because it's already happening, and you're already confused. I thought you were smarter than that." Rictor responded, holding up his index finger and wagging it back and forth. Mark could see him mouthing the words 'tsk, tsk' as if he was addressing his dog.

"Oh no, I know exactly what's going on. We're not going to war with the SHUR, I won't let that happen. We have too much to lose by doing that and so much to gain by working together."

At that, Mark watched Rictor scoff and heard an exaggerated gasp. "Those are treacherous words, Mark. It's starting to sound like you like them more than your own country. Whose side are you on?"

"Don't question my loyalties, Rictor. You don't know what it's like on the front lines. Let's see how long you last out there without your aides and policies. Big speeches don't really hold a lot of water when you're getting shot at." Rictor fell silent.

Mark could sense he was once again going to get nowhere with Rictor. Mark turned and entered the room. With a loud creak and a thud, the side door shut behind him. He took up his seat along the edge of the front row. Rictor didn't come in behind Mark. Instead, he made his way back to the main door.

Rictor made sure everyone noticed him when he entered. He made his way to the general seating area, some place that would cause a ruckus when he got up to make his speech. Mark was certain of that. Theatrics were something that Mark never took to, nor did he find necessary. The message should be able to stand on its own. If it couldn't, it either wasn't ready, or it wasn't right.

Mark put his glasses on his head, and with one hand, pinched his nose and rubbed his eyes. He fought off a headache he knew would come if he didn't get more sleep, or coffee, or both. He often wondered why he took on extra work that nobody asked him to do. The results of this wargame were not the only ones he had received. He had also inquired with his old Army buddy at the wargaming institute about several scenarios, well, thousands of scenarios, to see which held any promise of getting the two hemispheres to sit at the same table to begin discussions. It wasn't outside of his vision, but it wasn't inside his current job description. His job was to keep current countries investing in the NHN and not get the SHUR to speak to them.

He spent most of the night and early morning going over each case, mostly with confusion. There had to be a solution, he thought to himself. There were too many newfound riches coming to the SHUR now for them to be bothered with world relations. Many of the countries had spent so much time on the bottom that they had no interest in dealing with any country that they felt betrayed them and left them alone to rot in the past. None of his ideas came close to even the first stage of achieving his objective of simple discussion. Well, that wasn't entirely true; one scenario did.

He considered this idea, this scenario, a bounding scenario. One that tested the limits of the simulation. The radical input defied current human understanding of the cosmos.

The radical input involved an attack. An attack that devastated countries, disrupted trade but more importantly, caused mass panic. An attack that changed the world. It couldn't come from either half or a proxy. It had to come from an actor that nobody on earth knew about or thought about. The actor had to come from off world. He really desired for the sides to act as one and this off the wall scenario actually achieved it.

Mark halfheartedly laughed at that thought as he drowned out the morning remarks of outrage by the different leaders of the NHN. They were all saying the same thing, so there was no point in hearing it multiple times. The keywords he had to listen for to know it came from Rictor's camp were things like 'outrage', and 'disgust'. He had to pause momentarily when he heard the word 'traitors'. That was a new one.

Soon it would be his turn. But while he waited, he couldn't help but think that his lifelong dream would never happen. He could make the situation better, but that wasn't good enough for him. The simulation said that an alien attack was the only way to get the world out of the mess it seemed so intent to stay in. That didn't sit well with him. There had to be another way that didn't rely on an impossible event to cause death and destruction in order to stop death and destruction. He continued to wait for his turn. A dark shadow crept over his mind as his hopes for peace were all but crushed. It was a setback, to be sure. Could he remain undeterred at finding a solution to this world problem?

When the room finally died down and became his turn to speak, he laid out his plan. He did so with tact and the controlled tempo that matched the most experienced members of this cabinet. By presenting the facts, he countered the previous claims made by his political opponents. He had spent countless hours getting to know the ins and outs of this situation. His intention wasn't for the entire house to change and side with him, but rather to bring it close enough that no decision could be made today. He knew that with patience and proper care the right decision would be agreed to. He believed wholeheartedly that his idea was the right decision.

"So, what are you suggesting, exactly, Mark? Because it sounds a whole lot like nothing." Someone shouted from across the room. He didn't quite see who said it and didn't recognize the voice.

"Nothing can sometimes be the biggest gesture of goodwill that one can perform." Mark calmly replied.

"Then we look weak." Another voice added.

"We already look weak. And scared. We just sanctioned them without any pretense or action by them. Doing nothing gives us the opportunity to open negotiations. Then when we get them to the table, we can show our good faith and save face and remove these sanctions that had no foresight to begin with."

"They won't talk with us, they never do." This time Rictor jumped in. "Why is it that you are so fond of wanting to be friends with them? What do they have to do to our economy and our way of life for you to want to stop shaking their hands and take real action?"

"You mean drop some bombs, Rictor? No. The real action would be to shake their hands. They showed us how we should be working together. They have many things that we need from them, and we can't bomb it out of them. They know the same thing is true for them. That is why now is the perfect time to come to the table. They will talk – we just need to ask."

"Are you suggesting we couldn't win a war with them and take everything we need?" Rictor questioned. He was revealing more of his plan than Mark had expected. Of course, Rictor would make it appear not serious. But Mark knew his actual intent.

"Are you even suggesting War, Rictor?" Mark raised his voice, not a shout, but to show he was under control and serious about the path Rictor had suggested. "That's insane. And for the record, no, I don't think we would win. Nobody would."

The hall fell silent. Mark had little more to say. All he could do now was wait and see if what he said had been enough. The joys of politics. When the side conversations turned from whispers to muffled arguments and the shouts began once again, Mark decided there was no point in remaining.

His phone pinged with a new message. A quick glance revealed a longtime friend needed to see him. He used this time to leave to meet her.

He stood and searched the general seating section for his aide, Emily Watkins. Her bright yellow blouse stood out amongst the depressing blacks and grays of the business wear around her. Sitting next to her was Jennifer Stanza, just who he needed to see. He made his way over to them. "Emily, take notes for me please, let me know if there's an emergency. I have some things to take care of."

Emily responded with a curt nod and began trying to follow the different conversations.

Mark shifted his attention to Jenn. "Nice to see you, Jenn, enjoying the show?"

"Not particularly. In fact, I think it's time that I leave."

"Perfect, I'll walk you out." Mark and Jenn walked out the main entrance.

"Going to be another long night?" Jenn asked Mark.

"Another painful and useless long night. The counteraction to the SHUR's military movement should not be a military movement of their own, but rather, do nothing followed by an offer to sit at the negotiating table. Something we have not done in a long time." Mark began listing off the reasons it was going to be long.

"Didn't your war-gaming scenarios suggest that this would not work, negotiating? We all have access to that information." Jenn said back, questioning his stance.

"But a computer can't reliably take into account the instability and emotional response of a human brain. With all of the windfall that the SHUR had encountered, there are still several things that they need from us, and those could be held at risk until a peaceful solution is made. After all, we also rely on the SHUR for several resources as well."

"Going to all-out war with someone who owns all of something you need in order to fight that war isn't a great idea." Jenn stated again, clearly wondering where Mark's mind was at.

"Especially when that war is not expected to be won." Mark responded. He had a lot to think about. There was likely no straightforward solution to this current situation, and it may not turn out for the better.

CHAPTER 5

*Maggie–Advanced Individual Maneuvering Shuttle–Earth Lagrange
Point Four*

Captain Maggie 'Face' Lorrent sat in her cockpit surrounded
by the electromagnetic gel nicknamed 'the goo' making final
checks. The Light Gate hummed and glowed, ready to receive
her and the rest of Lucky's squadron. She looked down at her
status screen, which showed the readiness of the squadron. All
the fighters reported back at one hundred percent readiness.
They loaded six portable light gates on each ship. The nukes
were also ready, ready to be detonated and turn her and the
team into a million unidentifiable particles. A bit of anxious
tension made its way through her body, uneasy about the
prospect of blowing herself up to avoid getting captured. She
took comfort, like most fighter pilots, in the fact that her
abilities made that scenario an impossibility.

Maggie queued up the Kennedy Station Control, akin to air
traffic control Earthside, also known as 'Spin Control'.
"Kennedy Control, this is Lucky three, requesting formation
departure from Light Gate One." Kennedy Control was in the

process of directing the team to line up at the first light gate. This light gate was one of six of the private contractor controlled and operated light gates located in the solar system. Three of which were orbiting the sun at different stationary orbits near Earth's orbital plane, paired with three more farther out into the solar system. As they orbited the sun, the Earth light gates could reorientate, pairing with different light gates in the solar system as they became visible without the sun in the way.

"Lucky three, maintain formation and heading, standby for departure." Kennedy Station Control responded. They kept a clipped and professional tone, even with the excitement of what was about to happen. Nobody wanted to be the one to screw up, and that started with following all the communication protocols.

One other local light gate could serve as a backup to the other Earth light gates, allowing for reorientation. For this mission, the team would test the light gate for a flight past the sun, closer than the orbit of Mercury. It would not be paired with another light gate.

Maggie was looking through some other status screens when she saw the communications link from Ramat light up green, meaning Ramat was about to address the squadron. "Listen up Lucky's. We're on final approach. This light gate is not going to link us up with a far-end light gate. We are on our own. Trust your equipment. If something goes wrong, trust your training and we'll get you back. Everyone, perform final checks and prepare to depart. Lucky one, out."

This time, Major Charlie 'Wisp' Broadway came on the line. He usually followed up with a more down-to-business talk rather than something inspirational or motivational. "Remember the sequence, everyone. Earth light gate and re-accelerate with portable. Then two portables to return to normal speed. We'll assess from there for the return trip. Let your computer take care of the timing unless something goes wrong. You all know what to do. Lucky two, out."

Maggie checked over her AIMS portable light gates that were stowed around her hull. They blended into the outer shell, resting in a small crevice. It appeared as if they were a part of her ship. They consisted of the same material, an advanced nanocarbon. For this mission, Maggie knew that the Earth Light Gate was going to spit them out on their own, and they would have to rely on their portable light gates as part of the test. Maggie knew they were repeating the individual test she had already conducted, but this time, the entire squadron would tag along. The complexity, as well as hazards they could face, were exponentially greater.

Everyone spaced out to the sides, above and below her location. In the event something happened to one ship, the chances that it damaged or destroyed another one were lower. Not zero, but lower. It was also like this because they needed to begin and end their transition at precisely the same time. They would go through all together this time, a full flight of sixteen, in tight formation. Maggie looked all throughout her cockpit. Through her synthetic vision, she could see the formation. It was the first time they or anyone had been in a formation like this. Her jaw hung open.

"Face, are you seeing this? It's incredible." Maggie recognized the voice as Captain 'P' Parrant but glanced down to confirm that the private chat light was illuminated.

"Yeah, this is crazy."

"I feel like we're lining up for battle, you know, like the old days." He referred to ancient Earth history where each side would form up in lines and go head-to-head with their opponent.

"I wouldn't mess with us, that's for sure." After a brief

pause, she added, "Alright P, make sure you finish your checklists, we want this to go smooth."

"I'm on it, that and a bunch of other things."

Maggie wasn't sure what he meant by the last comment, but let it go for now. Things were about to get busy. She took one last look outside to take in the weight of her surroundings. If anyone hadn't yet grasped what they were about to undertake, they did now. With few exceptions of unmanned and even fewer manned single-ship flights, ships did not go through a light gate not linked with another light gate on the receiving end. And they certainly didn't do it in such a large formation. If one ship had even a slight deviation in direction or a thruster misfired at the wrong time, it could cause a collision, knocking others off course. The smallest error at the wrong time could disrupt the disassembly or reassembly process, which would be fatal to the pilot and ship.

The Lucky's began their approach. Their ships synced with the light gate, allowing it to take control of each one. The most important part of the transition and why the computers had taken over was how critical it was to be going the exact same speed and direction. A successful transition relied on it. Maggie kept a close eye on a screen she pulled up that showed her each fighter and their relative position and velocity to each other. If any of them strayed by even a fraction of a degree or a fraction of a single kilometer per hour, she would abort the mission. The computers were watching this as well, but experience acted as a backup.

She focused on the screens, with her finger over the abort cover. She pushed away the pressure and weight bearing down on her. Even in her environmentally controlled suit, she could feel her hands beginning to sweat. The problem, she knew, was that she had too few things to do and too much time to think about it. She much preferred actively flying and all the complexities of maneuvering. Sitting and waiting for something to happen, or not to happen, drove her insane. The prospect of traveling through the light gate still wasn't enough for her. That is why, as she concentrated on the distances and velocities so intently that she didn't even notice that time had skipped a beat for her.

For a moment, her brain lacked the ability to grasp what happened. Particle by particle separated from its host and attached to particles of light being accelerated. As soon as they broke apart and accelerated, they re-assembled as they passed the far end of the light gate, but now they were traveling nearly the speed of light. Attaching the individual person and machinery particles to the light particles impacted the characteristics of the light, slowing it, among other things. Without skipping a heartbeat, each ship in the formation had been broken down, accelerated, and re-assembled. Seamless, painless, but with undetermined lasting effects.

Because of her precise insertion into near light speed, her relative location and speed to her squadron had remained unchanged. She checked her squadron status screen instinctually. Her connection to the rest of the squadron flashed a red pulse every few seconds, indicating an intermittent connection between each of the ships. Theoretically, they should be able to connect with no issues. They were briefed that the ships might experience a partial connection drop as they tried to accommodate the unknown interference of traveling at that speed.

She expected to see the one icon that stayed red, her connection to the Kennedy. The sudden isolation in the vastness of space made her feel insignificant in a way she had never felt before. She gazed up into the unknown to try to lose that feeling. When she looked around, through the synthetic vision of her ship, she saw the other ships, but also absolutely nothing. An empty pitch black overwhelmed her senses. No stars filled the screen as they once did only seconds ago. Fortunately, she heard a crackle on the radio before she spiraled any further.

"…this is Luck…one. Audio che…" She could hear the male voice say, unsure who it came from. His speaking snapped her out of her thoughts, but also gave the computers some additional information to make a better connection with. The voice repeated, this time much more clearly. "This is Lucky one. Audio check, everyone report in."

Maggie responded first. "Lucky three, read you five by five." she responded, showing she could hear him loud and clear. Lucky three corresponded to her position as the safety officer and the test lead on this test. Luckys one and two were saved for the commander and the commander's wingman.

While she waited for the rest of the squadron to report in, she thought back to her initial reaction to transitioning. She almost broke down and lost it. Maybe a combination of the rush of adrenaline from the first transition and being overwhelmed with other tasks felt too much. She was getting behind the ship. A term used since the early days of flying aircraft, meaning that the pilot was too many steps behind and an accident was imminent. Or maybe the pressure of the test they were now doing was getting to her. Her reaction to each transition was completely different. She was in complete control the first time. At least she felt in control. This one, she wondered why it felt like it was getting away from her. She had never had that feeling before, not like that anyway.

She needed to get a grip. By slowing her breathing, she refocused. Now she could take in everything going on. She flipped through the different vision options. At the speed they were traveling, the normal view from the ship filtered out almost everything besides the ships that were traveling with her. When she flipped to the true view, which offered a more realistic representation of the outside world, she became mesmerized, but the feeling quickly turned into nausea. She understood why the scientists decided to filter everything out as the initial view. The colors and patterns of light were unlike anything seen before in nature. It reminded her of a program her little brother would use while listening to music. The different lights would bounce to the beat of the music. Only in this case, they were moving to the motion of the universe.

"It's all you, Face." Maggie heard Ramat call over the radio. Everyone had reported in, and it was time for the next phase of the test.

"Alright Lucky's. Log your ship status and prepare for faster-than-light transition. Once all ships are locked in and synched, we will begin the transition." By the time the check was done, the Luckys were in between the orbital paths of Mercury and Venus. Their fighters took over again, and a countdown began.

When the countdown reached zero, Maggie could look up and around her ship at the different view screens to see two solid black composite rings emerge from the center of her fighter. They slowly expanded to a circumference slightly larger than her ship so that they could smoothly pass over it. The two rings moved forward on the ship until they were ahead of the beginning of the teardrop. The two rings separated from each other, and at that moment, the backmost ring shot back over the ship with a blinding bright white light.

It would have blinded her if not for the viewscreens dimming and protecting her eyes, just before being broken apart. The first ring performed the same function as the permanent light gate near Earth. They separated individual particles, attached them to light particles, and accelerated them. The back ring fell away, now spent. She couldn't see this part because she was currently broken up into tiny molecules. But she knew what was going on. The frontmost ring instantly re-assembled the accelerated light and material particles as they passed through it. This time with their initial speed plus another near speed of light value, putting the Luckys traveling in formation at close to two times the speed of light. With another flash and a feeling of being born again or revived, she looked at a blank view screen with only her squadron around her.

"Luckys, synch up and report in." Maggie queried everyone as soon as she had done some quick checks of her systems. Her ship had a more difficult time synching up with the other fighters. She saw she had a good connection with Captain James Parrant and tried calling him directly. "P, are you synching up with everyone?"

After a few seconds, she finally got a response, her breathing returned. "Yeah, I'm having a little trouble. We're all headed off course a bit. We'll need to course correct."

"Copy. We must have been off trajectory when we transitioned."

"That and I think the techies need to do a better job calibrating these portables. Looks like boss is going a bit faster than all of us."

"Maybe they just wanted to give him an extra boost." Maggie joked back. That was more like it. She was relaxed again, but focused. Some relief washed over her, happy to not be sitting in that awful feeling any longer.

The computers on each ship were busy making adjustments to speed and trajectory until they could maintain a solid link. To make the initial link, they all needed to be close to each other but also not moving compared to one another.

She reopened the channel to James once the links were made. "I still don't get how this all works. You're the tech guy, how are we going this fast?"

"Magic." James responded, half kidding.

"I thought humans couldn't go this fast except for in movies. Aren't we breaking some laws of physics?" She understood more than she was letting on; they all did. They had to be familiar with the systems they were using. She knew James knew a lot more about it. Science fiction was his jam.

"Yeah, technically a warp drive is only possible in movies. Fortunately for us, that's not what we are doing. We're kind of cheating a little. You remember back when the SHUR found all of those resources? Well, some of them made all of this possible. Crazy amount of storage for both power and memory. These light gates rely on storing our precise sequence momentarily and using lots of stored power to do the whole disassembly-reassembly craziness. We sort of bypass the mass and acceleration limits by attaching ourselves to something that is already going that speed. We don't die because, well, we technically don't exist as people for a little while."

"That still blows my mind. And I don't like thinking that I die every time I transition. But still, my favorite part is these portable light gates disintegrating into a million little parts when we are done with them. I saw some of the tests for that. The way it breaks down and explodes out, I wish I had a missile that could do that." Maggie thought out loud.

"You know, this gel is pretty cool stuff too. It has some of that memory-holding material built into it. They don't advertise it like this, but it's pretty smart on its own." James said.

The outer teardrop shell of the ship masked the spherical shape of the cockpits. Quad SOP engines mounted around the spine of the narrow end gave the ship incredible power. One meter of electromagnetic gel separated the inner and outer spheres and acted to ease the intense G-forces the pilots could endure during maneuvering, as well as subdue the intense radiation experienced in space.

Maggie could see that all the links were green, and Ramat was opening a communication line to the squadron. "By the numbers now, Lucky's report." Hearing his voice continued to calm her nerves and reset her focus. He had that effect on her, on all the squadron. She could tell he was confident in their abilities, and that went a long way with her own confidence. He had developed his calm tone over a long career in atmospheric fighter jets. As Squadron Commander, she knew that the real weight of this test and the weight of his team's lives rested heavily on him. But even still, she couldn't tell.

Each member of the squadron responded, going down the line. A verbal response was mostly a formality. The craft themselves were in constant communication with each other, relaying status to the commander or anyone who wished to view the information. When Maggie's input came over the comms to relay her response, she also eyed through the communications menu to submit her status through the squadron computer. It took some time to master the retinal selection, but once she did, looking through menus and selecting different items was simple. It made actions like this less time-consuming.

The responses appeared one by one in a portion of the commander's heads-up display. Maggie could see the same screen he was seeing. Once all members had checked in, they all sat in brief silence.

Ramat opened his comm channel. "OK, everyone, begin making your observations." Due to the ships' relativity to each other and speeds, comms links between them were as if they were standing still. They needed to make verbal observations and capture any technical data and store it among the ships. Through the ships' link, they all shared all data, so in the event something happened to a single or even multiple ships, the others would contain that ship's data. Headquarters wanted the pilots to make real-time observations going through the second gate, mostly on how the procedures worked, but any observations were welcome.

They only had a minute to make any observations; at this speed, they would quickly fly past the sun and need to begin their flip and return trip.

Lieutenant Xavier chimed in. "Is it me, or are all the lights gone in the N view?" The N view, short for natural or normal view, displayed completely black screens besides his ship's systems information and seeing the other ships.

"Yeah, that's one of the things the briefings don't prepare you for. The scientists are working on an explanation. They seem to think that when we go this fast, we are no longer visible in the light spectrum. Likewise, lights are no longer visible in our spectrum. At least when captured with our instruments." Charlie responded. The ship's sensors were programmed to detect and show what was outside their ships, which wasn't nothing. It filtered out anything that it deemed noise or a distraction. Scientist discovered that space contained a whole host of things traveling faster than the speed of light, none of which were previously detected. Scientists couldn't provide an explanation for all of this yet. The answers could come later so long as they didn't hurt anyone, and the ships got them back alive.

This was Lieutenant Xavier, or X's, first trip at these speeds besides his solo, along with most of the other flight. He obviously was paying closer attention to the flying and not what was outside his ship during his solo. Along with updated procedures, these observations would inform new pilots, crews, and simulators on what to expect on their first light trip. "I also didn't feel anything, I blinked, and here we are."

"You didn't actually blink, that's just what your mind thought happened." Charlie responded again. He had made the most trips to light speeds out of anyone in the world, as far as anyone knew, anyway.

"Thirty more seconds, internal comments now." Ramat said into the comms channel. Maggie could tell that the boss liked the conversation, but those could trail on for a while. Time was something they didn't have. There would be more once they got back to the debriefing room. Now it was time to focus on the next steps.

Thirty seconds later, Ramat followed up. "One last time, confirm time sync and lock."

Maggie knew this was unnecessary as each fighter's indicators were green and crosschecked with each other, but they performed it again, anyway. There was some noticeable nervousness creeping in. Unsteady and shaky voices broke through the radio communications. This part of the mission was truly a first. A large flight going out, faster than light, but flipping and returning without a main light gate. No one had ever tried something like that before. The sense of inherent danger crept in. Any number of things could go wrong, with the best-case scenario resulting in the death of only one of the squadron members. Worst case, nobody would ever see any trace of them ever again as their bodies, broken up into tiny particles, were accelerated towards the vastness of space, forever.

Maggie checked the schedule, noting the time they finished the last task, which indicated they were early. They were very early. If something went wrong, it could throw the timing of a rescue off. As the safety and test lead for this particular test, it was her job to note any anomalies in the test and also confirm certain steps were complete. She prepared a message to send to Ramat, reminding him of the schedule, when she noticed that her in-flight recorders had been turned off. Hastily, she skimmed through the menus and noticed that everyone's recorder was switched off. She could also see that Ramat, Charlie, and James were in a private conversation. Nobody could listen in. Something was off; none of that last sequence was normal for a test of any kind, especially for one of this magnitude.

Maggie sent a text message to James. "Is something wrong?" the text read.

"Standby" flashed on her screen in response. That didn't help her feel any better. They were creeping up on the next scheduled event. But that didn't bother her as much as what was being kept from her.

They were in the kill box, one of the most vulnerable positions in the mission, and they needed to get out of it. They needed to follow the script. An ambush in this position, however unlikely, would be disastrous. Her mind went to the nuke in her bay. 'Oh shit. Am I going to have to use it.' She thought to herself. The other more likely possibilities of attack remained their furthest point when they transition back to normal speeds and again, as they transitioned to normal speeds close to Earth at the conclusion of the test.

Maggie racked her brain to figure out what could be going on. As she was in the middle of her next worst-case scenario, Ramat came on the comms. "Lucky's. Before we proceed, there is a new feature I recently had installed on your ships that you should be aware of. As you know, under no circumstances are these ships, more specifically, the technologies and pilots within them, to be caught by anyone, friend or foe. As you are also probably aware, the way leadership wants us to deal with that does not sit well with me and does not account for many of the possible outcomes of having a nice big bomb strapped to your ass." He paused to let the nervous chuckles subside. "Under your judgment, each of you has the ability to release the bomb to use as an unguided, unaccelerated nuke. Only detonate that thing inside your ship if it is the absolute last thing you can do."

Everyone understood this message wasn't to leave this little bubble. Besides the fact that they could all see that recording was turned off, this message was in clear contrast to what leadership had instructed and reinforced again and again. Their squadron commander had their respect, and Maggie knew that any of them would detonate that bomb in their bay without hesitation if given the order. Maggie now understood why they were ahead of schedule and went back and removed her note about being ahead, knowing it could potentially trip up any kind of defense if needed. She changed it to say that there was a link outage. Out of the possible worst-case scenarios she was dreaming up, what Trap said wasn't on her bingo card. Even with no gravity, she felt as though she relaxed and folded into her seat once again. Relief flooded her body with the affirmation that her boss had their back.

Ramat turned the recording back on.

With that, Charlie opened a channel to everyone. "Ready to proceed with the countdown to flip. On my mark, three… two… one… Mark."

In unison, each ship conducted a quick flip using their internal reaction wheels and thrusters and were promptly facing the exact opposite direction.

"Maneuver confirmed complete." Maggie said over the comms network.

"Begin deccel number one in three… two… one…" Charlie could not finish counting down because at that moment, the internal light gates began separating from their ships, disrupting the comm links. This time, the light gates moved to the back of the ship. Since they were to decelerate the ship, they would break the ship and crew up from behind and send the light-attached particles backward towards the second gate, against the current direction of travel. Once the light gates reached the rear of the ship, they separated and quickly moved from back to front. The flight of ships vanished and reassembled at a speed just below light speed.

"Deccel number one confirmed complete." Maggie said over the comms.

"Begin deccel number two in three... two... one..." Charlie said, again being cut off. The ships performed the same maneuver again, thrusting them into a normal speed. Everyone knew that this was the most critical time in terms of being a giant target. It took some time for the systems to recalibrate and begin functioning optimally following a transition. They all accelerated to cancel any remaining velocity and to head back in the direction they came from. Now that they were at normal speeds, they were temporarily sitting ducks. As much as a highly maneuverable space fighter could be, anyway. This confirmed their initial theories. Maggie made a note that they needed to change transition tactics and timing in the future, certain many others in the squadron had made the same observation. They needed to fix this tactical disadvantage before the enemy discovered and capitalized on it.

Maggie scanned the area with every sensor she had, quickly switching through different views and relying on her ship's computers to identify any other spacecraft. The tension mounted as the progress bar showed scans in progress that began close to her ship and slowly expanded. As they continued to all come back clear, she relaxed. The space was void. At least, clear enough that if a threat came up now, it would no longer be a surprise. After some brief maneuvering to test that all the controls of the systems were functioning properly, they realigned for their return trip.

They performed the same sequence, this time in reverse, with the plan to use a single light gate to accelerate back to just below the speed of light, and one more to decelerate them back to normal speeds.

Because the return trip only had one acceleration, they would coast for a longer time. As the time approached to set up for the final deceleration with the remaining light gates, Maggie came over the comms. "Is everyone ready to see earth again close up? It's time to button up and get ready for the final deccel."

After a few minutes, the squadron performed the final deceleration as planned. The timing of their maneuvers would put them around thirty minutes away from The Kennedy traveling at normal speed. "Deccel number one confirmed..."

Maggie breathed a sigh of relief. She began searching her screens and having her computer scan the area like she did at the far end of their trip. As she relaxed again, she noticed some bizarre readings. At first, she noticed the lack of friendly ships. The support ships were supposed to be much closer to their location. But there were no signs of them. The results of the distant scans returned. She struggled to make sense of what she saw, and so did the computers. At first, it looked like hundreds, if not thousands, of ships took the place of the dozen or so that were there when they left. Her heart sank as she realized what she was likely looking at. Maggie paused before continuing, trying to grasp what she was seeing. "What the hell is that?!" She muttered out loud, her words trapped inside her cockpit. Her jaw dropped as all the data flowed into her cockpit screens.

As their systems processed more and more data, a chaotic scene unfolded right in front of her eyes. All Maggie could think to say was "Boss, what is going on?"

CHAPTER 6

Riley–Earth Shuttle Landing Pad–Earth

Riley walked around the light shuttlecraft, periodically glancing at the pre-flight inspection steps on his tablet. He moved to the portion that had him checking that all the 'remove before flight' covers had actually been removed by the ground crew. He paused and absorbed the sight. Not just the physical shuttle, but what it meant. He made it. This was a good way to start his first official day of service. As he went through some of the more mundane items, his thoughts turned back to the previous weekend with his family. The sun, still rising over the treetops, countered the cool morning. The heat sped up his checks. He wanted to get into the temperature-controlled cockpit as soon as he could. He had performed these checks countless times, at least that's what it felt like to him, even though he had only been flying for a couple of years.

Atmospheric exit and entry flights were something he mastered while in school. He received his license and that particular certification. Because of this, command granted him permission to fly himself to orbit and dock with his new duty station, the Space Force Guard Ship Minotaur. The SFG Minotaur, also called The Minnow, was the first stop for most new pilot recruits as it was the main pilot training ship in the forces' fleet, hence the nickname Minnow. Nowadays, a skilled ground crew and extremely advanced AI diagnostic systems complete all these checks in advance, so they never catch any problems. Many pilots held on to this last check out. Riley did because it gave him some sense of control over the flightworthiness of his ship.

Riley grew up during the testing phase of some of these craft and read enough stories of things that went wrong because a human pilot didn't do one last check. If only they would have seen a bent impeller that ended up causing catastrophic engine failure. That was an extreme case, but he didn't want it to be him. The newer generation of pilots no longer received training on pre-flight checks, so they were unaware of what they were missing.

Even so, as Riley finished up his self-imposed checks, his work pad dinged, indicating he had a change in the status of his flight. This usually meant that the flight was delayed, so he cautiously checked the message. The message instead read, *Plus one passenger.* "Hmm" he muttered to himself. In all honesty, he had never ferried a passenger to a new destination before. He had only done brief flights up to orbit and back with some of his fellow pilots and even some friends occasionally. He would also do quick docks with dummy stations, intended for that purpose. As the thought crossed his mind that it could be a high-ranking officer or official, he quickly became nervous. But that faded as he thought through that some more. They couldn't be too high-ranking; they would have their own dedicated shuttle.

This was unusual, but his license allowed him to carry passengers so he wouldn't be breaking any regulations. The thought faded even more when he saw who was approaching. As he checked to see the name, a wire-framed young woman in an academy cadet uniform cautiously walked up to him. Her name tag read 'J. Starilla'. If ever there was a name for a space cadet, that was it, Riley thought to himself.

"Anything I can help you with?" The cadet asked Riley when she got close enough, a black backpack strapped snuggly to her back and a black duffle bag hanging from her left hand, freeing up her right for a salute.

Riley looked at her quizzically for a moment. "What brings you on board, cadet?"

"Summer immersion program, sir. I'm going up to The Minnow for the next month." Cadet Starilla said. A few curls of short black hair bounced as she spoke.

"Oh really? Not bad."

"We'll see. I hear it's a barren wasteland right now. Wanted to go to The Spin, but you can't win them all." Cadet Starilla quipped back without missing a beat.

Riley chuckled. "I hear that. She with you too?" Riley said while gesturing behind Cadet Starilla with his checklist.

As he did that, Cadet Starilla turned to see what he was talking about. She quickly glanced at the woman, who appeared to be Riley's age, approaching them. She returned her focus to Riley. Cadet Starilla turned back again, seeming to make sure they didn't know each other before answering. When Riley saw her do this a couple more times and blushed, the cadet finally muttered out, "Uh… I don't know, sir."

Riley noticed her cheeks turning red, as if she was about to get into some kind of trouble. "Don't worry about it. Stow your gear in the cargo hold and get loaded up, we'll be leaving soon."

Riley moved his attention to the woman quickly approaching. She certainly looked like she was on a mission and definitely not a cadet. There was something about her he couldn't quite put his finger on. Maybe it was the confidence she had in her step. Or maybe it was the long brown hair with artificial hints of red and blue that grabbed his attention. She appeared to be a similar age to him. There was one particular strand of red and blue that swirled down past her left temple, pinned between her face and glasses. Her form-fitting jean jacket was unbuttoned with a duffle bag strap, keeping it from flapping open. Riley thought there was probably a term for that type of jacket, but nothing came to mind at the moment. It didn't matter anyway. The chances of him ever seeing her again were slim to none.

"Room for one more?" She asked almost not bothering to stop.

"There's room for fifty more." Riley returned, pausing as he studied her, appearing as if she was about to board the ship. "But only if you're on my manifest. Sorry ma'am, rules are rules." The area was secure, although not strictly for the military. The spaceport was shared and often had crews that mixed between military and civilian for these types of short transports.

"Aren't those things meant to be broken?" She replied with a smile. "Look, if I'm being honest, I am a journalist, and I'm doing a story on the Captain of the SFG Minotaur. He's had a long career, and rumor is he's on his way out. I'm working on a piece to highlight the finale of his career. The process to get up to the ships was taking too long, so I'm down here asking instead."

Riley thought for a moment. Parts of her story could be true, but he also had done his research on the Captain of The Minnow, General Richard Sites, and he was not someone worth putting your journalistic time into. That is unless you were looking into something bigger that involved him, something scandalous. There were plenty of rumors about his off and on-planet ventures. He didn't want any part in releasing that story. "Nothing I can do, sorry."

At that moment, his pad dinged again. As he looked down, he saw another name added to the manifest. Not at all surprised, he read the name Jennifer Stanza.

The corners of Riley's mouth curled into a smile as he let out a chuckle, realizing she had played him. "Ms. Stanza I presume? Welcome aboard." She was on the manifest all along, biding her time until it got pushed to his handheld pad. Something about her attempt intrigued him. She technically didn't break any rules by asking and clearly had the drive to get what she wanted. The idea of having a contingency plan suggested an intelligence level above most. Or she enjoyed messing with what she thought as an easy target.

Her gaze dropped to the floor. Her jaw muscles clinched, drawing her lips into a straight line. She got caught.

She spoke again. "Sorry about that, I put in the request but wasn't sure it was going to get approved in time, or at all. I had to at least try."

Riley thought for a second, all with an amused smile on his face. He realized he probably looked confused and silly. He shifted his body and straightened his back, adjusting his posture before speaking again. With a reassuring tone, he said. "No problem at all. Just do me a favor next time. Don't apologize."

"Thanks, Lieutenant McCovee." She said as she looked at his name tag, reaching at and bending it up towards her so she could read it better, even though she could probably read it just fine.

Her confidence had clearly returned as she strutted up the lowered ramp, with Riley following behind her trying to avoid glances up the ramp in her direction. He kept his eyes glued to his pad while walking up, almost tripping as he acted like there was something important he needed to be checking on. It impressed him she understood the different ranks, even if she poked his uniform as she read his nametag. 'Stanza' he thought to himself. Her name rang a bell, but he couldn't quite place it.

Riley decided that finishing the checklist only opened the door for more last-minute changes to the flight schedule and manifest. No, he just wanted to get out of here.

Closing the ramp behind him, Riley made his way to the flight deck. Before he got there, he stopped at the passenger bay to make sure his two misfit passengers were getting situated. He also preferred to give a little pre-flight briefing in person instead of over the intercom if he could.

On this shuttle type, the flight deck rose above a winged box structure, sitting on top of the world with sight lines of the vehicle below. The smoothed edges helped with heat dissipation and aerodynamics but also gave it a more aesthetically pleasing look. The passenger and cargo bay extended below and to the rear of the flight deck, with some additional cargo and passenger space to the front. The reentry surfaces all had removable heat dispersing covers. They were replaced after multiple return trips to be refurbished, but for the most part reliably held off the heat of reentry once the ship needed to return to earth.

As he made his way to the cargo hold, he noticed the reporter helping Cadet Starilla into her flight suit and seat, currently working on the zipper portion of the suit. Riley made a mental note to tell the instructors at the academy that they should include some basic flight instruction for its cadets prior to them going on trips like these. It surprised him that the cadet actually asked. Or he assumed she did.

He glanced at his manifest again. Jade Starilla and Jennifer Stanza. Maybe Jennifer offered to help the cadet. Usually, nobody asks, and they end up screwing it up and getting hurt. He had seen instances of broken limbs because of being strapped in improperly or blacking out if the flight suit, which acted like a high-tech G-Suit, were to be worn incorrectly. The flight suit was fairly simple to don, essentially a super high tech adult version of a baby onesie, feet and all. It was also similar to that used by fighter pilots on the spaceships, although the primary concern and design consideration of these suits were to minimize the effects of acceleration G-Forces and safety in case of cabin depressurization.

Riley walked up. "What can I help you with?"

"I think we're good here." Jennifer replied as she finished and Jade sat down. She turned, looked at Riley, and gave him a quick smile before returning to her seat.

"I'm assuming you know how to get yourself in?" Riley more or less stated, implying that because she could help the cadet, she could also help herself.

"I should be just fine, thanks, Lieutenant McCovee." She replied as she returned a slight smirk.

"Riley is fine, Ms. Stanza."

"Jenn." She said, reaching her hand out.

They shook. After a brief awkward pause with Jade looking on, Riley muttered half under his breath, "I better get started with the safety briefing." And pulled it open on his tablet. Jade blushed as if she was watching a romantic comedy movie unfold in front of her eyes.

Ignoring the awkward looks and pauses, Riley began telling them about the safety features of the ship and their flight plan. "We have multiple options to reach orbit. Today we will be taking the mag rail followed by boosters to get us the rest of the way. Jade, can you tell me why we can't just use the mag rail?"

"Yes sir, the magnetic rail launcher can get things into orbit on its own, but not humans. The acceleration would be too much and would kill us."

Riley noticed the confidence in her voice. She seemed knowledgeable, but also shy around people. "Very good. We don't want that. OK. Now for the suits. When you see the lights turn green in the bay, helmets on until I say otherwise. There is a slim chance that we have a decompression event, in which case, these suits will save your life. Also, stay buckled up. We'll have an opportunity to float around if you want but otherwise, we're headed straight for the Minnow." He used the nickname for the Space Force Guard Ship Minotaur. "Any questions?"

They both shook their heads from side to side.

"OK then, buckle up and we'll get going." Riley said and turned to walk up the stairs to the cockpit.

As he strapped in, he commanded the auto sequence of the main computer to warm everything up to operating temperatures and pressures. The ship navigation computer also began communicating with the launch site computer. This process was mostly automated with minimal human input.

An automatic tug drove over and began the hook-up sequence. Riley came over the onboard intercom system. "Attention in the passenger bay, this is your pilot speaking, make sure you're still strapped in, we will begin the tow shortly. If you need any help, hit the call button on your armrest." Riley rarely announced the tow portion because the imperceptibility of the movement, but with a cadet and civilian onboard, he didn't want to take any chances of one of them getting hurt.

By the time Riley had donned his suit and strapped himself in, the flight computer had completed the remaining checks. He looked over the passenger compartment vid screen and could see that Jenn and Jade had also finished buckling up.

They were parked directly on top of the launcher tube

elevator and began a slow descent. They built the Mag into the ground to assist with the structure, security, and the removal of air from the initial tube. Riley looked out the cockpit window and couldn't quite see over the dynamic nose cone of the sled. That would take the brunt of the air friction as a combination of ship and sled made the transition from the vacuum tube to the outside atmosphere.

At the bottom of the lift, Riley could hear cracks and bangs. He knew this was the sled locking into place, and the tube they were about to slide through had begun the process of being depressurized. A countdown timer showed on nearly every display in the cargo and passenger areas, with a single countdown display on the flight deck. This was arguably the most dangerous portion of the flight for passengers, as the g-forces could cause serious damage to anyone not properly strapped in.

As the countdown reached zero, a click followed by a loud bang. The bang was the sled magnetically locking into the tunnel track as it was being released from the lift locks. Riley didn't notice the smooth acceleration at first, but the force grew rapidly. The seats were pivoting in conjunction with the flight suits squeezing and releasing, moving blood to different parts of the body as needed. They were in the tunnel, underground for what felt like a few minutes, but was actually less than one. The ride was exceptionally smooth, and the only sounds Riley heard were the creaks and cracks anyone would expect from a large ship. Anything that wasn't fully strapped down made its way to the back of whatever compartment that it resided in. The faint sound of wind built outside the ship as the tunnel transitioned to atmosphere. The transition had to be a slow transition because a sudden impact with the atmosphere from a vacuum would be fatal for most ships. If the ship managed to survive, the people inside likely would not.

Once the sled and ship transitioned fully to atmosphere, there was another short period of acceleration to reach the required speed. There remained a limit, again mostly because of the length of the tunnel and the ship's cargo, how fast a sled could get going in a vacuum and then transition to atmosphere. The principle being similar to that of a rocket taking off from a launch pad. It must deal with the forces of maximum dynamic pressure. The point of maximum dynamic pressure could crush a rocket like it could crush this ship if not accounted for.

Riley came on the intercom briefly. This wasn't too strenuous for him, mostly because he had done it plenty of times, but the transition could be a little nerve-wracking for anyone new to it. "We are about to finish the transition to full atmosphere and start accelerating again. It's going to get a little louder and rougher." His attempt at trying to calm them could have landed on deaf ears, as a loud bang and rumble made it feel like they were going to get ripped apart. He scanned his console to make sure all systems were still optimal. This was the last time they could abort and still stay on the mag rail for a rapid deceleration. Once they crossed that threshold and the acceleration took back over, if something happened now, he would have to perform an emergency landing.

Everything checked out, and they were ready to keep going. Riley could feel the vibrations from the ship hit a peak, which meant they were in full atmosphere now. His thoughts were confirmed when he noticed the acceleration picking back up along with the outside noise.

Unless you were an experienced crew member, it was nearly impossible to notice the transition from the Mag to free flying. Riley could tell, but he could sense every change being at the controls. There was a feeling of being let go as his body floated forward inside his suit and restraints ever so slightly. A moment before the solid rocket boosters lit up, Riley thought that it might have been a good idea to warn them about this as well, but that time had passed.

It was peaceful one moment, then with a huge kick, a sudden roar thrust them back in their seats, and they were on their way again but with an intensity unlike before. Riley loved that feeling and thought it would never get old. With the boosters igniting, there was a clear kick and more rapid acceleration, although not as pronounced as with the Mag, it felt raw and dangerous. They were, however, quite safe and reliable, being one of the oldest used technologies in space flight. Riley let the autopilot perform the next maneuvers, but he followed along with his manual controls. If something happened and the computer got disengaged or there was an issue, he wanted to be able to take control right where the computer left off.

After the boosters had been firing for some time, Riley began the starting sequence of the main nuclear engines of the shuttle. He typically started them a little sooner than the computer did, which the procedures allowed. This gave them a slight delta-v increase, or increased speed, and made sure the thrusters were working optimally before the solid boosters burned out and separated. This gave him more options; he liked having options.

When the boosters finally burned out, Riley felt a noticeable calmness throughout the ship. The pop of the separation of the boosters reverberated for a few cycles, and all fell silent again. Riley checked the trajectory and began making slight course corrections with the onboard thrusters to intercept The Minnow. Riley made the course corrections with cold gas thrusters mounted all around the shuttle. The firing of the thrusters went unnoticed. Riley instead noticed the rotation that the thrusters imparted, and again, the stopping of the rotation when the desired direction was reached. As he was doing this, Riley turned off the green lights in the cabin and came over the radio. But this time, he turned on their in-helmet microphones and speakers. He didn't like them on during launch because he didn't want any distractions. He relied on the call buttons if something went wrong.

"I'm starting to line us up with an approach to the Minnow. If you're not feeling well, please use the bags. Bonus points if you turn your mic off first."

The minor movement during this phase oftentimes led to most travelers losing whatever meal they had most recently eaten. There was a large enough disorientation that the brain and inner ear couldn't quite come together on a decision about what the hell the body was doing in relation to gravity. Then the brain would question, 'wait, where did gravity go?'. That's about when the helmets would come off, and the barf bags would come out. Luckily for Riley, these two seemed to have strong stomachs or the good sense to turn their microphones off before sharing their pain with the rest of the flight.

At that point, Riley came over the intercom. "If everyone wants to take a look out your window, you will notice that we are in space. Our maneuvering is done for now. We will be rendezvousing with The Minnow in about two hours. Enjoy the view." He quickly came back on the intercom. "If you need anything, you know where to find me."

Riley continued to monitor the ship and the radar. He had a small window up front, but that was mostly for emergencies in case the real-time video screens went down. Those vid screens could envelop the entire flight deck if he wanted, giving him a real-time view of anywhere outside the ship. He preferred to see out the front, but would occasionally swing a couple around to see different things around him, depending on what was going on. He had the forward ones on and a couple on the side for now to help with docking when the time came.

That's when the radar readings caught his eye. There was something off about them. There were way more ships on the scope than he expected. He double checked the status of the radar and the readings again. It should be the Minnow, some maintenance shuttles, and maybe fighters. There could also be some other transport shuttles like his.

What he currently saw looked way more chaotic. More traffic than all spacecraft put together condensed into that smaller area. The Space Force Platform Kennedy, or the Spin, should not be in view yet. But even so, that wouldn't account for what he saw on the visual display. Once he zoomed in as far as the cameras would allow, it didn't show a much better picture. His heart sank. There had to have been an accident of some sort. The data he saw made more sense if he considered an accident as the culprit. But that didn't explain why the Minnow looked much smaller than it should. He tried to piece together all the information and also build a picture in his mind like a puzzle to see if any of the floating fragments could make up the missing Minnow. That's when he noticed that there were several other large radar returns that his computers could not identify. The amount of debris couldn't be accounted for by the ships in that orbit alone.

His hands flew over the controls, pulling for any information he could to make sense of what he saw. There was a lot of debris and unknown ships in the area, which was the only information he had. The only conclusion that came to mind now was that there was some sort of attack. His mind tended to go in that direction. Whether it be his military training or upbringing. Only time could decipher what he saw now. Until then, he operated on that assumption.

He came back on the intercom, trying to sound calm even though he didn't feel it. Although he did feel oddly prepared for this situation. He had no question that he not only needed to do something, but also that he felt he could do something. "Everyone get strapped back in and stand by for maneuvering, there's been a change of plans. There's something going on out there."

CHAPTER 7

Ramat–Advanced Individual Maneuvering Shuttle–Earth Lagrange Point Four

All the Lucky's displays lit up with errors and warnings of new uncategorized debris, incoming distress signals, threat warnings from unknown ships, and impact warnings from debris along their flight path—the list went on. They had never seen so many different flags on their displays and flashing lights. There were some that they didn't even know about.

Almost nothing that Ramat saw was in the preexisting database of ship and debris locations. Ramat called the systems and sensor officer, Captain 'P' Parrant, to ask him what he could see so far. As the sensor officer, Captain 'P' Parrant focused more on analyzing what all of the ship's sensors were showing at any given time. Right now, Ramat felt overwhelmed with all of the data and needed someone to help him sort out what he saw. "P, what are we looking at?"

P replied quickly. "Sir, from the limited info, it appears that at least two ships have suffered explosions. They are venting atmosphere and are broken up. The Kennedy is one of them but looks to be intact still. The Mino looks to be in pieces. I am detecting at least three ships that aren't in our database in close proximity to the wreckage. They are their own ships, not more debris. Some of them are massive." Essentially, he didn't know what was going on, and someone or something looked to be destroying their fleet.

Charlie, his second in command, spoke up too. "If we are seeing it now, it means it happened a minute ago–it all looks pretty new." Since the Lucky's test took them out past the sun and back again through the orbit of Mercury and Venus, everything they were seeing would have been old and unreliable. The delay was because of their relative distance to the action. They reemerged far from the Earth Light Gate at Earth Lagrange Point Four, or L4, like they were supposed to, but even the gates were not close enough to the ships to get real-time data. The primary reason for the gates being far away made it so some catastrophic event with the Light Gate or ships re-entering normal speed didn't cause additional damage to space infrastructure.

In this case, one-minute old information would have to do. Things in space happened much slower than they did on earth. They wouldn't be arriving for another thirty minutes if they accelerated to their maximum speed. Ramat decided that if thirty minutes wasn't enough time to come up with a plan, no amount of time would be enough. He needed to think fast, but he needed to help the earth's fleet as quickly as possible. This put their ships close to their theoretical speed limit of one hundred seventy-five kilometers per second, or about 0.05 percent of the speed of light. This gave them time to assess the situation and come up with a plan.

Ramat didn't want his squadron to let their imaginations wander, nor did he want them to think he was frozen, so he came back on the nets. "Alright Lucky's, it looks like we may be up against some unknown attack. We will remain in a tight formation until we are fifteen minutes out, then break off into our four flights. I will identify targets for each flight as we get closer. We each have a free gliding nuke and your centerline guns, check the status of each." There were two centerline guns mounted down the center of thrust on the AIMS. These Gatling guns fired short bursts with an impressive rate of fire. They also had a large caliber incendiary cannon that had a low rate of fire but good accuracy at a larger range. This one had the ability for limited guidance and maneuvering built into the ammunition.

All AIMS reported back that they were ready to go. Ramat and Charlie opened a private chat with each other. "What do you make of this, Wisp?" Ramat said, with concern in his voice.

"It's hard to say. This isn't like the southerners to pull this off. I would rule out a terrorist attack because of the size of those unknown ships. No way a terrorist cell could build something like that without anybody knowing about it. It's definitely an attack though, the area of effect is way too big for it to be a collision or accident. Maybe someone's been building a force up by the outer light gates? There's not a lot of traffic out there. I just don't know who would do that." Charlie responded.

"Agreed. I want you to lead flights three and four and go straight for the two big ships on the inside orbit. I'll take flight two, and we'll go after the three ships on the outside orbits. Use one or two nukes right off the bat, released from a distance, and stand back. Ready your cannons for any small ships we may not have seen yet and prepare for a fight. Also, only comms between our squadron until we have opened up our attack. We're not sure what kind of intercept capability they have and if they even know we are out here."

"Roger that, sir, we'll get a battle plan worked up. Are you sure about using the nukes?" Charlie responded.

"No. But with the size of those ships, it's the weapon with the best chance. Be ready to shut them off just in case it's not what it seems. We should get some comms traffic by that point to see what's what."

"Copy." With that, the AIMS began flying towards the fight at maximum acceleration.

Charlie began issuing orders en route and had the different flights perform different assessments and simulations. They were trying to gather as much information as they could to determine the best course of action.

Over the next few minutes, they settled on a plan and were almost ready to execute.

Ramat came over the squadron comms one last time before their attack runs. "Lucky's listen up. We do not know what force we face, or what their capabilities are. But we have trained for every possible scenario we could have, and if I know anything, it's that you are up to the task and absolutely the right people for this job. Fly smart and kick some ass."

Ramat received a series of confirmations on his display that each fighter had accepted their orders and was ready to execute. The presence of smaller fighters remained unknown. Only the five large ships occupied the space around their home.

The four different flights broke off, changing trajectory to match that of their specified targets. On the inner orbit, Ramat could see flights three and four tracking towards the larger ships. He could see that they had locked their targeting on. After that, the connection was too weak to get consistent information. He had to trust that they had everything under control. Now it was time to focus on his flights and his tasks.

Ramat sent the commands to each of the ships in his flights. Ramat tasked three fighters from each flight with releasing a nuke on the three ships ahead. That meant there were two nukes per ship with two nukes in reserve.

"Flights one and two, P and I will launch ours first and target the farther ship. We want all six to impact at the same time. We don't know what their capabilities are, but we aren't going to give them any advanced notice. They may move out of the way if they detect the other ships getting hit. Get ready."

The computer on his fighter initiated a countdown. When the timer reached zero, his nuke released. He could see on his screens that there were now two nukes away. The second timer reached zero a few seconds later. Now there were six nukes coasting towards their unsuspecting targets.

"Looks like they're all away clean." James said over the comms.

"Flights, short reverse thrust, let's give them a little space." Ramat ordered, making sure everyone knew they needed to back off a little and create some distance between them and the bombs. The explosions of the nukes in space would be devastating, even with their relatively small size. Nothing has a good chance of standing up against the physical blast within close proximity, but it would be the debris cloud and Electromagnetic Pulse, or EMP, that it created that caused Ramat the most concern. Ramat assessed the risk of creating even more debris and decided that it didn't make much of a difference, given how much was already out there. The priority now was to hit back at whoever did this and make sure they couldn't keep on attacking.

The Lucky's plan relied on the fact that all five ships had remained in stable positions and had not moved outside of their predicted orbits during their observations and approach. Ramat's flights were all right on time. He couldn't tell yet if flights three and four were as well. Small course corrections from the nukes were possible with some built-in thrusters, but Ramat was not counting on using those. If their trajectories were off, it was because the big ships had changed orbits, and the nukes would not be able to compensate enough for that.

The sensor readings and comms traffic they had received up to this point continued to solidify his assumption that there was an ongoing attack, and that those big ships were an enemy. They also could tell that the fighter squadron and support ships that were supposed to receive them had hightailed it back towards the Kennedy to support the fight when news of the attack reached them. But they were destroyed once they arrived.

Ramat didn't take his eyes off the sensor screens. He was waiting for some indication that the nukes had impacted their intended targets. The time approached when he should have seen his nuke hit the farthest ship. The clock ticked down in the lower corner until it finally reached zero. Nothing happened. He waited a few more seconds. Still, nothing happened.

"P, do—" Ramat was cut off. Ramat's sensors, along with his screens to the outside, showed him two stunning bright flashes of pure white light. He had his answer. He continued to see secondary explosions that were less dramatic, but still as rewarding. His screen registered two more bright white flashes of destruction where the other two ships had been. It took a little longer for that information to make it to his ship because of the distance.

"We got four impacts. Both missed on the far ship; looks like it maneuvered just before impact. It must have gotten a warning as the nukes passed by the first two ships." James said to the two flights. "Still no sign of smaller fighters."

"Copy, P. Everyone keep an eye out. Target the remaining

ship as we get closer. It knows what we can do now, let's try the centerline cannons. Save the last two nukes in case more show up." Ramat responded. He didn't let it faze him that one evaded his attack. They got most of them and were hunting for the last one.

"Sir, I just got another reading. It looked like that last ship went through a light gate." James said quizzically, speaking directly to Ramat.

"Like a portable light gate? I didn't think anyone else had those." Ramat responded.

"Not exactly, the signature is different, but that's the closest thing I can think it is." James responded. After a brief pause, he continued. "It's gone. No trace of it at all, not even disposable light gates."

A stunned Ramat looked on. How did it do that? That moment passed quickly; however, there was a lot of work that needed to be done.

The Lucky's, on a high from destroying four of the enemy ships and sending the fifth one running, accelerated in to do some more hunting. When they flew closer, they couldn't see any smaller ships, and the larger ones had fragmented into various pieces, releasing what appeared to be atmosphere, water, and fuel.

Ramat opened his communication channel for a wide dispersal. "Kennedy Station, this is the Lucky's commander, we are clearing the area of threats, prepare for rescue operations." Based on the devastation he saw, they would need to look for survivors, if there were any.

CHAPTER 8

Riley–Space Force Shuttle 1703–Earth Orbit

Still horrified by what he saw, Riley changed course so that he no longer headed directly towards the now-destroyed Minnow. When he did that, he saw four flashes of white light. His sensors dulled them out so as not to shine too brightly to his eyes on the monitors, but he knew they could be only one thing: nukes. As the telemetry continued to stream in, he received radiation warnings, confirming what he already knew. The warning levels were low, and the ship had been hardened for that, but it made going out of the ship a much riskier endeavor if it ever came to that. The radiation levels would be dangerous to anyone out there without a proper protective suit. The emergency evacuation suits had minimal hardening for radiation, and that protection didn't last very long.

This gave him an idea. With all of this damage, there certainly had to be people that got thrust into the vacuum of space, ultimately to their deaths. But there also had to be some that had warnings and could get their suits on in time. He had a cargo and passenger ship, which was currently empty and could comfortably fit fifty more people. A limitation imposed for seating restrictions due to leaving the Earth's atmosphere. Now that he was already in space, he could transport at least double that at a time to transfer them to another orbiting platform.

Riley checked his fuel status. He did some quick calculations in his head and decided that there should be enough to get him to the debris and rescue some people. He should have enough fuel to get back to a ship, if there was one to get back to. At least the people would be safer inside his ship than floating out into space. He took stock of the ship, checking what equipment he had onboard and what its status was. There were only two Extra-Vehicular Activity or EVA suits that were designed to operate out in space and also had thruster packs on them. Technically, he did not hold an EVA certification, nor did he have any training doing this kind of activity, but he didn't think anyone would be checking. Plus, he knew he could do it. He doubted there were going to be many people in a position to help find survivors this quickly following, well, whatever the hell this was.

At this time, the ship received automated alerts from Earth, calling for a mandatory return to the surface. This was followed by some frantic-sounding space traffic controllers that were Earth-side, simultaneously telling him to come back and also asking what happened out there. Riley sent a quick response to the Earth controller but did it only via text. He didn't want to get into an argument that would waste valuable time. His mind was already made up. "Cannot return to Earth, performing search and rescue. Don't know what's out here or what happened. Going comms out." He ignored all future calls from them. There was no way he was returning to Earth right now.

He went over to the ship's comms. For the first time, he

realized that he had internalized everything, trying to take in everything going on his own. He had forgotten that he had other passengers. They either chose to turn off their mics or remained frozen in silence as they tried to access whatever information they could on their personal devices. He took another second to collect his thoughts and come up with a game plan. He needed to have it together when he let the other two know the situation and his plans to deal with it. "Cadet Starilla, Ms. Stanza, please make your way up to the flight deck as quickly as possible." He unbuckled and went to the bottom of the now-useless ladder, to make sure they were making their way in his direction. This would be much easier to explain when they could see what he was looking at.

Once they all got to the flight deck and strapped in, Riley began going over the situation. "There were four near-simultaneous explosions, here and here." He pointed to the screens depicting an overhead view of the local orbit they were entering. "They were definitely nukes of some size. Before that, though, there was a lot of destruction, including the Minnow. That ship is in more pieces than before it was built. Which means there are probably survivors. We're going to go over there and start searching. The next closest ship is the Kennedy, so we'll take anyone we can find there." He paused, hoping they would not object. He looked over their faces. Jade appeared to be focused. She had a look that she was trying to figure out what role she could play in whatever happened next. Jenn had a similar look. They did not look frozen, rather they were both processing the information they just received and figuring out their part in dealing with it. That was a good sign, Riley thought. "Cadet Starilla."

"You can call me Star, for short, if you want." Jade Starilla replied, trying not to be awkward.

"OK, Star." Riley couldn't help but smirk in his mind, even

in light of the situation. That would prove to be a difficult nickname to live up to. But if she had a chance, now would be the time to prove it. "Do you have any free space extra-vehicular activity training?"

"First time in space, so this should be fun." Star replied. "But I have about 500 simulator hours with this ship, well, the model before it, but its capabilities are pretty similar."

"Ok then." Riley replied. "I'll have you at the controls when I go outside. We'll fly in and search around, looking for beacons or any movement that could be a person. We'll get up close and bring them in through whatever airlock makes the most sense at the time." He knew Star didn't have any real-time flying a ship, but the simulators were so close to the real thing nowadays that he wasn't actually too concerned about leaving her to fly the ship with him outside. She would mostly perform station-keeping activities, keeping the ship still or maneuvering it slightly to get a better position amongst the debris. Typically, the computer could handle this task, but with the number of debris, it would likely not allow the close approach that he was planning.

"Jenn." When she finally pulled her head away from the screens and towards him, he continued. "I need you up here in this middle seat. It gives you the best view. You can take these screens, and these controls." He grabbed a set of monitors that were attached to a long arm and lowered them down around her as she sat in the center seat. They wrapped around her in a semicircle from side to side and up and down. He handed her the controls once the screens were in place. "These controls are pretty straightforward. This button zooms in and out, this button will rotate to look in a different direction. You have a 360-degree view. You can also hit these buttons to change to different cameras and filters. This camera will show heat." He switched to the thermal imager. "It may not work well depending on what is going on around, but it might come in handy. People in suits are almost always going to be a different temperature than the surrounding debris and space."

Jenn began messing with the controls and getting a feel for them, catching on rather quickly to their functions.

"We're going to get moving. This ride is going to be a little sportier than before, hang on." Riley said as he pushed the throttle up. They began heading for the wreckage of the Minnow.

Their original trajectory would have taken them about an additional hour to get to the Minnow, but with Riley's plan, he would cut it down to around 15 minutes. He accelerated hard.

"Why aren't we going right towards the wreckage?" Jenn asked as Riley steered a couple of degrees away from the wreckage from their perspective.

"Because when it's time to slow down, we'll have to turn and burn as hard. If we go right at them now, our exhaust will point right at them when we slow down. If they weren't already dead, they'd be barbequed after." Star clearly had studied and probably even practiced these types of maneuvers in a simulator.

"That's right, Star. I'll correct our velocity in the other direction, and it will make sure we don't blast anyone but also keep the debris as calm as possible. We should stop right next to any survivors." Riley added. Even so, it was easier said than done.

They were under several G's of acceleration for what seemed like forever, but in reality, only minutes passed before they flipped and repeated the process. Riley used the small control thrusters mounted all over the ship for fine-tuned control of where he wanted to go.

On the approach, Jenn spoke up in the flight deck. "I think

I see a lot of movement over here." She pointed to the main monitors. Riley manipulated his controls and zoomed over where she directed. It seemed to be dozens of people tethered together. Movement meant life.

"Nice work. We'll head there first."

As they made their way there, Riley began to unbuckle and head down the flight deck towards the cargo and passenger bays. He shot over his shoulder to Star. "You have the controls."

Star gave a questioning look, squinting and cocking her head, as if she was saying 'no shit'. That look quickly turned into an ear-to-ear grin. Riley could see a flood of emotions over her face as she seemed to become certain of herself and capabilities. Time was of the essence, the confidence she now radiated helped him let go of any reservations he may have had. Now she had her chance, and he thought she was ready for it.

"Copy that, I have the controls." Typically, an instructor pilot would be on another set of controls, ready to take over at a moment's notice. The current situation would not be that forgiving. Riley decided when he made the plan to trust Star. For all the shyness and relative inexperience, confidence was not an issue right now. The initial suit incident was the only thing that gave him pause, but Riley quickly shrugged that off. They all had the right intentions and he wouldn't want to be a part of an organization that could have any negative judgement against their actions today.

"I'm going to open the back. I'll close this airlock, but make sure you don't take your suits off." Riley said, closing the airlock behind him. There were a series of airlocks on each ship. The ships were compartmentalized, allowing people to survive in other areas of the ship in case of a hull breach until rescue arrived or the problem was resolved. It also made it so you didn't lose all the air on the ship each time you needed to go outside if you weren't able to pull the air out and save it. That was less of a common event these days, but it used to happen a lot, so crews had to carry enough oxygen to replenish the ship multiple times. This cut into the weight and size of allowable cargo, which usually translated into lost revenue.

Riley made his way down to the cargo and passenger compartment. He began cycling the air out of the bay, removing most of the atmosphere. He opened the rear door before the cycle was complete. The last molecules of air always took the longest, so he decided he could spare the air, but not the time. The remaining air left the bay with a rush and a brief hiss. Silence surrounded him. He pushed a button on his inner thumb to talk with the shuttle. "Star, spin the ship and begin approaching with our ass towards them."

He donned an EVA suit over his current suit by climbing into the back and putting his helmet through the open hole in the head. His main suit would provide the initial safety against the lack of atmosphere, and the EVA suit provided extra radiation protection along with a mobility jet pack to make it easier to get around. But it was not a sealed suite, so it provided no extra protection from the lack of atmosphere. He pulled straps on the side that closed the back up. With no time to figure it out right now, he noticed it didn't get as tight as he remembered they should get from training. He could control it with controls embedded into the thumbs and base of the pointer finger. This allowed him to still grasp objects while controlling his movements.

"Got it." Star took the controls, and as if she had done this a hundred times in real life, she expertly controlled the ship into a spin, stopping with the rear of the ship facing the survivors as she began simultaneously backing up towards them.

Riley took the grappling cable from inside the ship and instructed the computer on it to give him free slack so he could take it out with him as far as he needed. "I'm headed out, keep it stable." As he did this, he gave a slight sigh of relief at Star's first maneuver. She did good, and he knew he had made the right call. He could have interjected and tried to tell her how to do it but didn't want her to think he wasn't confident in her. Riley always leaned towards trusting people, and it paid off.

He flew out of the rear ramp as the ship sat suspended in space, dancing ominously around the debris. The survivors floated some twenty meters away now, all tethered together. Riley could see there were many more than he originally thought. It was going to take several trips. He searched quickly for what looked like the end of the line of tethered survivors. He figured the first ones out were probably the least familiar with everything, visitors or family members, and the last one out was probably in charge of that chain. As he was looking, someone caught his eye, waving frantically. 'That's got to be who I'm looking for,' he thought to himself and made his way over to the one flailing around.

When he arrived, he pressed his helmet up against the individual's and spoke. The helmets would transfer the sound waves into the other helmet. It was difficult to hear but was the only means of communication. He could only make out bits and pieces.

"I'm Captain… get me out of… hurry u…" The unknown voice gasped.

Riley decided to press forward with attaching him to the cable and hauled them in. There were about fifty people attached to this first string. He could fit more, so he mentally prepared to go back out. Slowly, he started reeling in the long string of spacesuits as they snaked along their route. He couldn't go too fast, or else he wouldn't be able to slow them down to catch them once they got into the bay, or they would whip around the ship and hit it hard, probably injuring themselves. As soon as everyone was on board, he instructed them to take seats and stand by, and they would leave shortly. As he turned to leave, someone grabbed his arm. While spinning, he caught sight of the angry face behind the faceplate, which was yelling something. Riley pointed to the comms station on the side of the bay where the two could speak by pressing small devices into their helmets. He didn't tell the man that Star and Jenn could also hear this conversation and were probably listening.

Riley heard an angry rant of nonsense for a few seconds before cutting in. "Sir, I cannot understand you. Who are you? Speak slowly and clearly."

"I am the damn commander of the Minotaur, General Sites, and I demand to be taken to the SFP Kennedy immediately."

"General Sites, I'm here to rescue you and anyone else I can fit before returning. And there are more people out there that need our help. I can fit more, so I am going back out. After that, then we will head to The Spin." Riley responded, trying to remain calm. Could he really want to leave the rest of the survivors there, his crew?

Riley added, "If there is some piece of critical intel that you need to pass on, we can do it through the ship."

"You will do no such thing – I must go now. I order you! The fleet cannot risk losing me." General Sites stated.

Riley could feel his blood boil. He could feel his face turn red as he clenched his fists. Would his short military career end now because of how he might handle this situation? How could a leader be that willing to abandon his people for his own skin? He hoped Jenn was listening and would write all about this. That last comment also made it clear to Riley that there was no intelligence that he had that would be immediately beneficial, or else he would have relayed it. So no, they would not be racing back so that this general could tell the SFG Kennedy a ship had destroyed his ship. There was too much at stake now with the remaining survivors, and this little tantrum, while wholly unexpected even from someone with Sites' reputation, did not help the situation.

With that, he removed the comm device, motioned that he couldn't understand, and turned and pushed off out the back of the ramp. He didn't have time for this. He quickly returned to get more survivors. His EVA suit was out of thruster propellant. Because he was the only one qualified on the manifest for EVAs before he launched earlier that day, it was the only suit ready to go. It would take too long to recharge it. He silently cursed himself for not thinking of that. He quickly removed the EVA suit and hooked it to a charging station and hooked a couple more up so he didn't run into this problem again. His own flight suit would work well enough for the short amount of time he would be out there. He put on a smaller strap-on thruster pack and headed to the airlock.

As he left, he spoke to Star. "Star, seal the hatch to the flight deck and don't let anyone in. Do you know how to block controls to the ramp?" Riley continued when Star confidently nodded her head. It looked like she already knew where he was going with this. "Good, don't let anyone mess with them, especially the General."

Riley floated down the ladder and back out of the airlock.

The next batch of people was much more difficult to get to. Riley thought it would be impossible, but he had to try. The ship couldn't maneuver any closer without risking serious damage to the ship due to the scattered debris. There was nothing for the stranded personnel to grab onto so they couldn't move to a better spot. Riley was low on maneuvering thrusters in his own suit and was counting on being able to use the tether to pull them back in. When he reached the end of his line, only ten meters separated him and the rescue of the next survivors. The body floated, unmoving like the others.

Riley thought it was a female because of the size of the suit; however, it could have been a smaller male. It mattered little at this point. He couldn't get to them, but they needed his help. As he looked down the line, he attempted to catch someone else's attention, but he observed that most of them appeared to be unconscious, too. He had to do something; he had to think of something. He wasn't sure what state they were in, but they needed help. Though he seriously doubted his thrusters were strong enough, he could try unhooking and pulling them back to the tether. He probably didn't even have enough fuel for that. His display showed only two percent fuel remaining.

When he moved around looking for something that could help the situation, a piece of metal the size of a softball that was floating nearby caught his eye as it went behind him. He was sure it was going to narrowly miss him, so he didn't try to twist out of its way.

A jolt resonated through the back of the suite when the debris had just passed. It had hit him. Softly, not hard enough to cause any damage, but enough to cause him to spin slowly. As he turned, he saw the same piece of metal floating off in a different direction. For some reason, the debris smacked into him anyway, hitting a protrusion on his back. Everything happened so fast; he knew he must have forgotten a few checklists. It also explained why his EVA suit was a little tighter than he remembered it being. He wore, like most shuttle pilots, a supersonic parachute attached to his flight suit in the event the shuttle had issues either during take-off or re-entry. The prospect of using it also scared Riley, so he never thought about it. But he could use it now. If he deployed his parachute, it might be long enough to attach to the end of the tether and reach the group of survivors.

He made a decision. He unhooked the tether and held it in his hand as hard as he could. As he did that, he took off his EVA suit and attached the tether to his flight suit and his EVA suit that was now floating shapelessly at the end of the hook. As he pulled the ripcord on his suit, the parachute slowly unfurled. He needed to help it the rest of the way because it didn't have the air resistance it normally would to assist it in fully unfolding. He disconnected the tether from him and attached the end of the parachute riser to the tether and the other end to himself. These parachutes only had two risers that fanned out near the parachute, so he couldn't connect more than the two risers together like he had. Riley attached the tether from the ship to one riser, extending the parachute flat in a way it wasn't intended, and attached the other riser to himself. It certainly was a unique sight to see, probably comical if the situation had been any different. He scooted along carefully to try to reach the closest unconscious person, hopefully still alive. When he got close, within arm's reach, he suddenly stopped. Once again, he found himself unable to reach. He looked over his suit for anything else that he might have missed. He saw his ripcord from pulling the parachute hanging by his side, still attached to his back. It was long enough if he attached it to the end of the parachute, it might work. He checked to make sure the ripcord wouldn't continue to get pulled out of its holder. It would have to be strong enough, at least until he got back to the parachute. After a powerful tug and it not budging, he trusted it would last for at least a few seconds of strain. His concern with fully unhooking now would be that the parachute would accordion back away from him, and he wouldn't be able to get back to it.

He quickly disconnected the riser and parachute combo attached to him and added it to the end of the ripcord. There was a convenient loop at the end of the ripcord, usually for someone's hand to pull, which worked perfectly for hooking in to. He slowly continued on the next meter until he could reach the closest person, floating motionless. He grabbed ahold of the arm, able to discern feminine features through the foggy faceplate as he pulled her to face him. While not completely trusting the strength of the ripcord, he pulled her closer and attached her belt to his harness before reaching for the parachute. He thought it was strong enough for him to pull all of that weight slowly, but it was too risky to have the winch pull them back in with that. Once he got to the parachute, he held on and commanded the tether to retract.

He returned with twenty-six more people about fifteen minutes later. Riley noticed a lot of commotion in the passenger bay. This was a new experience for all of them, and they were bound to have some questions. Hell, he had a ton of questions. He wanted to talk to all of them to figure out what they knew. They were trying to talk to him. But right now, in this moment, he needed to get them to safety, and he needed to reassure them that he was going to do that.

Riley didn't want to risk taking his helmet off so he spoke through his suit into the ship's intercom. "I know everyone is confused and probably a little scared. It seems that whatever those ships were that attacked are gone for now. We destroyed some of them, and at least one of them retreated. We need to get to the Spin as quickly as possible. Some of you are hurt badly. Anyone that is able to stand, help everyone else into a seat and strap down. This may not be the smoothest ride, and if I have to maneuver, I want everyone as secure as possible." He didn't know what else to say.

There was no way that he was the highest-ranking one

there, but he was the pilot in command of this ship. Everyone else had also gone through a traumatic experience and their mental state couldn't be completely trusted right now, as evident by the general. He could only imagine what they were all going through. He didn't hold it against any of them, except maybe the general. He hoped that his assessment of there being no more enemy activity was correct. They would be sitting ducks with unsecure passengers in the bay.

To his surprise, Sites was strapped in, ready to go. He didn't expect him to give his seat up or help the rest of his crew, but at least he wasn't waiting by the flight deck hatch. As he made his way to the flight deck though, he noticed that Sites was trying to unbuckle. He quickly cycled the airlock and closed it behind him, locking the controls, before Sites could get there. He made his way up to the flight deck and strapped himself in quickly. He made an announcement. "Everyone, hang on, we are going to start maneuvering out of the debris and make our way to the SFP Kennedy. Estimated time of arrival is approximately one hour. Please keep helmets on and suits pressurized in case of an emergency."

Star turned to Riley after he sat down and looked at him quizzically, "What happened there? You have an accident with your backpack?" Star asked Riley, glancing at his back that had a mess of cables and an empty slot where she thought a parachute usually was.

"Oh, that?" Riley responded. "I had to use my parachute and ripcord to reach the last group. I'll tell you about it later."

"Nice. Well, okay then, Ripcord. Looks like we got you a new callsign. Or maybe just Rip, I haven't decided what sounds better yet." Star replied.

Riley sat there, stunned for a moment. It had dawned on him, and there was no way that Star knew, his grandfather had a callsign of Ripcord, who they also called Rip for short. His mind flashed back to walking up the road by his house with his grandfather. He had to pull the ripcords of his team before it was too late. He froze. He wasn't quite sure how he felt about that connection. After a brief moment, he decided that what he had done would have made his grandfather and his parents proud, and so the new callsign was a good omen. Maybe it was the passing of the torch in a way. Riley noticed Star staring at him with a confused look, obviously waiting for him to respond. "Oh, yeah, that could work." He didn't know what else to say at the time. He did know that he needed to get moving again though.

As he made his way out of the debris field, Riley began contacting the Kennedy approach controllers. "SFP Kennedy, this is SFS 1703 with seventy-six survivors rescued. I need a place to take them. Are there any open docks there?"

A response quickly came over the radio. "SFS 1703, this is the Kennedy. Did you say seventy-six? Yes, we have a dock, docking bay three, make your way directly there."

"Copy, docking bay three. Affirmative, seventy-six survivors. SFS 1703 out." He purposefully neglected to tell them about Sites; he didn't feel like he needed the special treatment they would likely give him. He would have used his name to get a dock spot though if they turned him away.

"Wow, they are giving us a bay – that will make unloading everyone much easier." Star responded.

"Is there another way to get on and off the Spin?" Jenn responded.

"We could have gotten a docking port, which is what I expected. It would attach to the side door, and we would have to move everyone one person at a time. Civilians don't usually have to use ports, so not many know about them, but troops usually do." Riley said back.

"I guess I'm not too surprised then. They know we have

injured people, so it would be hard to get them off through a small door. Plus, the bays are all pressurized, aren't they?" Jenn replied. Riley could tell she knew more about the ships than she let on, or maybe he wasn't paying attention at first. Now that he thought about it, she seemed to make her way around the shuttle pretty well, and all of that maneuvering didn't faze her.

"That's right. They are also in the hub where there's no spin gravity, so it will be easier to move everyone out. This would be an absolute pain in the ass to get everyone out of here on the float." Star said before continuing. "Rip, I'll keep a lookout for debris along our route."

"Got it. I'm almost done plotting a course. I'll have to fly manually the whole way – there's just so much debris." Riley responded.

There were a few tense moments in the cockpit as Riley maneuvered around some debris that previously went undetected or was moving too rapidly for his sensor to pick up. There were moments of downtime. But Riley didn't let his mind wander. He had to stay busy and focused on what he was doing. People's lives depended on it. He couldn't get lazy or tired now. While Jenn and Star took turns checking on the passengers, Riley kept an eye on his instruments. Whoever was in the cockpit with him kept the conversation going. It was the best way that he found to stay alert while teetering on the edge of exhaustion. It was mostly mental fatigue at this point.

"What do you think we'll do after we unload everyone?" Jenn asked as they drew closer to the Kennedy.

"I'm not sure what they'll let us do. I'm going to try and go back out." Riley responded as he tweaked the controls one way to better line up with the docking bay.

The cockpit was silent from that point on.

When Riley landed in the bay at the Kennedy and lowered

the rear ramp, he came over the comms. "All passengers make your way over to the starboard airlock, it's lit up now, and exit calmly. The Kennedy crew will instruct you where to go."

After a few moments, he made a call to the bay controller. "This is SFS 1703, can I get a refuel? There are a bunch more people out there that are going to need help ASAP."

A voice came back over the intercom from inside the Kennedy's bay tower control room. "Affirmative. While you wait, you're requested to come up to the bay tower."

"Copy, on my way." Riley replied. That was strange, refueling didn't normally take too long, and while he could make a trip to the tower and back before they finished refueling, he had not experienced this before and didn't want to waste time.

As he unstrapped and headed down, he spoke to Star and Jenn. "Jenn, this might be a good time for you to get off. Star, I could use you, but if you want to get off now, you can."

They both shook their heads. "We aren't going anywhere. You know you can't do this without us, we make a good team. Besides, I definitely don't trust you two without me, alone, in a confined space, for hours on end." Star responded with a laugh. Jenn nodded yes, also with a laughed. She struggled to cover up her blushing. They all laughed together.

Without knowing what else to say, Riley kept talking. "Alright then, sit tight. Go over some of the data from that area and see if you can find any more spots where survivors might be holed up." Riley responded. Seeing that he wasn't going to persuade them otherwise, he thought he might as well give them something to do. As he headed to the cockpit exit, Jenn reached out and gently grabbed his arm. Since she was anchored to the seat, Riley's body twisted around. He fought to find something to quickly grab before he collided with her. He stopped himself with his face inches from hers. They both stared at each other for a moment. He waited for her to say something.

"Thanks for keeping me on. I know you could kick me off if you wanted." Jenn whispered softly, looking into his eyes.

"Star is right, I wouldn't be able to do this without you." Riley responded but quickly added, "both of you, you know." Blood rushed to his head, causing it to turn red. He didn't want it to seem like he was coming on to her, even though he was. He felt like she was doing the same thing. And apparently it was obvious, since Star already pointed it out.

"I'll be right back." Riley raised his voice a little louder this time to make sure Star heard, even though from her reaction to the whole incident, she could hear everything already. As he turned back to leave, he glanced over his shoulder one last time to see Jenn looking back at him. Relief that they would stay together for at least a little while longer.

Riley made his way out of his ship, grabbing onto handholds along the floor of the path until he reached a closed doorway on the inside of the bay, outside of his ship. There, he grabbed a personal propelling unit from the wall and clamped it onto a cable labeled "tower" in big red letters. The device was small enough to fit into his hand with a strap that attached to his belt. With the push of a button, a small electric motor began slowly flying him along the line towards his destination. The line ended on the outside of the door to the tower control room. As soon as he entered the dimly lit square room, he saw General Sites yelling at a colonel. He couldn't tell who the Colonel was from his angle; there were some rows of monitors and crew members trying to ignore what was going on. He didn't want to interrupt, so he kept to the side by the entrance. After a few seconds, Sites quit yelling, glared over at Riley, and tried to grab hold of something to push off of so he could make his exit. It would have been intimidating had he not been flailing around, trying to grab onto something, as if this were his first time in space. Even the head turn to give Riley a hard stare threw him for a spin that he couldn't compensate for. It was difficult—exceedingly difficult—for Riley to hold back a smile.

He caught the last of what Sites was saying. "That pilot better be cleaning out the toilets for the next three months if you know what's good for you."

Riley acted like he couldn't hear what was being said and stood at a rigid attention with his eyes glued to the opposite wall. He had to hold on to the railing with one hand to keep from floating away. Once Sites fully exited the tower, Riley breathed a silent sigh of relief that he didn't turn to him to finish getting out his anger. Once he collected himself from narrowly missing his first ass-chewing, he saw the Colonel looking at him with amusement and spoke up. "Sir, you wanted to see me?"

Colonel Archer turned towards Riley gracefully. "Sorry you had to see that, Lieutenant. If you didn't guess it, you're the pilot that's on toilet duty for the next three months."

"Sir?" Riley replied, stunned. "I know I went a little off course but figured for sure rescuing people would have been a valid excuse."

"Relax." Archer replied. "You're not in any trouble. He'll see the bigger picture when he calms down and probably forget about it by the time he gets to the chow hall. He's just flustered, or something like that." It came across as if Colonel Archer was trying to explain or defend the General's conduct, like he had done it before. 'Or something like that? That guy's a jackass.' Riley thought to himself.

He must have telegraphed the thought across his face. Archer spoke up. "Not a lot of people get along with him, but he was where he was for a reason, and his ship was just destroyed. That's gotta be tough on anyone." He paused. "Now for the reason I brought you up here. Between you and me, nobody knows you're a rookie pilot that's not even qualified in anything useful. But also, between you and me, with the pilot shortage we have now, we couldn't get anyone else to fly that thing. Lord knows we need to get back out there to get more people. Are you up to the task? I'd love to go with you if it weren't such a mess out here."

Without hesitation, Riley responded. "Yes, sir! I marked at least a hundred more people, and a few potential sites where they could be holding up. I sent out the locations to the Kennedy's main computer."

"Good. Your skills impressed me—you're doing us proud out there. I'm sorry I don't have anyone else to give you. Go get as many people as you can." Colonel Archer replied. "And take as many trips as you can. We don't know what we've gotten into, but something tells me it ain't over yet."

"Agreed, sir. Is there any news on what happened yet or who did it?" Riley asked.

"Not much yet. But word over the waves is that it came out of nowhere, and intel doesn't recognize any of the ships." Colonel Archer said. Letting the news sink in. "We have AIMS out doing patrol, so you shouldn't have to worry about getting into any trouble. Our fighters are what kicked their asses in the first place. I have a feeling that enemy isn't in any rush to go up against us anytime soon. Dismissed, Lieutenant."

Riley made a mental note that there were probably AIMS out doing patrol when they were first attacked as well, and that didn't seem to deter the attackers. He filed that away to look into when he had time.

"Well then, sir, just between you and me, some of the piloting was done by a cadet and the observing was done by a reporter." Riley said. And with that little bombshell, Riley spun and exited the tower. As he did, he noticed a brief grin out of the corner of Colonel Archer's mouth. *These must be desperate times if the Colonel does not care about that. Or maybe the Colonel thought he was joking.* Either way, Riley already left to make some more runs.

The single long day turned into two, almost three. When all was said and done, he stayed awake for well over forty-eight hours. He and Star would take turns taking naps on the out and backs while they were searching for survivors. They ended up rescuing over six hundred people scattered through the wreckage. Some survivors found pressurized compartments inside the remaining large chunks of the ship. Those were hard to detect, but Riley got some techs to tune his sensors to pick up the faint signals within debris. One hell of a first day, for all of them. The last batches of survivors were extremely hard to find and get to. Riley couldn't go on any longer, even though he knew there had to be more out there. He would get some rest and get back at it the next day. Before exiting the ship, Riley, Star, and Jenn all looked at each other. Hardly able to stay awake, there was a shared sense between them that their lives, and way of life, had changed dramatically forever. They made their way to a hub where some makeshift living spaces were thrown up in the spin gravity. Spare bed sheets hung from the ceilings in the corridors, providing more privacy than he expected. Riley, Jenn, and Star found a section that had a few free cots next to each other. There were only two other cots in their section, and both occupants were fast asleep. Riley could only imagine what they experienced today. Star picked an outside bed, leaving Jenn and Riley next to each other.

Star looked over at Riley and Jenn, already looking half-asleep, and said, "I can't stay awake another minute, you two have fun. But nothing too crazy, I'm still right here." With that, Star laid down and rolled away from the two of them. Riley thought she was already asleep by the time he and Jenn could respond.

Riley let out a quick, subdued laugh. "Sleep well, Star." Riley sat down on his bed; he picked the one on the other side, leaving Jenn with the bed in the middle. Jenn didn't sit down on her bed, though; she sat down next to Riley. Riley looked over at her. She was looking down at the floor, but slowly raised her head, and as she turned to face him, their eyes met. Riley didn't know what to do. With a clear sense of purpose, he knew what he wanted to do. He wanted to kiss her. He didn't know why he was so sure that's how he felt. But with everything going on, was it right? Was his breath okay?

He didn't have time to finish that thought. Jenn gave him the answer he had hoped for, leaning in to kiss him. It wasn't long, but it was enough to make him feel like everything was going to be alright. They hugged and held each other close. Jenn squeezed him like she didn't want to let him go. In that moment, Riley wished she wouldn't.

When they finally released, Riley looked at Jenn and noticed her eyes were watering, a single tear rolling down her face. She matched it with a smile.

"Is everything okay?" Riley asked.

"Even with everything going on, I'm allowed to be a little happy." Jenn reassured Riley. She wiped the tear away and stood up, still holding the smile. "I'm not sure what I'm going to do tomorrow, but we should probably get some sleep."

Riley nodded. He wished he could stay up later with her, but his mind and body would not let him. Riley laid down on his back, trying to reflect on all that had happened. As he drifted off, Jenn laid down next to him in his bed and put her arm around him and her head on his chest. They both drifted to sleep.

Riley woke up and looked at his watch. About eight hours

had passed, at least he thought that much time had passed. He didn't quite know what time they finally went to sleep. The memory of Jenn sleeping in his bed remained, an empty space now occupied by her absence. He looked around and didn't see her belongings, either. He saw a small, folded square of paper on his pillow, though. It had his name on it. Upon opening it, he examined the bottom and discovered that Jenn signed it, with a heart written below her name. Taking in every word, he slowly read the brief note, continuing to stare at it long after finishing. He reached in his chest pocket and took out the picture of him and his grandfather when he was little after their fishing trip. With a smile, he folded the note and put it along with the picture back in his chest pocket.

Commotion down the hall snapped him back to the present. He walked over to Star, who was still asleep, and nudged her awake. "It's time to wake up. Let's get some food and head back out." Riley said when she finally rolled over and looked at him. There was more work to be done.

CHAPTER 9

Mark—World Council Delegation Room—Earth

The entire committee in the Northern Hemisphere sat in the World Council Delegation Room. All one hundred of them, including aides and experts, sat crammed into the room, glued to the projectors on all the walls. There were reporters aimlessly trying to decipher everything going on. He had a hard time blaming them; with no data yet, nobody had any clue. Earth-based observation decks had picked up some explosions and some of the craft, but they couldn't identify who had done it. Each country pointed their fingers at the other within the Northern Hemisphere Nations, or the NHN. There had been some attempts in the past for other countries in the north to gain the upper hand and try to gain control of the alliance. But ultimately, they pointed their fingers towards the SHUR. Everyone was conflicted in believing that nobody in the NHN would be this careless and attack the collective NHN. But they also didn't feel that the SHUR had advanced enough capabilities to cause this level of destruction. The chaos currently going on in the World Council Delegation room reflected a subset of what was happening all over the world. Fear gripped earth. They were getting supplies, hunkering down for what looked like an all-out war that could follow. The looting and riots didn't take long. The lack of information did nothing to quell the unrest. Times were going to be tough, no matter what happened next.

Mark DeCanus periodically checked his phone. The ambassador had sent a message to Ramat D'Pol. Partially to see what was going on up there, but mostly to check and make sure his old friend was okay. Mark knew that he was in space at the time of the attack with his fighter squadron but had not heard from him since the event happened. He was worried for him but tried to keep it out of his mind for now; that wouldn't help him. Besides, Ramat was probably incredibly busy dealing with whatever had happened.

"We must stand strong against this attack. We must strike back on all fronts." Rictor Inagru, a representative from a small section of North America chair of several committees, shouted over the reporters on the screens.

"We don't even know who did it yet." Mark shot back, annoyed at Rictor for jumping to such a quick conclusion.

"This could be nobody else. The reports show that the SFG Minotaur was destroyed while the SFP Kennedy did nothing! General Sites thankfully made it safely on board the Kennedy. He should take over command!" Rictor replied, shouting again at the end of his remarks.

Mark replied, "Sites has no business being in charge of anyone. The only reason he got that ship was that it hadn't been fully operational yet and because you sold your soul to get him appointed there." The Minnow just began its pilot training mission, its sole purpose. Using his position and clever convincing skills, Rictor aided in Sites getting an appointment to the rank of Brigadier General. As Rictor planned it, there were no open one-star general positions, so he had one created as the commander of the SFG Minotaur before anyone even knew what was going on. There was an ongoing investigation into the matter, but it would not even matter by the time the final report got complete. There was not much to warrant his meteoric rise up the ranks, other than connections. General Sites was just a pawn in Rictor's secret agenda.

"Be careful there—you're the one that keeps on wanting to cozy up to the enemy. Maybe you're the insider? How else would the SHUR have known that the Minnow was defenseless? Only a handful of people knew that most of our AIMS were out on a test mission." Rictor snarled back as he leaned towards Mark with a menacing glare in his eyes.

Mark remained calm. He knew that this might get the attention of some of Rictor's truer, and gullible, followers. If Mark didn't play this right, it might even convince some that might be on the fence on the issue to side with Rictor.

"The SHUR are not the enemy here." Mark responded. He felt his phone vibrate in his pocket and heard a quiet ding. He checked it, eagerly awaiting word from Ramat. Instead, he saw the brief message from Jennifer Stanza. A lapse of panic at remembering that she had left to stay on the Minnow for a week quickly turned to relief knowing she was at least alive.

Mark, I'm OK up here. Working on the cleanup effort and figuring out what the hell is going on. It was NOT the SHUR. We saw some structures that were unlike anything we've ever seen. I'll keep you posted on anything else I find. -Jenn

Mark tried to decipher what it said. As he studied it and put the message in place with the other information he had, a picture formed out of the chaos. He was glad she was doing OK.

"The SHUR are not the enemy here." Mark repeated, louder and more confidently. He also used that time to gather his thoughts as they came to him. "It's verbal and physical attacks against the SHUR that will get us in more trouble than we can handle."

He briefly paused. Enough time for them to focus on him and think about what he had just said. But not enough for Rictor to interject. "Based on what evidence we have seen so far, and based on our wargaming, the SHUR would not attack in this way." Mark knew it wasn't them, he couldn't put his finger on it until this last piece of information from Jenn came in. There was something nagging at the back of his mind that was telling him that this could not be the work of the SHUR. Sure, they were getting bolder and had some advantages in space, but not that much. Not anywhere near to the extent that the world had witnessed.

Mark decided that this was his time. It was time to make the boldest statement that he had made so far in his career. He believed he had the evidence to back up his claim and the path forward to making a more unified world. There would certainly be opposition from Rictor and his followers. But from everyone else, when they heard and saw the evidence themselves, everything would become clear.

Mark dragged his chair to the middle of the floor in the stateroom in the most dramatic fashion he could and stood on it. He shouted out, "IT WAS AN ATTACK BY AN ALIEN SPECIES!" In an instant, he could only hear people shuffling to turn and look at him. This was the first mention of anything like this and the surprise in the room felt raw, and also sincere. Even the media, where wild claims were a regular occurrence, had not peddled this theory yet. Humans had looked for so long without discovering alien life that they all but gave up. Everyone figured it was because they were alone and so put the thought out of their mind that anyone would ever discover aliens.

He continued, a little softer now that he had everyone's attention. "It was an alien attack. It's the only explanation for the technology that we witnessed and has been reported on so far. As tragic as this is, We must not squander the opportunity to turn to the SHUR for open negotiations for peace and help. We don't know what we're dealing with here and could use all of the help we could get."

"You just want to use this to spin the same terrible plan you have been for years. To 'unite the world!" Rictor's hiss turning to laughter as he made the statement, holding up air quotes. His tone became more serious. "The only thing that will come of this is we join the enemy that caused the destruction we see now, and then become them. You're too blind to see that."

As both sides processed these two thoughts, arguments erupted throughout the room. Time is all that could calm them down. Mark, happy that he had introduced his idea, stepped down from the chair and began walking to the exit. He knew it would now be the center of discussion and would likely come to a vote in due time. He needed to go get more details on the attack and make sure he was right.

It was peculiar for him to think that not that long ago he was told that his grand idea of a unified earth was impossible because it required an alien attack to succeed. Now that event had occurred. The wheels in his head had never turned faster. He had been thinking of this day for many years now, when he could finally execute a plan. He struggled with the conflicting emotions of the cost of this event happening. The loss of life, although unknown right now, would be great. He didn't have any control over any of that. He decided he could both be upset and grieve for the events that took place, but excited for the opportunities that they presented. It was finally time.

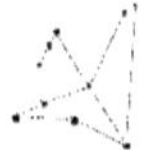

CHAPTER 10

Ramat–Space Force Platform Kennedy–Earth Orbit

Ramat had never witnessed this type of destruction before. The scale and magnitude were unmatched with anything he'd seen in his career. He sat in the small briefing room with a dozen or so high-ranking officers aboard the Spin. SFP Kennedy had been painstakingly moved back to earth orbit.

Ramat received a summons to attend a closed meeting discussing the damage assessment of the attack. They did not allow any staff or other personnel to enter, which was a departure from past protocol. It was another in a long line of briefings and debriefings that Ramat had been involved with since this whole ordeal started. They were running together. Between the briefings and flying patrol sorties, he was not getting enough rest. He knew that if he wasn't, neither was his squadron.

Ramat got the feeling that this briefing was going to be a little different. As they flipped through some new, close-up pictures of the wreckage, a new theme become clear. People down on earth and on the station, including Ramat, had guessed they were alien ships, but there was no actual proof to back it up.

These new pictures were telling a different story. The first picture was a shot of one of the larger chunks that remained after a nuke hit that ship. The shape seemed odd. The sheen and color of the material were unfamiliar to him. He couldn't quite place it, but something was off about it. It was a dull, dark gray that had small spots that were more polished than the rest.

"Did the explosions cause the metal to look like that?" one of the other officers asked, cutting off the intelligence officer who was giving the briefing.

"We thought that at first." the Intelligence officer responded. "There didn't appear to be a pattern until we looked closer. The shiny spots move and shift around, changing shape and size. It looks like they move to areas that are damaged and it starts to repair itself. It didn't seem too different from what our ships do until we saw larger chunks that came into contact would merge and start rebuilding the ship. At least that's what it looks like."

That drew some gasps from the room. Ramat knew his ship could repair minor damage from micrometeorites or other debris impacts, but not fully reconstruct itself. That had to be a new technology for Earth.

"That's just the beginning." the intelligence officer continued. Ramat could see a grin on his face. Ramat got this faint feeling that the next bit of news they got was going to change a lot of things. This intel officer had a secret he was about to share, and it was going to make a self-healing ship seem like nothing.

"When the unknown ships arrived, they began firing what is believed to be immensely powerful energy weapons."

"Their range must not have been very long because they

didn't do much outside of a few hundred clicks." Another officer said. Ramat assumed he was on a ship that was hit or watching from the Kennedy, which came out relatively unscathed. The Kennedy was about a few hundred kilometers from the center of one cluster of ships.

"That's correct. There was a whole lot in that range, and what they did hit, our armor didn't stand a chance. Some of the ships were civilian, as you know. What we are still working on is how they got to that specific spot with no portable light gates and no receiving light gates. They were in a perfect stationary orbit and didn't maneuver at all when they showed up. There was about a ten second pause before they started firing. Our intel says that there are no human ships or technology capable of doing that." That was not new information to Ramat, or anyone else in that room, for that matter. But Ramat knew this was building up to something. 'Freaking get to it.' He thought to himself.

"At first, we didn't think these ships could have come from outside the solar system. Our sensor system covers all of that and they didn't pick up anything."

"Captain." Ramat said to the intel officer, trying to be polite, but his patience was running thin. "I believe you are building up to something—it's better if you just get it out in the open."

"Yes, sir." The intel officer replied.

"This is the part where you tell us they are aliens." One of the other officers said with a laugh.

The intel officer took a deep breath and swallowed hard before switching to the next picture. They magnified a dimly lit cutout section of the ship chunk they were looking at before. In what looked like would have been a crew room, a body floated. A body, by all accounts upon first glance, shared traits with a human. It had a similar shape and size. The body was covered in a pale blue sheen of ice, making it difficult to determine the color.

"What are we looking at here?" Ramat asked. He could start guessing what it was, but he would rather the intel officer tell him.

"The torso and arms appear to be similar to human, there is one less finger on the hands. They are slightly shorter in stature. We haven't gotten one back into a lab to analyze its biology, but it clearly cannot survive in space without a suit. The atmosphere those ship pieces have been venting is similar to Earth's. As you can see, the legs appear to be more like a horse leg which suggests a world higher in gravity."

"Just say it." another officer in the protested. A chorus from the room quickly echoed the sentiment.

The intel officer switched to the next slide. A closeup of the face. "This is not a human body. This is an alien."

The questions were being thrown out in shotgun style, not even waiting for a reply. The room grew loud with lots of confusion. What did this mean? What does Earth do next?

After some time, when the noise seemed to settle in, Ramat spoke up to silence the room. "Quiet, everyone, quiet." He commanded the room with his voice and reputation. "Captain, do you have any other information for us? We need to start getting the word out before Earth starts tearing itself apart down there looking for the culprit."

"Yes, sir."

"Please continue." Ramat said. He needed to get what information he could and get it back to his people. His leadership, none of which were in this room, probably already had a version of this brief, but that didn't stop him from making sure everyone had the bigger picture.

The intel officer continued. "We know one ship escaped. The good news being, there were remnants from two large ships that we are meticulously going through to find out everything we possibly can. Which is exactly what had been ongoing for the last couple of months. After a closer inspection of the ships and their systems, it is abundantly clear that these ships are in no way of human design. The first body we discovered is being transported to a lab on a science ship being protected by the Kennedy and a flight of AIMS at all times. The forms were crystallized. Their outer skin that was visible appeared to be covered in short hair with flat, almost Neanderthal-like facial features. These are not your little green men with large heads we all grew up with." He added to try to lighten the weight of the information he delivered. "Because it is starting to get out that it wasn't another human country doing the attack, we have signed initial agreements to allow all nations, including the SHUR, to conduct inspections and share findings. There is a common team made up of each hemisphere's members. We also have another independent team conducting their own research led by Tobias Sinclair."

That got Ramat's attention. He knew Tobias; they shared the same close friend and were becoming friends themselves. They were both busy and working in different parts of the world so that made it difficult. But Tobias was a genius, Ramat knew. Each wanted to be the first to find and reverse-engineer a breakthrough. The north currently had a vast advantage in space travel because of the light gates, which the SHUR were still trying to master. In exchange for the SHUR providing much of the material required to make the light gates, the north allowed them to utilize the gates for science missions. The agreement did not include delivering the secret of how they worked.

Everyone involved with the recovery operation was on edge to begin with. After all, an alien species finally revealed itself and the first contact had been an unprovoked surprise attack on humans. The citizens of Earth were in shock, most of them outraged, but all of them scared. The headlines ran non-stop about a potential follow-on attack, or guessing when it would be, or that they would wipe Earth out. As if anyone knew the answer. How people on Earth were taking the news was something that he had seen little of. Ramat only focused on the military operations that he could control. He made a note to talk to Mark DeCanus when he got a chance. Mark would have a good feel for how civilians took to the recent events. This was no longer science fiction, so people immediately fell back on the pop culture they grew up on in books and movies. 'What else did they have to go on?' Ramat thought. The recent events had just proven the premise of almost all science fiction alien invasion movies.

Because there was a threat from an alien species, and there was a threat from other countries, each nation and the SHUR felt they needed to provide an armed military escort for the science ships inspecting the wreckage. There were at least five heavy military ships, along with the associated fighter spacecraft, that remained in the area at all times for each side. That was in addition to the civilian crewed science vessels. Military crews augmented the science teams on board to deter anyone from trying to capture the ship if they made a discovery. This only added to the tension because now the civilians that were focusing on the alien wreckage also had to be concerned about being killed. With tensions this high, a whole new disaster was one misunderstanding or one missed flight assignment away.

There were questions needing answers, a lot of questions. The leading question currently being who was the attacker? Because humans had short of given up hope of finding an alien species in any timeframe they could comprehend, they had not set up a real surveillance and defense network against such a threat. They would have to reconsider that point now. Ramat was among the team that was going to be looking into how to do that based on the little information they now had.

They also did not prepare their forces for this kind of attack. Most of the manned military vessels were located at L4. This was in part because of the increased desire for the use of the main light gate located there and a loose agreement among the members of the world that if a major conflict or accident were to occur out in space, they didn't want it clogging up an area near Earth.

Ramat recalled how Tobias Sinclair had begun his career, or fame depending on which article he read. He remembered Earth had nearly gone through complete launch shutdown decades prior. A collision in low Earth orbit between two satellites caused it to quickly spiral into many satellites. As the debris built up, the cloud became more difficult for satellites to maneuver around it, and impossible for new launches to take off safely. The brilliant mind of Tobias shined during this period. He made an ingenious breakthrough as a young teenager. Maybe he was younger, Ramat couldn't remember. It was almost Greek mythology at this point, since about thirty years had passed. After his inventions removed nearly all debris, he became world-renowned. It was actually a combination of multiple inventions and innovations that allowed him to solve this critical problem. The most substantial one was arguably the high-power laser system he designed. He set up high-power lasers around the world at ground sites which would fire in coordination at passing by debris. Over the course of a few hours, a small piece of debris in Low Earth Orbit could be de-orbited, while larger pieces or whole satellites took a little longer. The idea wasn't completely novel; it just hadn't been successfully attempted on this scale or in this particular manner. The trick came in the power storage and generation as well as phasing so that the lasers weren't affected by the atmosphere. Tobias himself developed new principles that formed the basis for his storage techniques and power distribution to the laser networks. These principles allowed the laser network to be working nearly non-stop on various pieces of debris orbiting overhead, while not completely draining power. It exceeded expectations. That got Tobias the funds, which led to some of the greatest inventions of the space age. From the modern hull designs and propulsion systems of many manned spaceships to the AI systems found on almost all computers. He was the one in charge of the initial assisted magnetic rail launch to space. He wasn't just the head of the company that created them, he was typically the most knowledgeable about them as well. His deep understanding of their inner workings, limitations, and the different purposes they can be re-utilized for made him the most knowledgeable. He was not an in-the-box type of thinker.

However, setting up the Space Force away from Earth to protect it from the destruction caused by humans engaging in space warfare with each other left Earth vulnerable to outside attack. There were many plans and policies that would need to be updated with this revelation, Ramat thought. New military tactics would need to be developed based on what little they now knew about this supposed enemy. New alliances would need to be formed. More importantly, what did humans do next? The answer to this question, the response to this attack, would likely be the single most important decision humans ever had, or ever would make.

CHAPTER 11

Danuibi–Center Staat Capitol Building–Razuud

Leader Danuibi got a faint sense of déjà vu as he sat at the head of the table in the Center Staat building. Not unlike he had on that fateful day so long ago. Yet he could still remember pieces of the attack as if they had happened yesterday. The city was well underway with rebuilding and healing from the tragedy that occurred. New construction replaced the sounds of crumbling dirt and buildings during the months and years in between. In place of fear and sorrow, there was now optimism and sometimes even laughter. The Razuuds were a resilient race and Leader Danuibi was proud of that. The war in orbit with the Tartins had also continued. Relentless attacking and defending. It felt the wear and tear on his mind and body. He struggled more and more with each day to do the simple task of getting out of bed. He needed answers and a path forward.

Shortly after the attack from space on his city, Razuud Intelligence Center determined the trajectory of the incoming attack and mapped it back to where it likely came from.

Factoring in galaxy rotation and orbital mechanics, they were not expecting the answer they got. A distant star system appeared to be the source. Leader Danuibi and his council deciding on sending a scouting mission to inspect the faraway place. The intelligence report suggested it was likely a hidden Tartin base. The scouting mission had returned, and they had unexpected news.

To maintain a sense of control and power in his world, Leader Danuibi decided to continue holding meetings at the Center Staat building in Rutaun. The memory of the streaking bright light and impact was still vivid in his mind. Even though it had been cleaned countless times, the room still felt dusty. That feeling may never go away. Not all the windows had been replaced yet. The metal slides blocked out all light and the view. The leaders seemed to like no view at all; it was a sense of comfort for them. But the leaders' presence on the surface remained important to portray calm amongst the workers. This particular meeting was with all the leaders, as before, but with the addition of General Drobbi, the commander of the failed expedition, to find the source of the attack on their planet. A seat for the General would not be found; he would be left to stand for this meeting. Leader Danuibi glanced over at Leader Darnwich. His arms were trembling and his legs were bouncing in his seat. He looked upset. He was stirring in his chair, uneasy with the briefing he was getting from the ship commander who had returned from the scouting mission to the distant worlds.

"How could this have happened?! There is no way that they could have been able to enact that much damage on us. We needed those ships to return!" Leader Darnwich was yelling as loud as his voice would carry. He was also using the amplifier built into his seat.

Leader Danuibi motioned for silence. "We need to hear the

account so we can make the proper decision moving forward. I'm sure the general was well aware of the need for those ships, but we were all also aware of the risks of sending them out. A point that General Drobbi made perfectly clear, but you supported still going out. Please, continue General Drobbi."

General Drobbi had a blank stare. He wasn't looking at anyone in particular, but through them. It was hard to tell if he was nervous or still reeling from losing most of his fleet in what was supposed to be a reconnaissance mission. Leader Danuibi wanted to show his support, but it only went so far as to get the truth. If the truth wasn't a good story, his support would end. He knew General Drobbi personally and trusted his judgment. He was hand selected for this reason. The outcome, as unfortunate and unexpected as it was, could have been much worse. General Drobbi's family's reputation was on the line and a poor outcome like this could have terrible consequences for them, including exile to the distant tunnels. Living was exceedingly difficult out there. Starting with the center of the city, supplies and resources were distributed, making their way out to the edges. The further from the center someone lived, the harder it was to acquire any resources and to have a job that could afford those resources. Closeness to the center was a status symbol as well. Leader Danuibi was now glad that he opposed this excursion, citing the danger of losing too many ships that were needed at home.

He knew that General Drobbi was also glad he opposed it. This could save him from that exile, if not from also losing his entire command. "As I was saying, Leaders, when we returned to relative speed, we were in the middle of the enemy ships, surrounded. They somehow knew we would be there. We were a quarter orbit away from the originating world of the terrible weapon. We believed we could get the intelligence we needed and return before we were noticed. Instead, we had to immediately go on the attack and fight our way out while we waited for our power to recharge. We caused massive destruction to their fleet, but then out of nowhere..." His voice trailed off. Still shaken by the near-instantaneous loss of three-quarters of his people under his command, he struggled to find the right words. A heavy burden for any commander. Almost a thousand lives, lost.

Leader Danuibi noticed the grief. "General, after your ships gloriously sacrificed themselves to allow your safe return, what else did you notice while you were there? The ships on the images don't look like anything we have seen from the Tartins fleet."

"Correct, Leader." General Drobbi spoke up, hesitating as he cleared his throat and mind. "They looked like an entirely new model. Their structure was well different. If you look at the images" General Drobbi motioned to the screen, showing captures of the engagement before he had to escape. "something is off. They are much more round and smooth than our ships. The color of the material is not like any we have seen before, at least in space. Our energy weapons were also much more effective against them at close range than the models we are used to seeing. It didn't appear that they had any type of shields. Their weapons were only partially effective against us, that is until..." Leader Darnwich cut him off. The general appeared relieved he wouldn't have to finish this line of thought and relive losing his entire fleet.

"But what about the massive destructive power of their new weapon?!" Leader Darnwich said, dashing the hopes of the General getting an easy out.

"Leader, that was entirely unexpected. Nothing has ever been even close to being able to destroy an entire ship in a single instance. That power does not exist. Did not exist. We cannot defend against something like that." He was getting upset again, mostly out of fear of potentially having to face that weapon again. His hands slowly opened and closed repeatedly as his breathing became shallow and rapid. His mouth was open only far enough to allow the air in and out.

"I can see your weakness." Leader Darnwich accused. His disapproval of the handling of the situation was evident in his demeanor, completely non-reactive. Leader Danuibi could almost see Leader Darnwich thinking of who would replace him. That would not happen as long as he had any say in the matter. And he had a lot to say. As if the General should have expected and been able to act on everything that had happened and come out with a more positive outcome. And as if he would have done any better. Leader Darnwich was one of the few who had risen to the level of a leader without first being a part of the military forces. His father had propelled his career to the top, with no experiences of how to handle military situations, certainly not stressful ones. He always had the luxury of time to weigh his options and seek advice. Sometimes even trying a few different ideas until one worked. Not General Drobbi. No, most of his decisions had to be made right there on his own, where the wrong decision meant lives were lost. Sometimes even the right decision meant that as well.

Leader Darnwich continued. "We must divert our fleets to that location and confront the Tartins head-on. If we destroy their secret fleet, it would be a massive blow and could turn the tide in this war."

He was so sure of himself that it was disturbing. He failed to see the major flaws in his plan. Leader Danuibi was eager to point them out so they could move on to coming up with a solution. "We lost two-thirds of the ships we sent. Even if we win, what's to say that same ratio won't apply? We already don't have enough ships to defeat them at home as it is, let alone with most of our ships gone. No. We will not divert any more ships to that area. General Drobbi will help develop tactics that can defeat that weapon and defeat their ships, and we will wait. In the meantime, we will continue fighting the war we have going on in this space. The one that if we lose, we lose our home world. Do we even need to cast a vote on this course of action?" He looked around the room. After seeing only blank stares and some hesitant head shakes, he dismissed the room. Everyone knew what to do.

After everyone had left, Leader Danuibi called up someone on his tablet, someone that he turned to in situations like these. When Artur Tibambae answered, he did not look surprised. After what had happened, he had been expecting a call.

"What can I do for you, Danu?" Artur said, forgoing the formal tone with his old colleague. He was never the one to follow long-standing tradition anyway. They had met when they were boys. While never openly admitting they were friends because they both lived in vastly different social circles, they enjoyed each other's company in private as children. As they grew up, their relationship morphed from secret childhood friends to secret colleagues. Leader Danuibi began his life as a politician after serving in the space fleet, while Artur started his career in the military ground forces, but quickly found a knack for the intelligence group. After many years of sneaking around doing the work that nobody wanted, they kept in touch. Leader Danuibi had Artur run the occasional side gig for him. Once Artur retired from active service, he could dedicate more of his time helping Leader Danuibi. Artur was far from done working. He began consulting for various large corporations and for the rich and wealthy to solve their most closely guarded problems. What Leader Danuibi's relationship with Artur did was give himself an in with some of the most elite Razuuds in their world.

Leader Danuibi never used this information to gain any favor but would use it to make sure that when the right decision needed to be made, there would be no one to stop him. This relationship also allowed Artur to go on special missions for Leader Danuibi when asked.

"I need to know about the source of those ships. As fast as possible. I fear our little shit friend is going to do something stupid, like run to his daddy." He said. They had grown up with Leader Darnwich's father, who was not nearly as bad as his son. The problem was, he was far more powerful and richer. After losing his other children to both respectable and less than ideal professions, he was always trying to please his only remaining son. "I have a strange feeling that these ships we encountered were not of the origin we think" he added. Leader Darnwich needed to confirm his suspicions, and Artur was his tool. There was something interesting happening, and he didn't want to be on the wrong end of it. If what he thought was true, Artur would find it and needed no more direction or potential miscues.

Artur had the special skills and equipment, but more importantly, Leader Danuibi's trust. Artur's ship had extremely sophisticated sensors and cloaking packages that were paid for largely by Danuibi's side jobs. If there was ever a ship that could evade detection and get the information he needed discreetly, it was this one.

"Sure thing, old friend. I'll begin immediately." Artur responded. The communication link was cut off before Danuibi could add anything else.

Leader Danuibi could only guess how long it would take to find out this information, and if it would be in time to be useful. But he couldn't think of that right now. Right now, he needed to get ahead of the current situation and figure out how to best use what little information General Drobbi returned with.

CHAPTER 12

Ramat–Space Force Platform Kennedy–Earth Orbit

Tobias Sinclair stood at the pedestal in the large conference room. Well, large for a space platform. It could hold about fifty people in theater-style seating, albeit a little cramped. It followed the contour of the curve on the spin hub. This gave it the added bonus of having enough gravity to keep him standing and everyone else seated. He was briefing the new 777th Fighter Squadron, previously the test squadron, on all the upgrades to the new AIMS. Since the attack almost over a year ago, humans had learned and changed many things.

"Your new ships will be quite menacing. To earth ships as well as those aliens we saw previously. The technology we were able to glean from their wreckage was quite outstanding." He paused. Ramat saw the looks of despair of his squadron over the fear that he might excitedly ramble on in super technical lingo, putting half the squadron to sleep. Most of the squadron had consulted with him on how to best implement the reverse-engineered technology, and so they were used to it by now. To Ramat, it looked like he was going to start again before pausing one more time until he continued. Maybe Tobias realized what the looks on their faces meant, or he remembered the conversation Ramat had with him before the briefing.

He had told him to keep it high level, out of the technical weeds. "So I don't bore you, let's get to it. The overview. Your ships have a much more capable light gate now. We couldn't duplicate their light drive technology quite yet, but what we did learn allowed us to miniaturize our existing ones. You can carry more light gates per ship, by a factor of three. We were able to gather a lot of information on the shields they were using. Because they were using energy weapons, they made the assumption they had shields to counter such weapons. We were able to adapt them to each ship, maybe not as good, but much better than being as naked as we were then. They had no defense against kinetic weapons, so we made some improvements in that area as well, in case they learned. Your cannons will carry a bigger impact, and you each get some more nukes for safe measure. There are also some other software upgrades and minor drive upgrades, but those will be briefed to you in the sim. Are there any questions?" He looked around, waiting to answer questions. "I know you're all tired and probably eager to try out some of this new tech. Please stop by my quarters while I'm still here if you have any questions." The room chuckled at that. Ramat, along with everybody in the room, knew that he was never there. He was always roaming the ship, checking on different systems and upgrades and tweaking them to squeeze the as much performance as he could. If someone wanted to find Tobias, they had to make a very focused effort to do so. Tobias bent his head with an empty smile, looking confused at first. His facial expressions turned to realization at what the light laughter meant. "Ah, yes, you probably won't find me there."

With no hands going up, Tobias walked off, not offended at all. He knew the training regimen they were under was quite grueling.

Ramat saw Tobias heading toward him. As usual, Ramat remained among the last to leave, making sure that his squadron was on its way out and getting some sleep. As he waited, Tobias approached him.

"Colonel, if you would, just a minute of your time?" Tobias asked. Ideas from Tobias could sometimes run off onto tangents that Ramat couldn't glean anything from, but he always made the time to listen. They had socialized several times before and got along quite well. Their personalities were quite different, but their love for their work connected them. In formal work settings, though, they remained professional.

"Of course, Mr. Sinclair, can we talk on the move? I'm being summoned by the Captain."

"Yes, of course." Tobias responded. "I was curious about this upcoming mission you are training for. In short, I would like to go. I think there will be a valid need for the level of knowledge that I have for these systems."

"Not to mention the potential new technology you could gain." Ramat conjectured, with a little smile on his face. After Ramat felt that the silence was maybe getting a little too awkward for Tobias, he continued. "I agree, your expertise could be especially useful. I'll bring the idea up to the Captain, but I'm not entirely for it. This is going to be a military operation; I don't love the idea of risking the lives of civilians unnecessarily. The chance of being stranded out there, or even worse, death, is going to be high."

"I think you have those two backwards, Sir, the worse part would be to be stranded. But that would certainly be where I could help out. Regardless, I appreciate your attention. Please let me know what he says." And with that, Tobias peeled off.

Ramat made his way to the command center on the opposite side of the hub to where he was now. The command center that General Sites had set up was not where the command center is supposed to be. In fact, it is supposed to be in the safest location on the ship, the center. He had moved it to be closer to his quarters. Ramat assumed it was so that he could have better control of his people, but also the comfort of gravity, so he didn't have to exercise. From speaking with Tobias previously, Ramat knew he didn't like the ship's captain, General Sites, but for some reason, Sites was fond of Tobias. It was probably because of the money he had. Sites was likely looking for a post-military career and was trying to suck up to him. He was, in a way, using this to his advantage. This opportunity would boost Tobias' company. It already had, to be sure, but Ramat was already coming around to the idea. Nobody knew the technology as good as him and nobody could get trained enough to replace him in the amount of time they had before leaving. Hell, there probably wasn't enough time ever. This was his technology that he adapted; if something went wrong, he needed to be there to fix it. That sense of ownership was one reason his career took off as well as it did this far, along with his pure genius.

When Ramat arrived at the command center a moment later, he walked next to General Sites' office and knocked sharply.

"Enter." Sites barely acknowledged them as if he was busy attending to other business. As Ramat entered, he begrudgingly tore his attention away from his screen with a sigh.

Ramat walked in with crisp turns and halted promptly in front of his desk, or at least as much as he could. Gravity wasn't quite good enough to make it perfect, but the experienced crew could make it look pretty good. As Ramat turned, he noticed that General Sites' office was also his quarters, and they were not kept neatly. He prohibited his troops from being this messy, not to mention the fact that it posed a flight hazard. He kept his mouth shut, though, not wanting to start a pointless battle. Ramat knew General Sites wasn't there to set any examples. "You wanted to see me, General?"

"Lieutenant Colonel, I mean Colonel D'Pol, yes, of course, please sit down." Sites said, appearing to purposefully get his rank wrong. Ramat received a promotion several months after the initial battle. There was a push, not by General Sites, to get him promoted to ensure he would be in charge of one of the fighter squadrons that was going to be heading out. He deserved the promotion regardless of his efforts the day of the attack, something General Sites tended to overlook. "Are you familiar with the rescue operation that were ongoing during the initial hours following the first attack?"

"Some, sir, our squadron provided escort for many of the transport ships." Ramat responded.

"There is one in particular." Sites continued as if he didn't even hear Ramat's response. "flown by two pilots, and a reporter, as it were. They recovered a large number of people and show great, um, potential. I'm assigning both of them to your squadron." He said, clearly struggling to find the right word. Ramat wasn't sure where the General was going with this, or the reasoning. As he thought about it, he recalled talking with Colonel Archer, the operations officer of the Kennedy, about a run-in with some pilots that had rescued General Sites. He connected the dots. He fought the urge to let the realization show on his face. They must be the same who General Sites referred to now. Although he didn't bring up the issues he had with them. Maybe Sites left that part out to help sell them being assigned to his unit. He didn't need to.

An order was an order.

At first, Ramat felt surprised and taken aback. He had heard of them, but he knew one of them had recently graduated school, not even flight school, and the other was not even close to being experienced enough to be a part of his squadron. Although he had to remember, this wasn't the test squadron it used to be. Being part of a fighter squadron opened him up to having some more inexperienced pilots. "Sir, are they ready for this? We typically require much more experience before accepting new pilots. And we are full up right now." He winced at that last part. He knew it would be easy for General Sites to fix that problem, and he knew he was going to take that opportunity right now.

Sites saw this and jumped in as expected. "Yes, Ramat, that's correct." General Sites said. He used his first name this time. That would normally be fine, even in professional settings amongst peers or from a superior to his younger officers. But that wasn't the case; it was to assert his dominance over Ramat, and Ramat knew it. "I need you to spread some of that experience around. Your team was the only one that saw the enemy directly in battle. You have done an outstanding job training the other squadrons, but it would be better if some of your men were imbedded in other units. Pick two to re-assign elsewhere and begin a training regimen for these new pilots. They'll need some work before we get moving. We will be undocking from the Kennedy soon and will be leading the fleet. Your squadron will be assigned on my ship, the SFG Catalyst."

Ramat was more than a little pissed. Not only did he have to take on two new pilots, but he also had to give up two experienced pilots of his own. As these thoughts were going through his head, he was able to keep it together long enough before there was another knock at the door. This sidetracked him from doing or saying something he would have regretted. It wasn't this one particular incident that got under his skin; if he was honest, it was actually a good idea. But no, it was the culmination of a bunch of shitty circumstances that centered around General Sites and most decisions, or indecisions, he made.

"Enter." Sites responded, the same way he had before.

Two young officers entered. One was a brand-new Second Lieutenant, the lowest rank for an officer. The other was a First Lieutenant. It dawned on Ramat that these must be the new pilots being assigned to him. They were fresh and eager. A look that only someone brand new had. Despite the overwhelming workload, they were going to get a trial by fire. He would have to move fast if they were going to make it. Another realization dawned on him. He recalled more from his brief chat with Colonel Archer. Colonel Archer had informed him about an interesting encounter with General Sites and these two new pilots. He mentioned they would face punishment for something they had done during the rescue efforts. This must be their punishment; those kids were at the wrong place at the wrong time. They had nothing to do with being assigned to him, so he would have to make the best of it. "These must be the two pilots." Ramat pointed out. He took a more welcoming tone with them. He knew he was stuck with them, and as unhappy as he was with getting them, it wasn't their fault, and he wanted to get off to a good start. Plus, they might actually be good pilots if the report of that first mission was correct. Ramat being nice to them in front of the General had the added bonus of getting the General to squirm in his chair. General Sites' face tightened up, with a little bit of a scowl forming. Seeing them handling this mix-up in assignments had not gone as the General had hoped.

"Correct. Why don't you show them to their new home?"

General Sites said. He had a dismissive tone that Ramat couldn't tell if it was annoyance or displeasure but he learned over time not to care about his mood either way. It was always foul.

His attention was drawn back to his screen, and it was clear that their time in his office was up. They all three got the hint, stood at attention, and saluted. General Sites glanced up and returned what some might call a salute if it were in a movie; most others that served would probably call it a disgrace.

With that, they turned and exited into the corridor.

Once outside in the hall, Ramat gestured for them to follow him. "I'm Colonel D'Pol, or Trap." Ramat looked at each of them in a hint for them to introduce themselves. He knew their story but hadn't gotten around to knowing their names yet.

"I'm Lieutenant McCovee." Riley said.

"I'm Lieutenant Starilla." Jade added.

"Nice to meet you two. I'll take you to the Lucky's break room. You can meet the rest of the team, and they can help get you settled. We'll need to get you folded into the training tempo as soon as we can."

Lieutenant McCovee and Lieutenant Starilla both nodded and followed along. It was, fortunately for them, on the opposite side of the General's office from the central hub. This reduced the chances of any accidental run-ins.

Shortly after they departed the general's office, Lieutenant McCovee spoke. "Sir, did you have the first space-to-space shootdown."

Ramat smiled and let out a small chuckle. "Yeah, LT, that was me. It wasn't as cool as it sounded, right place, right time sorta thing. If you're interested, I can debrief you about it when we get some downtime."

"Yes, sir." Riley said, responding almost before the offer

was finished. Ramat could tell that the kid probably knew a lot more about the interaction than he let on. But he would find out later. The trip was mostly silent after that. It must have been obvious that there was something on Ramat's mind, because the two new officers kept quiet.

When they were almost at the Lucky's break room, Ramat got a call on his duty line. This was an integrated line to his normal communication device, a small rectangular electronic device that fit in his palm but was all screen. The duty line was analogous to the 'bricks' of old that on-call pilots would carry. They kept the same name, but they no longer resembled a brick someone used to use to build a house with. The old, large rectangular chunks of plastic had limited communications capability. They were extremely reliable, but only if they were kept charged. Using it to talk to people with audible words was one of the last things it was actually used for now, but the name stuck over the years.

Ramat slowed to answer it. "Colonel D'Pol."

"Ramat, it's Mark, do you have a moment?" He responded to Mark DeCanus, an old friend of his.

"Yes, give me a minute, and I'll take it in my quarters. Talk to you soon." He put the phone back in his pocket. "Sorry about that, busy day." He gestured to the next door as they continued walking along the corridor. "Right in here."

As they entered, they saw the walls lined with pictures, plaques, flags, patches, you name it. This wasn't any ordinary break room; this was a legacy heritage room. Only a few were authorized these days because they were a distraction to operations and a waste of money to those that never experienced a quality heritage room or felt connected to a unit, like most of the Lucky's did. The amount of money put into one of these rooms wouldn't buy a single minute of time for an atmospheric fighter, but that wasn't the point. Comparisons like that were not allowed to be made for some undisclosed reason. But this room clearly had a story to tell. Flags and plaques from different operations the unit had been involved with and awards it had won throughout the many years it had been around lined the walls. While it hadn't always been called the 777th, its lineage dated back to the founding of the Air Force after World War II. Ramat knew that these were the real deal, not replicas. They were the actual flags and ribbons. The room was about half full, though many were in their bunks, which also lined the walls. The other half of the squadron was either out doing patrols or in the simulators preparing for the next engagement.

Ramat spoke. "Alright team, we got some new blood. Make them feel at home until we find a good place to put them. Wisp, can you take this? I got a call earth side." Ramat nodded to Major Charlie 'Wisp' Broadway.

Once he received a nod back from Charlie, Ramat turned and continued down the hall to his quarters. He entered his room and sat down at his desk to initiate his call down to earth. He made this call often, so it was on his quick call list.

Until his face replaced his name, Mark DeCanus read on the display panel.

"Mark, what can I do for you, old friend?" Ramat said with sincerity. They were old friends, and as far as secrets went, they didn't keep many from each other. The ones they did were only because they had to by law. It was a rare bond between service member and politician.

"Well, we have a bit of a dilemma down here. Rictor, as you know, in all of his infinite wisdom, managed to put Sites in charge of the most important mission in human history. Meanwhile, down on earth, he is trying to manufacture a coup that would return the world union to its former split country self, undoing my life's work. No big deal."

"Sounds like nothing has changed. Anything I can help with?" Ramat responded, knowing that General Sites being in charge did impact him in terms of the mission he was about to go on. He didn't know how much of an impact it would have. They were to go find the aliens, which they had a rather good idea where they were now, attack them, then return. They hoped Sites wouldn't be able to have any real impact on the actual outcome. The plan was to get Sites immersed with one aspect of an operation, forcing him to neglect all the others. This left them free to execute an effective mission.

Mark paused briefly. "I can handle Rictor down here – I have some measures in place that will take care of his nonsense in my absence."

"In your absence? Where are you going?" Ramat responded, not sure where this was going anymore. "I know you need a vacation, but I don't think this is the best time." He added, to lighten up the mood a little.

"Well, I will be taking a vacation, for your information, with you." Ramat paused before responding. This was unexpected news. He didn't like the idea of civilians on this mission, let alone friends. Not that they weren't useful, because they often were. It was an innocent life being put on the line, not typically what they signed up for. Before Ramat could respond, Mark continued. "I have been tasked as a diplomatic representative for this mission in the event that this new species wants to talk. Not that we know how to do that yet, I've heard the lab guys have been able to figure out a few words… I will be on your ship, trying to stop the first human interstellar, interspecies war."

"I didn't know there was going to be an opportunity for negotiations or even the ability to communicate." Ramat responded.

"There is always an opportunity for negotiations. We were

able to find enough about them that the linguists have been able to put their computers to the task of coming up with a translation to their language. It hasn't gotten anywhere yet, but it should. And before you go questioning whether or not I volunteered for this or not, well, I didn't. Rictor thought that if I were gone, he would be freer to exercise whatever plan he has going on, so he managed to get me assigned to this. Of course, I could have turned it down and then resigned. Since I'll never stop working, that wasn't an option." Mark said. That pretty much explained everything, Ramat thought. Ramat knew Mark left out a lot of detail, but due to their relationship Ramat could fill in the gaps. Mark relayed the important parts, and Ramat was not happy about what he heard.

Ramat figured they could talk about the rest when he got up there. Fighting it wouldn't do any good. Besides, who would he go to, and who would replace Mark?

"When do you arrive?" Ramat asked.

"Tobias has a shuttle waiting for me now. Should be there just in time for departure to the first light gate." Mark responded. Tobias and Mark had a relatively long history together. Mark was immensely helpful to Tobias when it came time to get senate approval to test out some of his space inventions, which most turned out to be instrumental in shaping how the world got to and worked in space. They always kept in touch and occasionally socialized whenever their busy schedules allowed. By extension, Ramat was also friends with Tobias, and the two hit it off soon after the meeting about 10 years earlier. Tobias was much more eccentric than Ramat would typically like, but he was someone that shared a passion for space. They had gone on for hours about that shared passion. Tobias also didn't care for politics, a trait that Ramat saw as a bonus. Ramat knew he could count on him without politics interfering, if ever the need arose.

"We'll see you soon, safe travels." Ramat replied. He was fairly sure this was Mark's first trip to space, so he knew it would take some getting used to. This was a raw deal for him; there was a chance that none of them would return. But the one advantage they had was that they had kept their friendship mostly a secret throughout their careers. This would be particularly important in navigating General Sites. If General Sites knew, there's no knowing how he would react, and it wouldn't be good. Only because Rictor wouldn't have liked it though. General Sites had no clue, and there was no harm in keeping it that way. Mark was smart and knew how diplomats and politicians worked. He may be what ends up saving this task force and maybe earth. He actually felt a little better now, knowing that he was coming along.

CHAPTER 13

Maggie–Space Force Platform Kennedy–Earth Orbit

Captain Maggie 'Face' Lorrent was mad. She was mad and frustrated. She didn't let it show in front of General Sites, but she still couldn't believe that she got pulled for executive officer duty. That was the last thing she wanted to do. Sure, she could still fly part of a shift each day to stay current. But she had to rotate that with simulator time. She was effectively getting half the flight time as the rest of the squadron on the eve of what could be the largest ship-to-ship confrontation ever. There hadn't been any real combat since the alien attack. Her undesired role as the coffee-getting, email-sending secretary, as known as the executive officer, wore on her.

She knew that in the military, sometimes she would have to suck it up and do the job. It being under General Sites just added to the disdain. As she sat quietly looking over the Lucky's roster to see who needed more flight time and who was performing well in the simulator, her old job, she could overhear a conversation General Sites was having. It was quiet where she was. General Sites had removed the closet from his room to put it in an executive office. He rearranged the room next door to his to be his new closet, much bigger than his old one.

"You see, General, I was able to get you in charge of this fleet. I'll be your man down here; just come back successful, and you can be practically guaranteed the presidency. Just think, the first president of the world!" Maggie looked down at her screen on the desk and saw who was on the line with General Sites. Rictor Inagru's name flashed with an active connection symbol next to it. He was getting overly excited about what he said. She could almost hear the evil, giddy laugh like some villain out of an old movie. She thought his idea was a little strange, given that the current construct of the world's leadership was not a presidency.

"Rictor, while I appreciate your confidence, I got myself here through my hard work. Don't forget that or think differently about it. That position will be mine with or without your help. Now, if you don't mind, I have to get back to planning a mission to save the world." General Sites said. Maggie saw the line disconnect, and she quickly removed that view from her screen and pulled up the latest messages.

"Captain Lorrent, look out for a message from Rictor. Delete it as soon as it arrives." General Sites said.

"Yes, sir." Maggie responded. She would do just that—after reading it, of course, and maybe saving a copy if it was important enough. Maggie had heard stories of General Sites, and her short tenure as his exec had so far confirmed nearly everything that she had heard. In the cases where the stories were wrong, it was because the reality was much worse. Maybe it was his condition, but he wouldn't even admit to himself that he did not actually get himself anywhere. It was either from the help of others like Rictor or the misfortune of others who had failed to realize he wanted the next higher job, not to actually do his own job well.

General Sites stood up, exited his office and quarters, and headed to the command deck right outside his door. Typically, they buried the command center, or CC, deep within the ship. There was no point exposing the leadership or the chief operators of the ship to a few layers of protection when they could be in the middle of the ship. General Sites didn't enjoy having to go so far away to get to the CC and also wanted artificial gravity, so he moved much of the CC to a few rooms outside his quarters on the Kennedy. He was actually going to be commanding the fleet from the SFG Catalyst because the Kennedy couldn't make the trip. He didn't want to do all of his work in zero-G, so he didn't plan to go aboard the Catalyst until they were about to depart.

There were few actual windows out to space in the entire ship, none in the CC. Any views that were worth seeing were video relays. The operators on the larger ships would fly with an extremely sophisticated augmented reality system. Depending on the task, they would control the massive ships using motion gloves and boots with augmented reality headsets that allowed them to view the exterior of the ship from every angle and guide the ship within feet of where they wanted. This setup was new to the larger ships. It was an eerie sight walking into the CC the first few times, seeing a bunch of crew members sitting around desks with glasses on. The concept was so new that the previous consoles were still in place with the screens turned off. The systems were still running in the background, waiting to take over if there was an issue with any of the crew's gear. If the crew were being perfectly honest, they loved the new system.

Maggie followed General Sites out of his office into the remote CC. She saw everyone working away, blissfully unaware that he was looking to catch someone doing something they shouldn't be. Maggie knew the crew liked this new system, if for no other reason than he couldn't see what they were actually doing. And they had an excuse if he was trying to get their attention. 'Small victories' she thought to herself.

The AIMS pilots hadn't begun using this form of augmented reality yet because of the maneuvering. Maggie remembered trying to test some of the helmets and glasses out, and they couldn't quite seem to keep the view flowing during certain maneuvers. Once they figured it out, though, it could be a tremendous advantage. For now, the inside of fighter cockpits was a seamless sphere of screens. Most ships were similar in construction, either scaled up or down depending on the mission. So, the larger battleships were a larger version of a fighter, a slight teardrop shape with SOP engines mounted on a pivot point where the teardrop tapered down. The outer portion where the engines mounted was all in one piece. The smaller end of the teardrop held the power generation and fuel. When a thrust vector needed to change, the engines would swing the entire outer surface, leaving the middle hull and cockpit sections to decide how to best compensate for g-forces. The engines would pivot around the teardrop depending on what maneuvering was taking place. The biggest difference between the fighters and any ship larger was that the cockpit in the fighters rotated independently of the outer shell and middle hull. This allowed the fighters to make much more extreme maneuvers without killing the pilots.

For long duration trips, there was some gravity for a good portion of the trip. As General Sites sat in a chair that oversaw the remote CC, Maggie continued to the exit. Outside the remote CC was a hall filled with other rooms and offices. One of the first ones was to the Flight Standards Doctor, Major John Belintes. This position was a doctor, but not the kind that would take care of any sick crew members or treat injuries. This person would make sure that the ship adhered to work and rest cycles, gravity cycles, and so forth.

Using the back of her hand, Maggie knocked sharply on the door a few times.

"Come in." She heard a muffled voice from behind the door.

When she entered, the doctor stood up and greeted her. "Hi Maggie, are you ready to go over the plan for this trip?" He asked.

Maggie had spoken to him briefly several times but never got into too much detail. These weren't the types of tasks she enjoyed doing, but now that she was the exec, it fit her new job description. "Yeah, John, let's see how much time I'm going to have to spend in the gym on this trip." Maggie joked back to Major John Belintes. She knew that the longer they were on the float and not under accelerating to create gravity, the more time they had to be in the gym exercising and taking supplements to ward off bone loss and other side effects of zero gravity. Because humans couldn't get a giant spinning module through a light gate or get it moving fast enough if they could, they had to have a way to create gravity while moving through space. Instead of spin gravity, they used acceleration gravity.

"It shouldn't be too much. General Sites has made sure we have provisions to spend most of our transit time under at least partial moon G." John responded. They both knew it was because he didn't want to have to spend time in the gym—the same reason he moved the CC to the ring on the Kennedy. More gravity equals less exercise required. John continued, "The newer SOP engines can sustain a constant low-level thrust for a lot longer period of time using less fuel. The plan has us burning most of the way after we go through several light gates and flipping halfway to burn again before we need to jump back through light gates." Because they were going to be using so many light gates, the fleet had enough fuel to burn almost constantly for the short coast phase. Gravity was essential for maintaining the health and morale of the crew. For exceptionally long trips, though, the acceleration would have to be spaced out because the fuel would not last long enough.

"We shouldn't run into any issues with gravity cycles. We won't have more than a couple of days without gravity before we arrive. You may have to be careful if you spend too much time in your fighter though. We'll have to track the accumulated zero-G for you guys. You might have to be grounded for a day every week or so to make sure you get enough gravity. We need everyone in top shape for the fight to come." John said.

"I know." Maggie responded. "We just can't afford too much downtime—they need all the time they can get training. We might have to do more simulators than we would like. The new people just don't transition from simulator to the real thing very well."

"If we don't keep up a good schedule, we'll have to return to earth, or else everyone won't be able to walk when we get back."

"That assumes we make it back." Maggie responded. There were a lot of firsts on this trip, and the chances of something going wrong would increase every minute they sped away from earth. They were going to go right through the earth light gates and use several more of their own portable light gates to accelerate to several times the speed of light. The trip out would be long still, so there would be some periods of acceleration, but comparatively, their speed would hardly move; it would solely be for gravity creation for the crew.

"Don't be so doom and gloom, Maggie." John said back. "After all, it was your test mission that made this possible. We wouldn't know if flying formation like this was possible using individual light gates unless you did it. Too bad your welcome back was that alien attack and not a party."

Maggie could tell he was trying to cheer her up and make light of the situation, and it was sort of working. Even so, did he really think that General Sites would turn around and go back to earth before meeting the enemy, all because the crew might be short on their gravity rations? There's no way that would happen, not even General Sites would do that.

Changing the subject, Maggie continued, "How are you going to track the fleet, especially if we aren't able to establish a link or get separated?"

"We have what, six other ships? The Carrier, three battleships, and two support ships?" John responded. When she nodded, he continued, "That shouldn't be a problem. I have techs keeping track of all the ships. I'll be on the carrier with you guys and will coordinate from there. I'll keep track of the three fighter squadrons on there, and the techs will keep track of the fighter squadrons on their own battleships. The supply ships will stay back a ways, so they may be on the float more than us. They have a smaller crew but will have to exercise more. Those ships are set up better for that anyway. I'm more curious to see those triple centerline railguns in action on the battleships."

"Those are pretty impressive." Maggie responded. "Well, it seems like you got a handle on this. Send me a message with the details, and I'll get it to General Sites. He was interested in the plan."

"Will do. Feel free to stop by anytime." John responded. Maggie got the sense that he was inviting her over for something other than work, but she was far too busy to think about her personal life right now.

As Maggie walked away, she couldn't help but think back on the attack force they were sending. The attack force was going to be the biggest in the world's history. In total, there were going to be three battleship-class ships, which carried three centerline railguns each and also came equipped with a fighter squadron each. There was a single star carrier-class ship which was actually slightly smaller than the battleships. It only had some close-range defense but massive kinetic and energy shielding. The real power in the carrier, though, was the three squadrons of fighters it carried. There were also a few other supply ships and repair depots. Those were minimally manned, but housed a massive number of supplies that could handle most repairs along with food and fuel for the duration of the trip. These ships actually had the most powerful engines of them all. They needed them to keep up in normal space because they were the heaviest when fully loaded.

There were too many things to think about leading up to the mission kicking off. Maggie walked into the CC and saw General Sites sitting at his command chair. He had his headset on so he could hear various communications channels, but he did not have his augmented reality glasses on. He was looking back and forth between his blank screen and everyone else's in the remote CC.

Maggie approached General Sites. "Sir." she said, standing to the side of him but where he could still see her.

"Yes, Major?"

"I just received the final gravity standards brief. Looks like he has a good plan to keep us out of G trouble." Maggie stated, hoping it would be a quick interaction.

"I'll be the judge of that, Major." General Sites responded. Maggie had one more question to ask him. She didn't want to, but she knew others needed to know. "Yes, Major, is there something else? I have a lot to do before we depart."

"Sir, do we have orders published? Several of the commanders are asking about them." Maggie said. She couldn't find a better way to ask the question. She knew he held the plans and execution close, unwilling to relinquish any notion that someone else could carry them out. Typically, a good commander would help establish a plan and order of operations and allow his team to execute it. And would build that plan based on input and feedback from those under them. That was not the case in this situation. General Sites felt that he needed to manage every aspect of the operation. With an operation this large, there were going to be many things that were left off if only one person was overseeing everything. Fortunately for him, he had a good crew. They picked up the slack for him, and he was oblivious to that fact.

"Those that need to know the plan know it already. Everyone else can follow orders as and when they are given. Tell any commander that does not like that to return to earth for a replacement while they still can."

Maggie nodded. She figured the response would be something like that but needed to try anyway. Maybe, just maybe, he would shed some more light on how they were going to go about this mission.

General Sites interrupted Maggie's train of thought. "Is everything ready for departure?" Sites asked, presumably to Maggie, but he was looking off into the CC, so he could very well be talking into the communications net. Sites insisted that his Vice Captain, Lieutenant Colonel Mary Ann Barker, not be present for most situations. His excuse was that he wanted her well-rested if she was ever needed. Maggie felt that General Sites had never had that intention. She thought he specifically chose someone with a much lower grade than him, so that he had no problems ordering them around. It also gave him the leeway to do whatever he wanted. Maggie saw him do that repeatedly, oftentimes to the objection of Lieutenant Colonel Barker. Lieutenant Colonel Barker was more than qualified to captain the ship; indeed, the Catalyst was her ship until the task force took it over to be part of the fleet. She was supposed to remain captain while General Sites was in charge of the fleet, but he decided to take over both jobs.

Maggie put on a headset from the closest console to listen in case he was talking to her. She didn't want him to sit there waiting for her response. Making him wait never went well. As she put on the headset, she could hear his Operations Officer, now Colonel Archer, speaking. He was sitting at the console next to hers. "We are waiting on one last shuttle from earth, scheduled to dock in about 15 minutes. It's one of Tobias' shuttles, so it's getting here pretty quick. All other preparations are complete." Although Colonel Archer was now only in charge of the active external flight operations, he had a familiarity with the logistics and other tasks because of his previous post as the Duty Officer. He kept tabs on his old job and team to have a better idea of what was going on around him.

"One of Mr. Sinclair's shuttles? Lucky bugger. Is it that Mark De something or other?" Sites asked, seemingly back at Colonel Archer, but he was not looking in any direction in particular.

Archer quickly pulled up the manifest on his console and responded. "Yes General, Mr. Mark DeCanus, Diplomatic Representative to Earth, and cargo."

"I'd rather just take the cargo." Sites said matter-of-factly, looking around to see if anyone heard what he thought was a decent joke. He glanced back at his blank console when everyone remained busy and didn't hear him. The truth was, most of the people on the ship liked and respected Mark, and though most of them heard the joke, it certainly wasn't funny to them. "What crew compartment is he staying in?" Sites added, trying to move on from his own internal laughter or imminent embarrassment.

Archer did a few more gestures on his console and spoke. "He's going to be right next to the Lucky's, eh, the 777th Fighter Squadron, sir." Maggie could see him tense up at the nickname. Maggie knew General Sites was not a fan of nicknames, especially that one. "I will contact Colonel D'Pol to send someone to escort him." He added, with the assumption that he was looking for someone to get him to his room and seat quicker.

"Very well, Captain Lorrent, please assist in getting him to his quarters as quickly as possible. Meet me in the CC on the Catalyst. We will leave when you arrive." Sites responded.

"Yes, sir." Maggie responded and turned to leave. She made her way through the maze of corridors and airlocks until she arrived at the Lucky's squadron room in the Catalyst, which was far less impressive than the one onboard the Kennedy. She had made that trip so many times she could probably do it with her eyes closed. The room had a shared area with a small table in the middle. It was a cube with three walls lined with beds that swiveled depending on if there was gravity or not and also doubled as acceleration beds. They could conform to the person in them and provided some protection from the small amount of g-forces the massive ship could produce. Another wall had storage but also had a pull-down projector where the team would go over mission videos to critique. Of late, it had mostly been used to critique the new pilots, Riley and Star, who had only been with the squadron for about six months. At the moment, the screen was used to watch the latest action movie. Maggie found Colonel D'Pol sitting in a seat by the entrance, partially enjoying the movie and partially working on his tablet.

"Sir, I need a couple of escorts to help me get a DV from the dock and brought to his quarters." Maggie said, shortening the term for distinguished visitor or someone of high importance.

"Sure thing, Face." Ramat said as he looked up at her. "Listen up, Rip, need you to go to the cargo bay and get a DV. Follow Face and help move his things. It sounds urgent?" Ramat asked at the end.

"Yes, sir. We are departing as soon as he is in his room."

"Good to know, Face. Rip, get him in his room and buckled up quickly, then get yourself back here. Everybody, we are leaving as soon as Rip gets back. Make preparations for departure. We can finish this movie another time. Understood?" Ramat quickly asked.

"Yes, sir." Riley responded, and quickly made his way to the door and into the corridor with Maggie leading the way. Riley grabbed Star on his way out. There was an unspoken rule among newer members of a ship that they never traveled alone. Even though Maggie would be with them, there was no telling if she were going to be pulled away to something else. Maggie wasn't surprised and knew that Riley and Star had become close friends, considering what they experienced together during the invasion. They typically never went anywhere without each other.

After weaving their way through the ship's corridors for a short while, the three of them finally made it to the cargo bay area. As they approached the cargo bay door, it opened, and a man in a suit was floating there looking around, presumably for some sort of sign as to a direction he needed to go. Fortunately, Riley made it to him before he could go off in the wrong direction.

"Mr. DeCanus, this way, sir." Maggie said down the hall,

grabbing his attention.

As they approached, Riley reached out his hand. "I'm Lieutenant McCovee, I'll be taking you to your room."

Mark gave Riley a strange look as he followed him.

"Lieutenant McCovee, nice to meet you—you can call me Mark. By chance, do you have someone in your family that goes by the nickname Rip?" Mark asked as they made their way back through the halls.

Riley also had a confused look on his face. When he responded, it was clear to Maggie that it wasn't because he didn't know anybody by that name, but because the question threw him off.

"Yes, actually, that was my Grandpa's nickname a long ways back. I was named after him and my dad. Riley McCovee the third." Riley responded.

"I've heard that name in old war stories my father used to tell me. His name came up quite a few times.

"I'd like to hear some of those if you have time later on?" Riley questioned thoughtfully. He wasn't making small talk anymore; he was genuinely interested. There was truly little he knew about his Grandpa's past and was eager to learn while he had the chance.

"Sure thing, Riley." Mark responded.

Once they arrived at Mark's room, they assisted with getting him strapped in and gave him a quick rundown on the safety procedures and what to do if he heard any sirens.

"If anything happens, one of us will come over and assist you." Riley said.

"They'll take good care of you, Mr. DeCanus." Maggie asserted in the hopes to calm any nerves he might have about this trip. She left to make it to the CC before General Sites blew a gasket, wondering where she was. "Let Colonel Archer know that I'm on my way from here." Maggie added, directing it to Riley. When he nodded, she continued on her way to the CC.

When Maggie made it back to the CC, she reported to General Sites. "Sir, Mr. DeCanus is all set."

"Very good." General Sites responded. He came over the fleet-wide communication system. "Fleet, prepare for immediate transition." He nodded to the crewman that was at the helm, indicating that he wanted him to accelerate towards the light gate so they could begin the transition. He realized that they all had headsets on and couldn't see his gesture. Realizing this and hoping nobody noticed his head nods and hand gestures trying to get someone's attention, he spoke to the CC room out loud. Maggie noticed and tried to contain her laughter. "CC, everyone enable pass-through so you can visually see me or use your old consoles." Most of the CC crew were already in that mode and witnessed a clown flailing around but acted as though they had seen nothing and faked turning their pass-through cameras on. Maggie could tell this because many of them had the same painful expression she did when it happened. The pass-through mode would allow them to see some things outside their headset in a partially transparent view. It enabled them to monitor their tasks but still know what was going on around them in their real environment. Most of the crew in the command center knew they were not going to be transitioning immediately, and that they were already going the necessary speed for the transition. Therefore, nobody did anything when he asked. The fleets were all on automated programming, for good reason. The lack of reaction must have annoyed General Sites. His face twisted, growing a deep scowl as he grabbed his armrest. Maggie braced for an ass chewing, but nothing came out. She hoped that the fear he must be feeling about the approaching transition and beginning of the mission took over and silenced him.

After over thirty minutes of coasting, the fleet entered the light gate. It was an extremely tight fit for the entire fleet. All six massive ships had to squeeze simultaneously into a space about the size of four football stadiums. The ships' AI could keep them all in line. They would spread out once transition was complete, but the initial pass through the earth light gate was going to be sporty.

General Sites blinked. When he opened his eyes, the screens were blank. "What's happening?" General Sites asked with more than a little panic in his voice.

"This is a normal part of transition, Sir. The views are getting updated with our new speed filters." Maggie responded. As she spoke, the screens flickered back on and showing a highly modified and filtered view of outside the ship.

Colonel Archer came over the command communication line to General Sites. "Sir, all ships have been re-linked and are reporting no issues."

Without acknowledging Colonel Archer, General Sites came over the fleet comm channel. "Prepare for immediate additional light gate transitions."

Again, this confused the crew. He didn't need to say anything; it was all automated and part of the plan that each ship captain and crew knew. It also would not be immediate. The fleet needed to disperse first. After they were clear of one another, each ship would begin a synchronized effort to use portable light gates to attain much faster speeds. After several transitions, the fleet could arrive in under three weeks.

All the crew members on the Catalyst were thankful that this process happened without the General's intervention; otherwise, they were confident that they would not reach their destination.

CHAPTER 14

Riley–Space Force Guard Ship Catalyst–In Transit

Riley crashed down on his bunk, at least as hard as the acceleration gravity would allow. The gravity produced by The Catalyst felt somewhere between earth and lunar gravity. Scientists and doctors determine that to be the sweet spot to keep humans healthy for longer duration stays in space. The small rapid thrust from all the engines fired so close together that sophisticated sensors had a hard time detecting a change. Even though it shouldn't have been noticeable, the human brain called bullshit on that which registered as a disorienting feeling to Riley. Nevertheless, there was a positive psychological and physical effect to have gravity on a long trip through the stars.

His bunk was the only area of privacy he had. They had concluded debriefing a rigorous simulation where their squadron was pitted against ten of those same ships they encountered at Earth. Riley wasn't there with the squadron when it happened, but he saw enough of the aftermath to understand the importance of doing these simulations. He hoped the odds would not be stacked against them like that again. He pulled the flap down to cover his area of the bunk and opened up his touchpad. It was a newly issued device. It could connect to all the ship's systems that he had permissions for, which were a lot. Much of the internet was on the ship's storage systems. It had two small handles on each side, attached to two round tubes about the thickness of his finger. When he pulled them apart, it unrolled, revealing a large screen that glowed. He rested it on his knees and pulled open his messages.

As expected, he had a new message from Jennifer Stanza. They had stayed in touch ever since that day on the launch pad prepping his shuttle. He found himself always looking forward to hearing from her. There was something between them, something that Riley didn't want to lose, and he thought she didn't either. They had an obvious attraction for each other that neither had fully acted on, and Star would always tease him about it. The two of them, well three, shared a bond that you can only get while going through something difficult together. The more difficult, the deeper the bond, Riley had always been told.

Following that first night together on the Kennedy, they hadn't seen each other again. They had tried to meet up, but the schedules they were on and all the chaos that early on never allowed it. Any downtime Riley had, he would open his chest pocket and pull out her note. It wasn't poetry, but it was direct, and he liked that. "I like you, stay in touch." with a heart drawn at the bottom above her name. Stay in touch, he did.

He was looking forward to an opportunity to see her, with nobody else around, when they got back. If they got back. They typically had written each other at least once a day; there were also fairly frequent video messages. They began as innocent exchanges, seeing how each other was doing after the events or how their day was going. They gradually turned more serious, which made the communication delays all the more painful. Riley wasn't quite sure what he was feeling, but he knew it was getting serious. Even though they hadn't been with each other in person since that first day, he liked everything about her. He couldn't stop thinking about her. As soon as they were through the first light gates, they could no longer have any real-time conversations. The comm drones could take a lot more risk and go much faster when relaying messages. That was not fast enough for Riley.

Riley replied to Jenn. Before he stopped the recording, he paused for a second, as if deciding whether he should say what he was about to. He decided it was probably for the best. "I have one more thing. The trajectory we are on, the star we are headed towards, is giving me this weird feeling. It's familiar in some way. I have limited resources up here, but I'm going to start looking into some things. I'll let you know what I find out." He knew he didn't have to ask her for help because he knew her well enough now that she was going to be curious and want to know herself. He didn't give Jenn any more information because he also knew how she operated. She wanted to come to her conclusions with no one impacting her point of view. So he left it vague. If there was something to find, she would find it. He stopped the recording and got to work.

The direction they were headed didn't sit well with him. Something was off. This bothered him frequently lately, and he didn't understand why. He tried to block it out by doing what he normally did after he read Jenn's messages a few times; research. This time he was going to see if Star would help him. He had been trying to work it out on his own so far, partially because he enjoyed doing things alone and partially because he didn't want anyone to think he was crazy.

Riley was a history buff and thoroughly enjoyed the era of initial space travel. He always felt he could learn something from how people back then innovated and took extreme risk to accomplish an amazing feat. Something that was not as common today, he felt. Although, if those original explorers saw them today, they would probably think that he was crazy. He also enjoyed learning about the formation of the military space force, which followed well after space exploration began.

Military space operations got their roots in the first half of the 21st century, when different countries began establishing their own space force. Their initial missions were mostly to defend space assets that were limited to Earth-orbiting satellites, from both physical and cyber-attacks. Riley was beyond excited that Tobias Sinclair, THE Tobias Sinclair, was on the mission. Tobias's Artificial Intelligence company played a key role in the advancement of North America and many of its allies. The threat shifted to manned spacecraft, going after other manned spacecraft and other space targets of opportunity and high value. Despite existing laws against this, they were largely ignored.

The first space dogfight occurred between Russia and China. At least that's how those countries were assembled at the time. It was much slower, much more cumbersome, and anticlimactic than some would expect. Those who are accustomed to fast-paced, head-snapping space dogfights from the movies would have found it disappointing. However, that encounter taught us more than the previous twenty years of manned spacecraft building.

Many things needed to be changed; the entire idea of what the ship needed to even look like was no longer correct. That was what led to the tear-drop shape with the rotating bodies. Why spin an entire ship around when you only need to move the engines? This was another one of Tobias's innovations, along with some other material advancements. Nobody could see outside anyway, so it didn't matter which direction anything was facing. Human comfort wasn't even the biggest consideration; it was in what orientation would allow for the best maneuverability that humans could survive through?

There were only a handful of other space dogfights since the first one with a lot of posturing and chest-beating in between. Ramat, Riley learned in childhood, was in one of those few space dogfights a while back. They taught about Ramat's expertise and spaceship handling at school and at pilot training. Needless to say, Ramat was a legend in space dogfighting. He had the first space-to-space kill. He killed the spacecraft but rescued the pilot because nobody else would have gotten to him in time.

As he breezed through the military space history, which he was already fairly familiar with, he made his way to the history of faster-than-light travel.

"Star, can you help me with something?" Riley asked Star as he leaned over the edge of his bunk down into hers.

"Are you still trying to figure out what the parachute is actually used for?" Star joked back.

"Funny." Riley responded. His expression drew serious. "No, actually, something's been bugging me about where we are going. It's familiar for some reason. Look." Riley hoped out of his bunk, which would have hurt in Earth's gravity but was a nice gradual fall to the main floor where Star was at. He showed her his tablet. "I've been looking through observation records from all of our space and ground telescopes for as far back as there are records, and there's no indication that anything is out there. But there is also almost no data on this particular heading."

"Space is big – we've only mapped a small sliver of the sky

so far. It just so happens that we started off looking in the wrong place, I guess." Star said back, but Riley could tell that she was getting hooked now.

"Maybe. But even after the attack and we figured out which direction they came from, we still could hardly tell there was something out there. But we should see something."

"Well, if we just looked at them from this far away, they would never know." Star responded. The wheels were turning between the two of them. "Us being here and spying on them shouldn't be enough to send an attack fleet, would it?" Before Riley could respond, he realized it was a rhetorical question because Star answered herself and kept on talking. "No. You would have to be provoked in some way. But we never sent out anything capable of attacking past our solar system. They have all been science missions and—"

"TEST PROBES!" They both nearly yelled together, causing everyone in the room to pause momentarily and look at them.

Riley continued on the train of thought that he thought Star was on. "Speed-of-light test probes, the first tests!"

"That could be devastating if we accidentally hit a planet. But we were supposed to check for things like that to try and avoid impacting a potentially habitable planet." Star said.

Riley feverishly tapped at his tablet. "Look, here's a list of all Sputnik light-speed attempts." Riley pointed. It was a long list. He zeroed in on Sputnik 75, the first known successful near-light-speed probe.

Near-light speed was anywhere from ninety-five to ninety-nine percent of the speed of light. It was becoming increasingly common for manned flight to travel at these speeds throughout the solar system. Large ships holding over twenty-five people were also starting to utilize this technology. These advancements came in the mid-21st century when

Doctor Boris Von Procter made an outstanding, and with most remarkable things, accidental breakthrough regarding the production and storage of energy.

Riley hit a few more buttons and removed some of the flights. "Here are all the successful attempts and their trajectories. Star pulled out her tablet now and was looking for the flight data for each. "I'll start at the bottom, you start at the top, and we'll work our way to the middle." Star said.

After a few moments, they both finished their section, both coming up empty. "I got nothing." Riley said.

"Same. I thought that idea sucked, just didn't have the heart to tell you." Star joked with a chuckle. She stopped mid laugh looking at Riley.

Riley had a look on his face, like this wasn't over yet. He was still thinking about something.

"The original ships were large and were mostly batteries. A massive amount of energy was needed to operate the Light Gate. The Light Gate had, what, five major components. Power storage, power generation, the scanner to analyze the ship, data storage, and finally the disassembler accelerator re-assembly thing, MDAR, I think." Riley said.

"Yeah, we all know that now. Hasn't changed much. I did a project in school on the MDAR. Would have finished it the next semester if you hadn't dragged me out here to do all of this lame space travel stuff." Star responded, laying on the sarcasm.

Riley liked that about Star. She was unapologetically humorous. She found a way to lighten the mood even in the most tense situations. He still had an idea, but he needed more information. "Did you see a mission partially work? Like maybe part of the ship got boosted, or it only got some of the energy so instead of just below light speed, it got halfway?" Riley asked.

"Oh, I see. You think that maybe some of the missions that failed actually worked? With what we know now, we should be able to see that in the data."

Now Riley was looking over Star's shoulder as she typed away.

"Easy, not too close, you're taken, remember." Star said. Riley got the hint and leaned back a bit, but he would not back up any further.

"Is it that obvious I'm taken? Do you think it's going a little fast?" Riley questioned, hoping Star could shed some light on the situation with a girl's perspective.

Star looked up and stared at Riley in either a look of disbelief or amusement as she spoke. "You guys were together for what, eighty straight hours, telling all sorts of stories. That's like twenty or thirty dates without any action. I would say you're taking it too slow."

Riley thought for a moment. He had never considered it in that way before. She wasn't wrong. Star got right back to work.

After a few minutes of Riley not being able to follow what Star was doing, she yelled.

"Got it!" Everyone in the room looked at her for a moment again before going back to what they were doing. "Got it." She said a little quieter. "I'm not certain, but it looks like there are a few partial successes that were first categorized as failures but may have actually worked." She highlighted the ones in question. "If we plot their courses." She typed a few more commands.

"And account for their potentially slower speed and the rotation of the solar system and the other solar system around the galaxy." Riley added, knowing the program should already be doing that.

Both of their eyes went wide.

"We need to tell the boss!" Excitement and terror

consumed Riley in that moment. And they both shot up so fast that they left the ground momentarily before floating back to the deck. They both left the squadron room and went into the hall for the short walk to Ramat's office and room.

Ramat had his door fully open, which was typical for him. He wanted the feeling that anyone could come and see him at any time. It automatically closed in emergencies or during the increasing frequency of drills that General Sites loved to do.

Ramat was sitting at his desk, leaned over towards his couch, talking to someone. As Riley and Star advanced further, they could see someone sitting on the small two-person couch, in a relaxed posture, with his legs crossed. Riley recognized him as the man he went to pick up before they went through the Light Gate at Earth. It was Mark DeCanus, he remembered. He had seen him around a few other times over the last couple weeks during the outbound trip but hadn't yet had the chance to talk to him about his Grandpa.

Riley knocked at the door.

"Come on in." Ramat said, with a welcoming tone.

"Sir, do you have a minute? I found something that I'm not sure what to do with." Riley responded as he entered. He glanced at Mark. He also hinted that it was important enough that it should probably take priority.

"Of course. You remember Mark DeCanus, right?" Ramat asked.

"Yes, sir." Riley said, and he nodded a hello over to Mark.

"He's the Ambassador representing Earth on this mission, in case we need any type of diplomacy out here." Ramat replied. That helped fill in the gap for Riley as to why Mark was there.

"I can come back another time, Ramat." Mark said, using Ramat's first name, indicating to Riley their status as close friends.

"Sir, you might want to hear this as well." Riley responded. Riley realized that if he was right, Mark's services were going to be needed after all.

Mark nodded with a confused grin on his face.

"Sir, Star and I found something in the database. We were looking through old faster-than-light attempts, you know, back with the old Sputnik probe trials?" Riley paused, waiting for some signal that everyone understood where he was starting from. The Sputnik trials were incredibly famous, considering where they were now, and what they were doing now wouldn't be possible without them.

"Yes, Rip, everyone knows about the Sputnik trials, get on with it and tell them the good part." Star interjected, letting her excitement get the best of her.

Riley continued. "Something about the direction we're heading didn't feel right. We checked the vectors of all of the light-speed trials to see which direction they went."

Ramat interrupted. "The tech guys on Earth did that a while ago – they didn't find any correlation."

"We didn't either." Riley said. Before he could continue, Star cut him off.

"Unnntillll." Star drew out the word.

Riley took back over. "We looked back at some of the failed missions. We looked back at some of the data based on what we now know about the signals that are emitted when transitioning and a few of the tests didn't fail."

"At least not fully." Star cut in again.

"That's right. This one in particular." Riley said as he put his screen on Ramat's desk and began tracing a line from earth off of the screen. "This one got at least part of a charge before disappearing. Also, not all of the mass was accounted for in the debris that remained behind."

Both Ramat and Mark were leaning forward now. They

looked like they hadn't quite made the connection yet, but were eagerly waiting for the point to be made.

While Riley expanded the view on the screen, Mark almost fell out of his chair, leaning forward. Star jumped in. "That vector is the same flight path we are on now."

It was obvious to both of them now. The slow realization dawned on their faces as they tried to grasp what this could mean.

"What if it wasn't a random attack? What if this probe hit their world at near-light speed?" Riley added.

"That would be bad, and also make this make a lot of sense. Ramat, we need to check this. If it's verified, we need to send this information to General Sites. I'll send it back on my channels also. We need to let them know that we possibly started this. We could have attacked them first." Mark said.

After a moment of silence, Ramat said, "And we have less than a week to stop the first interstellar war from breaking out."

CHAPTER 15

Jennifer–Pentagon–Earth

Jennifer Stanza entered the main entrance of the Pentagon, like she had done so many days before. This day wasn't different except for the package she carried. She concealed it in her folder, the same folder she typically carried into the media briefings which occurred every other day. Sometimes it was more often if there was a major update on the progress of the outbound mission. The mission that Riley was on.

"Hi George, how's your daughter doing? Recover from that cold she had?" Jenn asked the security guard as she passed by his station.

"She's doing just fine, Jenn. Nice article last week, anything new coming out?" George responded.

"You know me, there's always another story." Jenn responded, doing her best job of hiding the fact that there was indeed another big story, but it likely wouldn't see the light of day.

"I can't wait. Say hi to your pops for me." George replied, and Jenn turned to walk away waving her coffee cup at him because she didn't have any free hands.

Jenn had a genuine connection with people, if given the time to build a relationship. Not that she was one to use other people, but she always enjoyed having people she knew everywhere she went. They might be able to help when she least expects it. Such as this instance. The folder she brought in would typically be flagged and searched, but that was not something she wanted. She had figured out a soft spot in the security and how to get through it.

After she sat through the briefings, the real purpose of her visit began. Being a reporter was great, her dream job, in fact. But she was unlikely to reveal what she was doing to anyone. At least not for a while. This was bigger than some story. In fact, her experience and skills as an investigator allowed her to dig up and uncover everything she had.

She hadn't responded to Riley yet with her findings, but she also didn't think it was safe too. She had a backdoor channel to the ship if she needed to, but she didn't want to use that yet. Her boyfriend, or at least that's what she thought Riley was to her, had asked her a question in a roundabout way in his last message. It had been nagging at her for a while.

What could she find out that he wasn't able to with the limited resources he had on the ship? What did she have access to that he didn't? When she received a hidden message from Mark DeCanus, she knew where to look. The message said that the Earth scientists had looked into previous light speed events and tagged anything that had a path towards the source of the ship that attacked Earth. The report said that it had come up empty. She didn't believe that. She wasn't sure why, but something else was off. How did Riley and Star find something with limited resources on their downtime that an entire team of Earth's top scientists had missed? She didn't doubt their ingenuity and the drive to find the truth. She knew what they were capable of and witnessed it firsthand the day of the attack.

That's why she was on her way to see her father now. Something she regularly did as well after many of the briefings. Those trips were usually just to check in and say hi. This time was going to be different. General Stanza, her father, was one of the few members of the war council and was the overseeing officer in charge of this mission. While General Stanza didn't always see eye to eye with Mark DeCanus, he respected him and his reputation. Enough to introduce him to his daughter when she said she was interested in politics. When Jenn thought back on it, it felt forever ago. In reality, it was going on shy of seven years. Her dad had set her up to shadow him for a high school career event. Jenn couldn't get enough, but she wanted to take a different approach to changing the machine, and so went into political reporting. That fact that she still stayed in close touch with Mark was a secret that they didn't share with anyone except her dad.

Jenn's and Mark's relationship began out as a mentor and mentee. In her high school political science course, the teacher paired each student with a member of the political world. General Stanza had recommended Mark to Jenn's teacher. At the onset of conversations with Mark, she realized the work he was trying to do and so did her paper on the merging of governments. The paper was far too short to capture all the detail required, but it got the point across. Merging governments remained elusive to humans throughout history. Once Jenn seriously wrote during college and as a freelancer after college, they had a better use for each other than mentor and mentee. They became friends. She would keep an ear out for him and he would alert her to big breaking stories before they broke. Or set her up so that she broke them. It wasn't always to help Mark out or to help Jenn out. They had an unspoken agreement that if something wasn't right, they would make it known to the world. It didn't matter if it made them or people they knew look bad. So not all the stories that Jenn wrote were flattering to Mark or to his party, but that was something he was okay with.

But all of that, this friendship and working relationship, led to this. The file that Jenn received from Mark was the tip of the iceberg, and she may have found everything hidden under the water. Jenn made her way to the upper levels, close to the center ring, like she had so many times before. She stopped at various acquaintances' desks to make small talk, not alerting anyone to the importance and purpose of her step. She finally made it to her father's secretary. As she approached, the secretary nodded, indicating he was in his office and currently not in a meeting. Jenn knew this, of course. She knew his schedule and arrived precisely when she wanted to.

Jenn knocked gently on the door. The knock was completely out of character for most of the people that visited General Stanza, so he recognized it right away.

"Come in, sweetheart. I read your piece this morning. Nice work, it didn't make a lot of my friends happy, but they are just too single-minded. What's new with you?" General Stanza said, he could have continued talking, and normally did, but Jenn knew she probably looked like she was bursting at the seams to say something. Her stance showed she had a more specific, urgent reason for being there.

Jennifer went to close the door and as she spoke. "I have something important for you. Nobody else can be trusted. It has to do with the task force. Don't ask how I got it. Just take it and know that it is the truth, not like whatever the hell Rictor is going to try and shove down your throat." As she spoke, she handed her father the envelope of information she had been carrying. She was simultaneously relieved and worried.

Relieved that she was no longer holding on to the information, and worried about the outcome of what this information could bring.

"Easy there. I wouldn't ever question you. Rictor on the other hand..." General Stanza joked with a smile out of the corner of his mouth.

"I have something else that I didn't put in that report. I got locked out of a database I use sometimes when looking into people. This report says that our teams on Earth checked every trajectory of past missions and compared them with where we are going now. But it didn't, or at least that's what we are led to believe."

"What are you getting at, Jenn?" General Stanza asked as he shuffled through the package.

"The data, some of it, had been silenced, erased. We have sent probes in that direction before, but that information was intentionally left out. I was getting close to finding out who before that went missing too."

"I see. You just promise me you'll stay safe. Don't go digging around any place dangerous." General Stanza responded.

"You know me, Dad." Jenn said with a smile on her face. They both let out a small chuckle, knowing that was exactly what she was likely to do. "I trust you. But there's more." Jenn stated. "Rictor. He worked on the science team early in his career, long before politics, that searched for habitable planets. Because of that experience, he was given the position on the faster than light programs to decide what were safe directions to point and what were no-goes. Now he's in a position to decide if we go to war or not based on all of that. The data I'm finding has all been tampered with. He's up to something big."

"That's pretty serious stuff, Jenn. I trust you, but it seems you may have already broken your promise of staying out of dangerous places." After a long, thoughtful pause, General Stanza continued. "I'll take a look into that personally. It will be handled."

She knew he would handle it. She wished she knew what her dad was going to do to whoever was behind the cover-up. She really wanted to be a fly on the wall in whatever room that decision was made in. She would have to settle for figuring it out the way she normally did, good old fashion investigation.

"Who else has seen this?" He responded.

"Just me and a few others on the ship. Colonel D'Pol and Mark wrote it. Riley is the one that found it." Jenn stated deciding it wouldn't do any good trying to hide where she got the information from.

"I see." He responded. "How is Riley doing?" He asked. Jenn was glad he was changing the subject, and glad he was changing it to this.

"He seems to be doing good. Have you seen anything?" She asked, hopeful that he had more information that he could share. They hadn't met yet, but he had read the reports and heard Jenn talk about him most times they met.

"Not much more than you, I'm afraid. You probably know more than I about how the crew are doing. I mostly just see the overhead reports from General Sites. As informative as they are."

After a long pause, Jenn got up the courage to ask a question. "Dad, what was it like, between you and mom early on, you know, with you gone all of the time?"

The question didn't seem to faze him, almost as though he was expecting it. Maybe not now, but at some point in the future. Jenn's parents got together at the beginning of her dad's career, but she never was old enough to see what her mom went through with him, not there all the time. By the time she was old enough, he was a high enough rank that he was mostly home, even if home changed every couple of years.

"It wasn't always easy. There were good times and bad. She had to count on those close to her when I was away. I'll always be here for you." Jenn knew that would be the short answer, but for some reason hearing it out loud made it harder. He continued while she was still processing what he had said. It wasn't a lot of words, but their impact was deep for her. "Does he know how you feel?" He added.

Jenn slight slump in her posture told her dad that she wasn't sure if he knew. An imperceptible movement to most, he dad had a sixth sense when his little girl was off. "I don't know. I think so. I hope so."

"Then you have nothing to worry about. If it's something you want and he is there for you, all you have to do is be there for him." After another round of silence, he continued. "And if he hurts you, there isn't a safe place in the space force for him." He finally said. Both of them laughed. The mood had gotten a little too low for what they were both used to around each other. Ending the conversation on a high note cheered Jenn up.

"I'll get right on it, Jenn. Don't worry." Her dad responded, nodding to the envelope she had given him.

With that, Jenn winked and turned to walk out of the office. She knew her dad was indeed going to handle this, and it likely would not be pretty for those that had done wrong. She got many traits from her mother, including a sense of adventure and breaking rules. But it was her sense of right and wrong that she got from her dad and neither of them liked it when someone did wrong and put their loved ones at risk.

CHAPTER 16

Ramat–Space Force Guard Ship Catalyst–In Transit

Colonel Ramat 'Trap' D'Pol was sitting in the squadron room, making minor last-minute adjustments to his plan of attack once they entered normal space. Based on the timing, he knew that should be soon. The plan of attack that he was preparing for was not an attack at all. It was to get his team out as quickly as possible and fly in defense of the fleet while they attempted to talk with whoever they encountered. If that failed, they needed to defend the fleet long enough to recharge all of the batteries and realign the ships for a return light gate transition. While he was about to brief the squadron, he heard a crackle on the intercom followed by General Sites' voice: "This is the task force commander speaking." General Sites began. His words were being broadcast through all ships in the fleet. "We are beginning preparations for the transition to normal speeds. We will be within range of the alien home world where we have just received confirmation from the war council to proceed with our attack. I will show this enemy why it is not a good idea to mess with Earth! Battle stations, everyone.

General Sites, out."

The voice cut out and the crackling stopped. Ramat was stunned for a moment. "What the hell was that?" Ramat said out loud, not intending for anyone to hear. He tried to open a communications line to General Sites, but it didn't go through. "He blocked me? What is going on?"

"Something wrong, sir?" Captain James 'P' Parrant said as he slowly approached.

"Yes, P, this shouldn't be the plan." Ramat responded. "Rip, Face, get over here." As soon as he said that a loud wailing siren alarmed, indicating a transition was imminent. "Stand by, get in your couches."

"Damnit, not enough time to go see what the hell happened with our message." Ramat said to Charlie.

Charlie's face had twisted into an angry scowl. "Something shady is going on." Charlie responded.

Ramat thought of Mark. He might know what nonsense threatened this mission and all of their lives. This was his arena, after all. Ramat could tell initially that Mark was skeptical that a diplomatic approach would work but knew that they had to at least try. "Mark, do you know what's going on? There is no way that is the response we should have gotten." Ramat spoke over the comm unit. Mark was in his room for the transition while the Lucky's were all in their squadron room, which was now the ready room. They were all ready to launch in their fighters as soon as they completed the transition. Two of the team were already outside, completing their transition in case there were enemy spacecraft as soon as they arrived. These were essentially fodder to hold off any enemy long enough in the event the fleet needed to transition back through light gates to make a quick escape. The two fighters would fight to the end to buy time for the fleet. Ramat didn't like the idea, but he knew it may be necessary.

"Yes, I have some idea. I have something for you. Can't send it to you yet. I'll come over as soon as we transition." Mark responded quickly.

Ramat thought Mark must have been referring to his back-channel comms path that he established. If it was important enough that he didn't feel comfortable relaying the response through the ship, it was probably something big. Ramat's mind raced, but couldn't figure out what the next step might be.

Ramat would have preferred to use the secret comm channel that Tobias had set up for them, but that was only at his desk, and he needed to get the information now. So, everything he said was over the ship network. If General Sites was looking for someone that may have leaked the information, Mark would be at the top of his list of suspects. He probably heard that conversation.

Ramat knew he needed to get to Mark first, for some reason, he knew things were about to go downhill quickly. "Wisp, get three guys to come with me to Mark's room as soon as we complete the transition. I mean, the millisecond we complete it, we're not waiting for the all clear. Mark is in trouble. You stay behind to handle any tasks which we'll probably get in order to keep us busy. I think someone is going to try and keep us distracted until we make first contact." Ramat knew Charlie wouldn't take any bullshit from anyone. If the tasking made little sense, he would ask so many questions about it they would forget the original task, or he would flat out deny it until someone provided a proper explanation. That wasn't exactly the military way, but it got the job done. He was supposed to follow every order, but he only followed the right ones. Charlie always felt that the difference between the right order and the wrong one was up to his interpretation. Sure, he didn't always have the big picture and the reasoning behind some orders was beyond his grasp, but he knew when that was the case, or at least when he was told that was the case, he would comply. This time was going to be quite different from anything anyone had done before, so his experience in determining which order was correct or not would only provide a vague guide.

While Charlie was getting three crew members, Ramat headed for his locker. He reached in and pulled out a lockbox. He never checked this box except right before leaving on a mission. It was more for good luck than for actual use, although he knew it still worked. With a thumb on the screen, he heard an audible click as the indicator turned from red to green. He opened the lid and pulled a pistol from the box. Safely tucked away in his flight suit, he started wishing he wouldn't have to use it. It was a violation to have a firearm on board for several good reasons, but this was one rule Ramat did not care for much. He made his way back to the ready room.

From experience, he could hear and feel the ship complete the transition to normal speeds.

"Let's go." Ramat said, gesturing to Riley, Star, and Captain Maggie Lorrent. Captain Lorrent was to be the muscle, if needed. She wasn't exceptionally large in stature, about average in most regards, but she was well-trained, with a documented, and word-of-mouth history of being able to handle herself in close quarters hand to hand 'situations'. Hence, her call sign of 'Face'; apparently anyone that went up against her got their face adjusted. While there was some talk about it being because she was incredibly attractive, nobody wanted to test which was the reason for her callsign. Ramat knew the truth, and so he pitied the poor soul who ever thought it would be a good idea to ask. Riley and Star came along mostly because they already knew what was going on and didn't need to be brought up to speed. There was no time.

They all unbuckled and were out the door, not waiting for one another to push the crowds of people. Everyone would go to their battle stations soon. They were going to retrieve Mark. They didn't know what or if there would be any trouble. But Ramat thought it was a possibility and so they were ready for it. As ready as they could be.

A voice came over the ship-wide speakers. "Transition Complete." Followed by. "All crew, battle stations. All crew, battle stations." With that, hatches flew open, and crew members began hastily making their way through the corridors in an organized chaos.

When they approached Mark's room, Ramat could hear muffled voices through the door. One could be Mark's and was sounding labored, stressed. The other voices were escalating in volume and desperation. "Get ready, follow me." Ramat whispered as he entered the room.

He didn't expect to see the military police attempting to handcuff Mark.

"Stand back! This man is under arrest for treason. Stay where you are." the military cop ordered to Ramat and the others.

"What's going on? He's done nothing!" Ramat responded, holding up a hand to stop his team from advancing for now.

"Ramat, the message." Mark struggled to say. He was currently being wrestled with hand restraints being put in place. "It was manipulated by Rictor and the General. I have new orders that put you in charge. I must get out of here." Mark pleaded. "Let me go, the fate of the mission is at stake. You're making a huge mistake." Mark continued, this time talking to the military cops.

Clearly, the time for diplomacy had passed in this room. Ramat floated motionless for a moment. His military career, all that he had done, hung in the balance. Would he decide to stand by and do nothing, which would likely lead to him getting rolled up in the bad side of this mess, anyway? Or would he do the right thing? Help a trusted friend in need and potentially change the fate of the human race, forever.

It was only a split second. All of those thoughts rushed in over Ramat, but the decision was easy. He typically knew the right thing to do in a situation, and even though the circumstances were extreme and the consequences were worse than he had ever faced, he did not shy away from taking the chance. Not now, not ever.

Ramat signaled to the others to surround the two guards. "Boys, you really don't want to do that. Let him go, and we'll forget the whole thing ever happened. He's right, you're making a huge mistake." Ramat urged, speaking calmly. If he could, he wanted to diffuse the situation peacefully. He knew that likely would not work, hopeful that his team surrounding them would do the trick. He resisted the urge to reach for his pistol.

"You know we can't do that. We have orders right from the fleet commander." One guard said.

"Of course, you can. You don't know the whole story, but Mark here is right. General Sites has been feeding misinformation. The grounds for this arrest are unfounded. Let him go, and we'll sort it out. Nobody has to get hurt." Ramat repeated. He became increasingly aware of the time that had passed since the transition was completed. The longer this took, the more likely they would get caught, and the more inevitable it was that General Sites would attack the aliens. Something needed to happen, and it needed to happen now. He was growing impatient, and it showed on his face; he could feel it in his palms as he reached for his gun. The acute smell of the room mixed with their perspiration from moving to meet Mark so quickly caught up with him.

"Call this in." One guard said to the other.

"I've been trying, radios are jammed." The other returned.

"That's right, you can't get a signal out of this room. You're not getting back-up. You're outnumbered. Turn him over. This is your last warning." Ramat said to the two cops, turning his tone aggressive to make sure they got the hint. Their faces struggled with what to do. They both looked confused, as if they were truly contemplating the dilemma, as they should be. Because they were on a spacefaring vessel, they were not permitted to carry guns. They had shock sticks, which were out and ready now. However, due to the sensitive electronics throughout the ship and the risk of fire, they had turned the voltage to the shock sticks way down. So much so that it would have little effect on someone in a fight with adrenaline coursing through their body. Which was exactly what was about to happen if something didn't happen soon.

As if to push the guards into making a decision, Ramat couldn't resist any longer and drew his pistol from his flight suit, casually holding it at his side but visible for both to see.

The two guards looked shocked. At that moment, Mark pulled down hard with his hands. Each guard had a hand on their shock stick, and another on Mark's restraints. This forced the two to be pulled down and towards each other, while launching Mark up. One guard maintained a handhold on Mark's restraints while the other had no choice but to let go. The one that let go was quickly in close company with Maggie. She maneuvered behind him, putting him in a rear choke hold as Star distracted him. The guard was unable to strike her with his shock stick from behind in this position. While Maggie was holding him, Star worked on restraining him with a set of zip ties she grabbed off of the cop's utility belt. Indecisive on his next move, the guard contemplated whether to remove Maggie from his back or prevent Star from reaching his belt.

The wild, violent movement of the guard made it difficult to get the zip ties. The zero G and not having anything to push off of or hold on to made counteracting those movements much more difficult. The fight in him faded as he became unconscious. His body relaxed and so Maggie relaxed her grip.

The other cop released Mark and tried to aid his friend. Noticing this, Riley thrust off the side wall and into the guard with all the force he could manage, cutting him off. This knocked them back into the corner of the room. Ramat began putting his gun back into his flight suit as he made his way towards Riley and the other cop. He joined in the scuffle. With the other cop already in restraints, Maggie began helping with the second cop and made quick work of tying him up. They gagged the two guards and tied them up in the closet. They had little time.

The four Lucky's, with Mark in tow, exited his room, closing and locking the door behind them. They headed towards the Lucky's ready room. It had only been a couple of minutes, but by this point, most of the crew were at their combat stations. There were a few stragglers, but nobody paid any attention to them.

They quickly made their way back to the ready room. They had transitioned to normal space, and the fleet crews would be working feverishly to gather all the different telemetry that the sensors were picking up and determine what was out there in terms of an enemy. All the information would be significantly delayed because of their proximity to the enemy from where they reentered normal space. While it was not ideal, this gave them the time to determine the strength of the enemy fleet and finalize an attack plan. That was the original plan anyway.

Once back at the Lucky's ready room, they all entered and shut the door behind them.

All the crew of the Lucky's were in their ready positions. If called, they would quickly move to their AIMS while their orders were being uploaded to their flight computers. They could review the orders as the spacecraft finished getting prepped and during the transit away from other ships. Although there wasn't much time, the pilots quickly became accustomed to distilling the most important information and deciding how to deal with it.

Ramat looked around and saw X, Lieutenant Xavier. X was not listed on the on-call roster and Ramat planned to use him as back-up. He was also one of the more junior members, so the job he had in mind was perfect for him. In case guards were sent to look for them, he didn't want the team members who helped Mark escape to be exposed in the hall. At least, he didn't want them exposed until they could execute the takeover of the ship.

"X, stand guard in the hall. Don't let anyone in. Don't get hurt, but if you get taken to the brig, I won't hold it against you." Ramat said. He knew he was putting his squadron on the line, and if his plan failed, he would take full responsibility, but he had to take tremendous risks right now for the good of the crew, the fleet, and Earth.

"Yes, sir." Michael said as he went to the door and opened it up. He looked around in the hall, stepped out, and shut the door behind him. They manually locked it from the inside and jammed the lock to prevent manual override from the outside. Something that Ramat knew the guards and probably General Sites could do.

"Mark, what do you have?" Ramat said, eager to see the information that could likely destroy his career.

"It's all here." Mark said as he opened up the display. He scrolled through the information and went right to the order. The order was short and sweet, and all that Ramat needed.

It read: *Colonel Ramat D'Pol, you are hereby appointed the rank of Brigadier General and are to assume the command of the task force immediately, by any means or force necessary. You are to remove General Sites from command and place him on quarters if he complies, or the brig if he does not. The information you provided made clear that we do not want to go to war with this new species. Do everything in your power to avoid a conflict but exercise caution and good judgment.*

- North America War Council.

This came right from the top. Ramat was going to have to play this close to the chest.

"Sir." Maggie broke in. She had been monitoring the ship comms traffic. Since she didn't have access to the guard's channel, they wouldn't know if what Ramat had done had been discovered yet. If they had, it would only be a matter of time before General Sites sent another team to capture them. Maggie could monitor the sensor station comms, and what she heard was alarming. "We are closer to the enemy, or the other aliens, than we thought." She quickly corrected herself. They weren't the enemy anymore, apparently. She would have to get caught up on why part later. "There are a lot of ships out there, we were only able to identify some of them. There is also some sort of battle already taking place near the planet. Nobody seems to know what's going on. What do you want to do?"

Ramat was going to have to decide, and quickly. He needed to take command before General Sites made the first move to attack. He paused there, clearly in deep thought, but only for a second.

He began. "Face, get me Major Thompson on the line, he's the head of ship security. I'm going to need him on my side and to escort me. Next get me Colonel Archer, the duty officer. All fighter squadron commanders will listen to him. I need them to stay put and not go on any offensive. They would be the first to strike, so if we can delay that, we could delay entering on the wrong side of this conflict. Once you do that, get back to the bridge with General Sites. Everyone else, with me, we're taking the command center."

CHAPTER 17

Maggie–Space For Guard Ship Catalyst–Razuud System

Captain Maggie 'Face' Lorrent walked through the hatch to the CC room. General Sites sat in the command chair, looking over the multitude of screens in front of him, seemingly not noticing her entering. She hoped that was the case and made her way to the closest empty console. She didn't want to tip the general off. So she acted as normal as possible. The upcoming battle could explain any noticeable nerves. He didn't seem to be focused on anyone. She wasn't sure if he knew where his entire fleet was, let alone what was going on with the enemy ships and the unknown ships or the crew on his own ship. He was trying to work on a tactical plan, which was normally developed below his level. Someone should have brought up solutions for him to decide on. Because he micromanaged the battlespace, everyone else that normally developed those plans was sitting idle, waiting. Or that's what Sites thought. Maggie knew they already had plans, good plans, ready to go when shit turned sideways, which it likely would.

Maggie was looking around the room when she caught

sight of General Sites. His face twisted in ways she didn't know were possible and turned bright red. She looked down and saw that he was on a communication channel with someone, but she couldn't listen in without him knowing.

"He WHAT!?" She heard General Sites cut loose on whoever was on the other end. "How does someone like that escape two guards? How incompetent are you? I want you and Major Thompson, soon to be Captain Thompson, in the command center now! And find Mark DeCanus!" He shouted the entire one-sided conversation. It was difficult for everyone in the command center to act like they couldn't hear and to continue with what they were doing.

His poise and control did not reflect a picture that Maggie expected from a general. She anxiously waited for when that time would end. A serious threat in space rapidly approached. This action should not have taken precedence over the current risks. When they entered normal space, they were much closer to the alien planet than intended. If they could slow down, they would be within range in a few hours. General Sites refocused and spent the next few minutes finalizing his attack plan and pushed the order to the operations teams and squadron commanders.

Colonel Archer would typically see the orders at the same time so he could prepare the ships for movement to include getting fighters out into space. After the attack, General Sites always treated him like an afterthought. Luckily, all the flight crews still had Colonel Archer's respect, so nobody left the ships without his say so.

Little did General Sites know, but Colonel Archer already got orders from the new commander of the fleet, telling him to deny any action for any maneuvering of the fleet. At worst, Colonel Archer could stall any action for several hours from taking place, which should be enough for whatever Colonel, now General D'Pol, had in mind. Maggie trusted Ramat, but this was still an enormous risk for her. If something went wrong or it didn't turn out, it would not end well for her or anyone involved. General Sites likely wouldn't even transport their bodies back to Earth. She wanted to see the look on General Sites' face when they finally confronted him.

Maggie took stock of her surroundings. The crew, their state of mind, anything that might help turn things around once Ramat came through the doors. That's when she noticed the sensor operator next to her. She was rapidly looking back and forth between her screen and General Sites. Her motions became more and more exaggerated as the seconds ticked by.

Maggie quickly glanced at her name tag and rank. "Lieutenant Bradly, what's wrong?" Maggie asked. Maggie could see by the sign above her station that she was the lead sensor operator. She knew all the leads, and she was not one of the normal ones.

The agitated Lieutenant snapped her attention to Maggie, bursting at the seams to reveal the information on her mind. "We were told not to bother him, but the number of ships approaching us is massive, much more than we were expecting. Much more than we can handle. And we don't recognize half of them."

Maggie glanced at what she was seeing. The enemy could easily wipe out the human fleet. It became exceedingly clear that the two different groups were engaged in combat with each other. The ships appeared to be breaking from the main engagement and this worried her. They stopped attacking each other and instead focused their attention on her own fleet.

"How much time until they are within range?" Maggie asked quickly.

"At this rate and if General Sites does nothing, within the hour." She responded.

"You need to tell him." Maggie turned to General Sites. "General Sites, sir, there is some new information coming in that you need to hear." Maggie said while motioning to Lieutenant Bradly.

"General Sites, sir. There is a situation." the sensor operator said, with some fear in her voice. More so out of how the General would respond and less because of the situation they were in.

"What could it possibly be this time? I told you not to give me any more reports. We already have a plan, and that is what we are going to execute. We cannot change it anymore." General Sites responded. "Didn't I just put you in that position? Don't make me regret it."

"But sir, both groups are headed our way. We will be within range of their known energy weapon within the hour. Our plan doesn't account for both groups coming to meet us." Lieutenant Bradly said, beginning to find her voice. She was getting a little mad that the lives of the fleet were being considered so lightly. "If we don't do anything now, our fleet will get destroyed, and we'll all die!"

Just as the sensor operator was about to continue and probably be cut off by General Sites, Maggie turned with a sigh of relief to find General D'Pol entering the command center. A contingent of military police, along with members from his squadron, Mark, and Major Thompson, made their way through the entrance. Maggie turned back to General Sites in time to see a twisted look flash across his face.

General Sites turned to them before speaking. "It's about time Major Thompson. Can you explain to me why it was so difficult to apprehend this man, Mark?" He said Mark's name with a hiss, as if it left a foul taste in his mouth.

"I can do that." Ramat stepped in. "General Sites, you are hereby officially relieved of duty. These police officers will escort you to your quarters. If you do not wish to go to your quarters, they will forcefully take you to the brig." He paused before saying. "Please choose the second option."

"What is the meaning of this, Colonel D'Pol?" Maggie didn't blame him for not noticing the new General rank Ramat had. At this point, she was simultaneously sitting back, enjoying the show, and ready to act in case there were any members loyal to Sites hanging around. "You have no right or authority here! Get out of my command center at once! Major Thompson, arrest this man, all of them. Anyone that is working with him!" General Sites yelled.

"That's General D'Pol to you, Sites. I have orders from the war council on Earth to relieve you of command. You were not forthcoming to them about the information we sent to them regarding the reason for the alien invasion and are incapable of commanding this fleet. I no longer have the time to waste explaining anything to you. We have a war to stop." Ramat responded forcefully. There was a tone that General Sites could not mistake, and certainly couldn't match. It was a command presence that Maggie knew Sites would never admit to not having, and certainly not even being capable of. Maggie hoped he felt alone in that moment because he was.

"Rictor, that slimy little shit, he's going to pay for this. I did nothing wrong! You can't do this to me!" General Sites responded, his voice elevating an octave or two.

"Get him out of here, Major Thompson." Ramat said, nodding at Sites.

"With pleasure." And with that, Major Thompson and the security detail removed General Sites from his chair, kicking and screaming, and left the command center. A couple of security guards remained behind as a precaution. The possibility remained that a diehard follower of General Sites lurked in plain sight, waiting for the right time to attempt another takeover.

"Looks like he picked option two." Riley said from the back of the command center.

RAMAT

Ramat gave a slight smile to Riley before turning to the crew in the command center. He opened a line of communication to the entire fleet. Even though the rest of the ships had already been prepped on what was going on, Ramat needed to demonstrate to the fleet that he was in charge and had a plan on how they were going to proceed next. He looked over and nodded at Maggie. "Team, this is your new task force commander speaking, General Ramat D'Pol. As you may already know, there are two forces bearing down on us. One we know of and have encountered before; the other is completely unknown. But what you don't know is that the known force should not be our enemy. You see, it was us who attacked them first, although we did not know we did it. We unknowingly destroyed part of their home world, and they were simply retaliating, much in the same way we are doing now. We have an opportunity to break the cycle before it begins. Our goal is to reach out and communicate with this new species. At the moment, our team is dedicated to establishing communication with them, and they are almost ready to do so. I still expect a fight on our hands. But with whom, I do not know. What I do know is that we have some of the best ships, crewed by the best crews that Earth has to offer, and if there ever was a team that could succeed, it's this one. Stand by for new orders. Everyone, to battle stations.

Trap, out."

Without missing a beat, Ramat looked for the Lieutenant he saw speaking up to General Sites. He could tell she had a big picture idea of what was going on and needed her insight and input to come up with a response plan to the current situation. In fact, he was going to need everyone.

"Lieutenant." Ramat said, looking over at the sensor operator. She still had her gaze fixed on where all the commotion happened and hadn't snapped out of it yet.

"Yes, sir?" She responded with a look of fear and surprise in her eyes.

"Give me a layout of the battlespace." Ramat responded, noticing some hesitation in her voice. She was about to speak; her voice came out shaky. This wouldn't do, Ramat thought to himself. The entire crew sat terrified in their seats, either from working under Sites, or in fear of the situation. He made a judgement call and assumed it was from working under the former commander. The fear of death never outweighed the fear of working under an insufferable boss.

"Listen up, everyone." Ramat bellowed in the command center. He didn't send this message to the entire fleet. Ramat intended it only for those who worked directly for General Sites. He could tell that Sites had done a number on them. "I need everyone at their best. Any transgressions or trouble you thought you were in while interacting with General Sites, it's over, done, they are gone. I am going to need and rely on all of your expertise. I need you all thinking independently again. Don't worry about telling me what I want to hear; that will get someone killed. Tell me what is actually going on and give me your best assessment. You are all in your positions because you know what you are doing. It's time you acted like it again." And with that, the feeling in the command center was noticeably upbeat and focused.

Ramat turned back to the sensor operator. "Lieutenant, sorry for interrupting, you were about to give me a layout of the battlespace. Please continue." He was trying to convey that he needed the information she had and that it was important.

"Sir." she began again, this time with confidence. "There are two separate fleets that currently appear to be engaged with each other. The unknown fleet is larger in number; however, we don't yet know their capabilities. They are approximately five hours away at our current speeds. Still out of accurate missile range and there would be low confidence of a dumb bomb impact, similar to back on Earth." She said. "More pressing, though, they each broke off several ships on a direct intercept course with our fleet. That contingent will be within range of their energy weapons in less than 45 minutes now."

With that, Ramat understood. He didn't quite get everything she was saying when he first walked in. Now he knew that the timeline for making something happen was tight. "Thank you. Comms, get me the Engineering department." The engineering department held the linguists and the communications engineers. The linguist was responsible for figuring out what this species' language sounds or looks like. This person will be the translator. The comms engineer had to figure out how to get the signal out in a form that the alien species could understand. They could intercept some traffic back on Earth during the initial invasion, and so they used that to come up with a way to copy it. They hadn't quite figured it out yet.

"Engineering. General, you wanted to speak?" Said Sergeant Viso on the other line.

"Yes. What's the timeline for getting that new language signal and translation online?" Ramat responded. He didn't want to put the emphasis on urgency until he knew how long they were going to need. They already knew they needed it as soon as possible but were not yet aware that there was an actual deadline. Better not to tell them if they were already complete. Ramat was hopeful.

"We are very close. The shortest amount of time is probably two hours, sir." Sergeant Viso responded.

"We have forty-five minutes until we are within range of enemy weapons. Let me know as soon as you have something. Even if you haven't fully tested it yet. Out." Ramat said. He knew that telling them to get it done in thirty minutes wasn't going to work. Some things took time. They knew what they were doing, and now they knew the dangers. If there was any way they could go faster, they certainly would be doing it now.

For the first time, Ramat realized someone was missing. The ship's Captain, Lieutenant Colonel Mary Barker. Known to him as Mary Ann. "Where's Colonel Barker and Mentle?" Lieutenant Colonel Mentle was the Operations Officer, the second in command of the ship to Lieutenant Colonel Barker. Ramat asked to no one in particular but expected an answer.

He got his answer from an unexpected source. The security guard spoke up from behind him at the door. He was hesitant at first. "Uh, sir, I know where they are."

"Go on, Sergeant." Giving him permission to speak. Not that he actually needed it, but he could tell that the sergeant was unfamiliar with the customs in the operations center and didn't know his policy. Ramat had a policy everywhere he was at. It didn't matter what rank you were or what job you had, if you had information or an idea that people needed to hear, you needed to speak up. With and especially without permission. This allowed all the best ideas and concerns to be heard with no one worrying about getting stepped on and chewed out.

The sergeant spoke up. "They are both in the brig. Well,

sorta, they are both locked in their quarters with all comms locked out. Something about disobeying a command and attempted mutiny or something like that. I only know because I had to stand guard one night. I don't know anything besides that."

"Holy shit!" Ramat exclaimed to the room. "What the hell did Sites do?" Ramat rarely lost composure in front of his team but was struggling extremely hard to understand what was going on and how Sites could do all of this. "Never mind the why right now. Sergeant, get both of them here as quickly as possible."

"Yes, sir!" The sergeant said and took off out the door as quickly as he could.

While he waited for them to return, he needed to come up with a plan to extend the time as long as possible before they were within range of the alien fleet. "Helm, halt acceleration, reverse course, and align the vector to put the approaching fleets with the known alien force between us and the unknown alien fleet. We want to give the comms guys as much time as possible to figure out their language and means of sending it. We also don't want to start attacking everything we see; that could prove bad for us."

"Yes, sir. Reversing thrust. Setting intercept vector behind the known alien fleet." The helm responded. One of the last elements of a navy ship kept. Mostly, though, space operations were nothing like anything else ever done on a ship, and all positions and techniques needed to be new. The helm didn't steer a wheel or anything like that. The pilot simply input some commands into a computer or adjusted a few settings, and the ship's computer did the rest. Fine-tuned controls were done with the augmented reality gear. The vectoring was almost counterintuitive, especially when in reverse thrust. In this situation, where the ship needed to slow down and move away from the unknown alien fleet, they needed to point the exhaust of the thrusters directly at the unknown alien fleet. This would slow them down and move them away from their ships. Ramat had to do it in a way that positioned the known fleet between them and the unknown fleet. He figured this gave them the best chance of survival.

As the Earth Fleet began to slow and maneuver, the time before being within range of the enemy's energy weapon increased. The alien ships were accelerating, so there was a limit to how long they could postpone this engagement. When the time to intercept counter stopped moving at one hour thirty-three minutes and slowly counted down each minute, they knew they had reached the equilibrium. They could not match the enemy ship's performance, and they appeared to have maxed out theirs. The unknown enemy fleet was mostly stationary in the battlespace, seemingly to be in a position to clean up the mess of the two fleets that were about to go head-to-head. Luckily for the crew and the fleet, they hadn't yet realized that they were about to attempt to become allies.

The only lingering question for Ramat remained this: What if they have a quick exchange with the aliens and they find that, while they shouldn't go to war with each other, they also shouldn't go to war with the unknown aliens either? This may be an impossible situation to get out of without some sort of confrontation, the exact reason he warned his crew. A battle was going to happen, it was a matter of who it was between.

CHAPTER 18

Danuibi–Battleship Ryceen–Razuud Orbit

General Drobbi sat strapped into his command chair, buried deep within his Razuudian ship. The Battleship Ryceen, which meant flowing water in their ancient language. His ship was not physically the lead ship because it needed to stay protected. The rank structure in space battles did not allow for the leader to be taken out of action without serious consequences, so they often buried the command ship amongst other ships for layered protection. This held even more true now that Leader Danuibi was on board.

Leader Danuibi immediately requested to board General Drobbi's ship when reports began coming in that alien ships had recently arrived in their solar system. Alien ships from the same direction as the failed mission returned from.

Leader Danuibi knew that General Drobbi wanted revenge and hoped that his presence in the situation would deter him from doing anything drastic. Leader Danuibi was also expecting to hear from Artur soon. 'Where was he?' Leader Danuibi thought to himself. He received word that Artur had sent forward a comm drone with news of his arrival, along with some unexpected news. As Leader Danuibi sat in a makeshift command chair set up next to General Drobbi, he reflected on the message he received from Artur before learning about the aliens entering the system.

"Leader Danuibi, I need to speak with you, in person, immediately. The alien fleet is on its way, if they aren't already there, but there is more to the story than you think. I do not trust the information to this comm relay and must speak to you in person. Do not attack them unless you must." Danuibi knew something strange must be going on. Why shouldn't they attack them? There was nothing he could do or say short of removing General Drobbi from command that would get him to stop his pursuit without actual proof. He needed Artur to get to him and get to him quickly.

Leader Danuibi heard General Drobbi issued commands. "Divert my battle group to intercept the new targets. General Grayson will be in charge in my absence. Full thrust."

"Where are we going?" Leader Danuibi asked. He knew the answer, but he wanted General Drobbi to know that he was questioning his intentions.

"Leader, if this is the same enemy that took out my expedition, I want to be the one to enact revenge. We are the best suited to test out the new tactics. They think they have the jump on us, but they are mistaken." General Drobbi responded. There was a hint of irritation in his response. His whiskers and corners of his mouth had an almost imperceptible twitch as he spoke.

"Very well." Leader Danuibi wasn't sure what else to say at that point. He didn't want to let General Drobbi in on the secret yet. It could turn out to be nothing, after all. Artur was good at his job, the best, in fact, but he didn't always have the big picture in mind.

As soon as they broke off to intercept the newly arrived force, something else strange happened. The Tartins also broke a fleet off. "Where are the Tartins going?" Leader Danuibi asked. It was hard to tell, but he knew the sensor team could tell their precise heading.

"Check the Tartin fleet heading." General Drobbi said into his microphone. After a few moments, he spoke to Leader Danuibi. "They are also heading towards the new target."

"That would indicate that they also don't know who that is. Which means it is not their fleet. General, it is at this time that I should inform you that this new fleet may not be the threat we expect. I am waiting on additional information, but I urge you not to engage with them." Leader Danuibi said.

"Leader, while I appreciate your input, your presence on this ship is merely out of respect for your position. I will do what I must to carry out my mission. If you do not like my way, I ask that you replace me. Unless there is more information you can share with me, I intend to turn that fleet into stardust."

After a tense moment of contemplating the situation, an eerily timed call from the sensor team broke the silence.

"General Drobbi, sir, and Leader Danuibi."

"Yes, comms." General Drobbi responded.

"Sir, we have a docking request. He insisted and was able to override our codes. We can't see the ship and cannot engage it with any weapons. What would you like to do?"

General Drobbi looked over at Leader Danuibi. He sat with a veiled smile. "I take it you know who this is."

"Yes, General, and I suggest you do as he asks." Leader Danuibi responded. There was only one ship he knew of that could dock undetected in the middle of an active battle, and only one pilot skilled enough for the task. So Leader Danuibi knew it had to be Artur.

"Allow it." Drobbi responded.

That Artur was intercepting them in the middle of a battle said something about the information he had. Seeing as though they were approaching the alien ships, the timing couldn't have been better.

A few moments later, the ships docked. General Drobbi and Leader Danuibi got out of their chairs and headed to General Drobbi's quarters, where they were told to meet. They found Artur sitting on a spare chair off to the side against a wall in the cramped room.

"What do you have for me? It needs to be good – we are about to engage the enemy ships." Drobbi said, making sure he knew Artur needed to cut to the chase.

"Oh, it's good." Artur replied. "I was able to observe this planet we recently attacked, Earth. The native population calls themselves Humans. Not terribly different from ourselves. Their languages are difficult to translate, my computers are still working on it. However, I was able to determine that much. I was also able to get ship logs from what appears to be a military database of sorts. With their records, a mission was never sent in our direction. The only thing that made it our way appeared to be some type of reconnaissance mission. It didn't even look like they knew we were here. The humans sent out many probes of this nature in seemingly random directions. I think we may have been hit by a reconnaissance probe. We've seen it in our testing before."

Drobbi sat in disbelief. What are the chances of something like that happening? His room's comm link rang. With a startle, Drobbi responded. "Yes, comms?"

"We seem to be getting another incoming communications message. It's from the enemy ships this time." The communications officer said.

"What could they possibly have to say to us? Do they want

to work together to destroy this foreign threat? Nonsense, we will take care of it ourselves." General Drobbi responded, beginning to come to his conclusions before even hearing the message.

The communications officer cut off his train of thought. "No, General, it's from the other enemy, the one that just arrived."

"The humans? What do they say?" Now he was intrigued. They still couldn't understand or convert the sensor data they brought back. It wasn't exactly a priority for his race at the time. Artur had a better system and could make more progress on the translation. They assumed they would not have to deal with them for some time long in the future, meanwhile they had an ongoing war with the Tartins.

"It is not entirely coherent, very primitive. I'll forward you the message. They attached some other raw telemetry data." The comms officer responded, trying to be as brief as possible.

"Very well, send it over." General Drobbi and Leader Danuibi looked through the data. It became clear to them and hit Danuibi like a hammer. He felt angered at first. Were so many of his people killed due to bad luck? If the data wasn't manufactured, it was a tragedy, but one that did not need to lead to further killing and another war with a new species. The information that he received from Artur was being confirmed by the unknown alien species, the humans.

Leader Danuibi looked over at General Drobbi, who was also finishing up the reports. "General, I'm inclined to believe what they are saying."

After a moment of silence, where General Drobbi appeared to be in deep thought, he spoke. "I am as well. The information your source gathered confirms that they are telling the truth, at least part of the truth." He paused. "But why would they come all the way out here to tell us that? What is their true purpose? You don't send a fleet of ships for a peaceful mission. Nothing in their message explains that."

"I also agree. But I don't think it's enough of an unknown to not at least talk with them first."

"We can try, but we'll keep our guard up. We'll need to get a message back to them quickly; the Tartins will have received the same message."

Leader Danuibi thought about the dilemma for a brief moment. "The last thing we need is for the Tartins to gain a new and powerful ally. They'll be quick to turn this into their favor if we let them. It's best to keep this new species on our good side or at least neutral until we can sort it all out."

Leader Danuibi had a small hope that by giving them some information on the Tartins that this new species may side with him and even help. The Razuuds had been at war for too long; although many would not admit it, they were slowly losing. One more decisive loss would likely be the end for the Razuud way of life and how much it had progressed, and they would regress back to the way of the Tartins. So, out of desperation, he had no other choice, and no other hope but to try to side with the new species. He allowed himself, briefly, to think of a future meeting with them, the humans. But for right now, they were quickly approaching a battle that could determine the fate of his species.

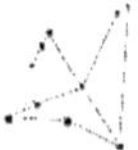

CHAPTER 19

"Sir, there is an incoming reply. We just finished translating it." a communications officer said to Ramat.

"Thank you. I'll look at it right here." Ramat responded. He was sitting in his command seat in the command section; there was no reason to be anywhere else until this was all over. He sent Maggie and Riley back to the Lucky's ready room. He couldn't help but wish he was going to be out there with them. But he belonged in the CC now. It was going to take some getting used to. A problem for another day.

When Ramat opened up the data file that contained the message from the known alien fleet, he first went to the reply message file; it was a text file. All it said was, "*Message received, accepted.*" That was short and to the point. Did they accept our explanation or our cease-fire, or both? Hopefully both. He turned to the data files that contained some more information. His eyes widened as he read more and more. The information was more than he had hoped for, almost too good to be completely true.

"Comms, are your techs and intel looking through this?" Ramat questioned. He hoped they weren't still operating like they did under Sites, totally dependent on his orders.

"Yes, sir, so far they can confirm much of the information is accurate, to the extent we know. We can only take their word about the Tartins, though, without any independent information."

"Very well." He breathed a sigh of relief. He had no other reason but to believe what they were saying for now. If what he was seeing was even partially accurate, the decision to aid the known alien fleet, who are calling themselves the Razuuds, in a fight against the unknown aliens, who they call Tartins, was quite a simple one. If it was to be believed, the Tartins invaded their home world some time ago and began raiding without so much as trying to open a dialogue. The Razuuds have only stayed on the defensive and protected their world. Ramat understood he was being fed a one-sided dialogue, but it seemed possible, considering his species was about to do the same thing. The thought of that made him grimace.

Nearly a year ago, the Razuuds deployed a scouting party to investigate the location they believed the attack came from. They attempted to figure out what the weapon had inflicted so much damage on their home world with the hopes of stopping it. At what they believed to be a safe distance, they entered normal space, only to find themselves directly in the middle of the Earth fleets. They thought they had no choice but to engage out of self-preservation. A few terrible coincidences brought these two alien species together, the humans and Razuuds. What brought the Tartins and the Razuuds together was a separate matter altogether. One that would be investigated if his fleet made it out of this alive.

"What are we going to do, Sir?" Lieutenant Colonel Mary Ann Barker asked Ramat. He snapped out of his train of thought. Speaking for nearly the first time since returning to the command center. She was also understanding everything that had been kept from her. She was going to need to be brought up to speed quickly to be effective in whatever happened next.

"First things first. We need to send this information back out to Earth, and our intentions. Fastest means possible." Ramat responded.

"And our intentions are what exactly?" She asked back, hoping she knew the answer already.

"Make some new friends, and some new enemies. If what they are saying is true, there is no reason we should be fighting them, and several good reasons why we should be helping them. We have no idea what we are getting into, but we don't have a lot of options right now. The way I see it, we either stand and fight with the Razuuds, or try and run and be chased down by the Razuuds and Tartins. The outlook is much better with option one." Ramat said back, thinking through his plan as he spoke. It was the only option where he could save as much of his fleet as possible. If for no other reason than saving human lives, he had to side with the Razuuds.

"Information sent." The comms officer interrupted. They had a message drone equipped with enough portable light gates to get it back to Earth in a fraction of the time than it took to get here, days instead of weeks. It was standing by for whatever message needed to be sent. The importance of the message dictated using this valuable resource now.

"Next." Ramat continued. "Let's show both of them we mean business." He called to Colonel Mentle, the operations officer for the fleet. "We need to get four squadrons of fighters out and accelerating towards the Tartins. Lead the charge with nukes. Same tactics as we used on Earth, but this time, have some fighters do quick hops with their portable light gates to get close behind them. Have them release the nukes and hop away. With any luck, the Razuuds did not pass on how badly we can hurt them. Also, have each SFG launch missiles in range or not. I want to confuse them and to get them to focus on something else."

"Roger." Mentle responded. She got onto her comm channel and began relaying orders to the different ships. This was going to be a massive coordination effort, and it was all up to her to keep it organized as much as possible.

CHAPTER 20

Riley–Space Force Guard Ship Catalyst–Razuud System

The Lucky's ready room bell rang three times sharply as Maggie and Riley entered the door.

"We're getting the call to saddle up!" Captain Maggie Lorrent yelled through the squadron room of the Lucky's. Everyone was ready to go. They were as prepared for this moment as they were ever going to be. It was a short walk down the corridor where their AIMS were waiting.

All the Lucky's were getting called up. Major 'Wisp' Broadway was now in charge of the Lucky's with Ramat getting tagged for fleet command. Riley, Star and the rest loaded into their AIMS. All while glancing at each other nervously. This was the first actual combat for some of them, but it would be like nothing any of them had ever experienced before, simulator or otherwise. They did not expect this scenario at all. Humans had just learned of their first alien species, now there was a second one, and they were going to war with them. They were all watching the situation unfold while they were waiting in the ready room, so they knew what was going on outside and what they would be up against.

Charlie broke in over the squadron comms. "You all know what to do. Stay calm, pick your targets, and watch each other's backs. Let your training take over and we just might make it out of here." Charlie was a man of few words and was direct and to the point. This was the first motivational speech he ever had to give. Not that he really had to, but he knew they needed to hear something from their new leader to get them focused on what they needed to do.

As soon as Charlie got a green indication from all the squadron ships, meaning they had all checked in as ready to depart, he contacted the Catalyst control tower. "Catalyst control, this is Lucky flight, number one, requesting squadron formation takeoff ASAP."

A voice came back over his intercom, which was being relayed to his squadron. "Lucky number one, immediate formation takeoff approved."

There was a brief pause before a more familiar voice came over the same channel. "Kick some ass, Lucky's!" An enthusiastic Colonel Archer said. He was finally getting to get some of his ships into the fight.

"Copy that, Sir." Charlie replied over the comms. "Lucky's, take off in three, two, one, depart." With that, the crew released all the magnetic locks and propelled their spacecraft forward off the surface of the deck, starting slowly at first. The magnetic field was strong enough to push the fighters out of the airlock before their cold thrusters took over to get them the rest of the way out of the bay. Once out, they all fired up their main pulse drives and headed towards the enemy.

This wasn't a normal flight. They wouldn't be sitting long before they saw action. As soon as they were clear of the ship, they were going to do a rapid combination of light gate transitions. They would go through one set with a limited power setting. As soon as they reassembled, they would go through another set to return to normal speeds. Once they jumped in behind the enemy fleet, they were to release their nukes and repeat the process to get back to the fleet. They needed to get a clear sight picture away from friendly ships before that time.

All the fighters that deployed accelerated away from their mothership. It was well-coordinated and being executed much smoother than Ramat expected. This was the first large-scale fight that any human space force had ever been in. The first of anything rarely goes as well as one would hope. At least this time, they had an experienced ally who was providing them with some guidance through this event.

Just before the Lucky's had a clear sight picture, Charlie's message board lit up. He had an urgent incoming message from Ramat. He had to make a double-take because it said fleet command. A commander rarely got a message from fleet command in a tactical situation unless it was important. He looked at the message. The more powerful sensors of the larger fleet ships were picking up what looked like swarms of smaller ships. The telemetry was being fed to all the fighters since their smaller sensor suites couldn't quite detect them yet. As he was reading, sensor updates populated his ship, along with messages and new orders. This was followed up by comms traffic within his squadron net, and also among the squadron commanders' net.

Charlie was the lead for the Lucky's and was being directed by Colonel Jennifer Mentle, who was the fleet operations officer. Colonel Mentle came over the squadron commander communications net. "Everyone listen up. We have a swarm of small and maneuverable ships that broke away from the larger ships of the unknown enemy fleet. Current estimate puts it at around one hundred. As soon as you are able, jump behind them and launch the nukes, and I will sector off the battlespace for each squadron to take care of the smaller fighters. The primary mission once the nukes are off is to get back here and protect the fleet. Those fighters, because of their quantity and unknown capabilities, are our greatest threat. We are currently requesting information from the Razuud alien fleet about these smaller ships. Stand by for more information. Good hunting."

Charlie began making electronic orders to distribute to his squadron. They were assigned the lead sector and would likely encounter the swarm of ships first. The nuke impacts were going to be occurring shortly after release. Once this happened, they were to maneuver in front of the SFG Catalyst.

"OK team." Riley heard Charlie speak into the squadron comm network. "You have your new orders. Prepare for rapid transition in five, four, three, two, one."

When Riley last closed his eyes, he had his battleships and carrier behind him and a large fleet of enemy ships in front of him on his scope. When he opened his eyes, everything was behind him and the planet was in front of him. He had jumped to a large percentage of the speed of light and back again to normal speeds in the blink of an eye.

"Everyone, pull around and line up shots with the large ships before they realize what happened." Charlie said over the squadron comms link.

Riley pulled back hard on his flight controls and began to steer his fighter towards the target highlighted on his display. A countdown until the release of his nukes ticked by in the corner of his display. This indicated to him that everyone was lined up and ready. He felt a small shift in the fighter as the countdown timer reached zero and the nuke released below his ship. He turned away with the rest of the flight and pointed back towards his own fleet.

"All bombs away. Executing light transition." Charlie reported.

Riley noticed something happening to the larger ships. They weren't moving differently, but some panels on the outside facing them shifted. "Looks like something's happening to the big ships. We need to get out of here now." As Riley began speaking, the transition sequence began. Riley could see a bright flash off to his right side before everything momentarily went dark. When his vision came back a split second later after the transition, he noticed at least two of the fighters from another flight off to his right were now missing.

"What happened to those fighters." Riley asked on the open channel.

"Looks like one of those ships got a shot off with their energy weapon before we could all get away." Maggie responded. Her fighter could get some more readings before they left and match them with the previous weapon signatures.

"Damn. Well, they're about to get a heck of a lot of payback." Riley said as he began flipping his fighter back around.

Many fighters stayed behind during all of this and released their own set of nukes. The hope was that they would get caught in a nuke sandwich, and maybe some of the debris would take out several smaller ships that were now swarming their way.

The Lucky's lined up with the sector they had been assigned. Sector one, right in front of the carrier where Ramat was leading.

If Riley didn't know any better, he would have thought that Ramat was using his old squadron as personal bodyguards. He didn't blame him. They were the best squadron to be in that position due to them having the most pilots with space combat experience.

Once in position, the Lucky's waited. It was an intense few minutes for Riley. He felt it was probably intense for everyone. He made a call to his lead, who he was the wingman for, Captain Maggie Lorrent, Face. "You seeing anything different, Face?" They all were looking at every detail of the sensor data, trying to find some weakness, some indication of the capabilities of the enemy, anything that could help them get an edge. They wouldn't find any.

"Not on my screens yet. Just make sure our ships stay linked as best you can. There's no telling what kind of interference we'll see. If something goes wrong and you lose power, sit tight, I'll find you."

"Same to you." Riley responded.

"We'll make it back home." Maggie said back.

Riley wasn't sure if she was encouraging confidence in him or wanting to believe it herself. The position they were in right now, he went with confidence and briefly closed his eyes. He thought of home. His grandpa, his parents. Jenn.

When he opened his eyes, the sensor suites began going haywire. The nukes had detonated. Some appeared to be on target, others missed. At first glance, it appeared that about half hit their mark. Which meant half of the main ships were still heading straight for them, fully operational. It didn't appear that many of the fighters got hit. During the time they waited, an updated estimate of fighters was around 125, which was larger than the original estimate. Riley kept an eye on that counter and watched as it continued to rise. The odds kept getting worse. Following the nuke strikes, they were now registering 110 fighters. More than what was first thought but getting better.

Riley made observations out loud to Maggie. "By sheer numbers, we seem fairly evenly matched. But the enemy fighters appeared to be smaller."

"Which likely means they are more maneuverable." Maggie responded. "Be ready for a lot of jinking from your ship."

That was about all they could gather. They couldn't tell if they had energy weapons or conventional, or what type of armor or shielding they had. This first encounter was going to be purely trial and error. Not exactly how anyone wanted to enter a potentially deadly engagement.

"Alright, look sharp, looks like the brunt of the fighters are headed towards our sector. We're getting some help from the other squadrons. Expect missile weapons range in ten seconds." Charlie said into the squadron net. Riley noted his calm tone and had a slight sigh of relief being reminded that there were a bunch of other human ships out there that had his back.

At that moment, all hell broke loose. Seemingly hundreds of more fighters broke off from the larger ships. And the fighters that were already deployed launched what appeared to be missiles. Each fighter dropped four to five missiles that rapidly accelerated towards them. It was hard to tell at that moment if they were targeting the human fighters or the larger fleet ships.

"Holy shit, do you see that!?" Riley nearly yelled over the radio link to Maggie.

"Make sure you're locked in tight, Rip. Set everything to detonate at proximity, we'll need to take out multiple of whatever those are with each shot to stand a chance."

"Yes ma'am. It looks like our new friends are engaging too." Riley noted out loud, a hint of relief in his voice that they were getting some help from someone who knew more about this enemy.

"Just focus on what you have in front of you, and we'll make it through. Get ready for the first wave."

Some of the many fighters that were released were already

in a fray with the Razuud fleet, who had launched some fighters of their own. But unfortunately, the vast majority were heading towards the human fleet.

The enemy missiles that were launched were approaching rapidly. The Lucky's were almost in range. Charlie came over the squadron comm net again. "We got a lot of activity now. Each fighter coordinate a ten-ship lock on, release, and begin evasive maneuvering." This gave the squadron ships the command to coordinate a lock on of ten targets each. The ships coordinated and each one picked ten different enemy fighters. With 160 ships targeted in his squadron alone, they might get out of this on top.

They all released their missiles a moment later. Riley could see the rocket engines firing with his natural vision. Each fighter, in a pair of two, wingman and lead, began evasive maneuvers. Riley acted as Maggie's wingman. Their ships coordinated their maneuvers. They weren't identical, but it kept them in proximity to each other. The movements were too fast for the pilots to make on their own, so they were augmented with the artificial intelligence. The series of random jinks and jags with variations in acceleration were almost not noticeable in his pod because of the goo.

"Switch the decoys to automatic. There'll be too much going on to trigger them manually." Maggie called out.

"Roger." came a few other voices back over the line. Riley did the same. He didn't have combat experience like she did, but she had been training him since he joined the squadron after the first attack. It felt like ages ago now. The decoys consisted of an advanced chaff, which released electromagnetic, EM, pulses that mimicked the ships' EM output. Since they didn't know how the missiles tracked, they also released smart flares that mimicked the SOP engine output and heat signature of the fighters. They would soon find out if any of these worked.

The anticipation was mounting for Riley. His heart rate, which he was finding difficult to maintain at a low rate with his breathing alone, raced as they approached. This was it, all the training and briefings and sim time, for this moment now.

Time was up. His AIMS abruptly performed evasive maneuvers. The enemy missiles were getting closer. It became clear which of the human ships were being targeted.

"All of the missiles are targeting our fighters." Riley said over the squadron intercom. He had been watching that closely, and that was good information to know and spread. It was possible that the enemy thought the missiles weren't powerful enough to damage the larger ships, or maybe it was to clear the way for the enemy fighters and larger ships to get within range of the larger human ships with their more powerful energy weapons.

Their mission was clear. Riley would not let those ships through. Before the enemy missiles were getting to be within range of when the chaff and flare would normally release from the AIMS, the enemy missiles all emitted a powerful laser from their noses. Before any countermeasures were released, the lasers struck the unprepared fighters. The lasers connected with the energy shields of the human fighters.

"My energy shields are absorbing a lot, but they won't last much longer before they overheat." Star said, deciding to launch her chaff and flares manually. She wasn't the only one. They manually released countermeasures as they started taking laser fire. That lessened the amount of direct laser damage they took. The missiles shifted their fire towards the decoys. The large number of ships, countermeasures, and missiles in the battlespace made it difficult to maneuver without taking damage.

Maggie and Riley sat a little further back and hadn't

experienced any hits yet.

"Rip, release decoys now and target the closest missiles with your Gatling gun. I don't know if they exploded yet, but they aren't trying to maneuver much." Maggie told Riley. Riley was thinking the same thing and wanted to get ahead of the game if they could.

The missiles were easy targets. They didn't seem to maneuver and had slowed their speed considerably so that their pass took longer. This was likely to get more laser shots at them before passing by. As soon as they saw this tactic working, Riley saw a message go out over the all hands to everyone's heads up display from Maggie on what to do. The other fighters caught on to this as well and began taking the missiles out. Once the energy shields on the AIMS were depleted, the physical shielding remained, capable of withstanding a brutal beating, even from an energy weapon. However, they preferred to save that for when they encountered the enemy fighters. It also appeared that the missiles only fired energy weapons and never exploded. That was one less thing to worry about.

At this point, the missiles that were currently engaging the Lucky's and the other fighters were getting picked off quickly, but also were apparently running out of energy because their rate of fire was decreasing. The power output was also decreasing. Unfortunately, the new wave of fighters entered the effective range of the devastating weapon and also launched missiles of their own. In addition to this new threat, the Lucky's were about to make the first fighter on fighter engagement with the enemy.

"Get ready to join the fray, everybody. Check your six, fly smart." Charlie said to the squadron.

It was then that he remembered to check how well their missiles had done. The missiles they launched were quite effective at thinning the enemy lines. They had taken out about fifty of the original fighters. Riley did some quick mental math. He figured their missiles were about thirty percent effective at max range. This would be important information later. He sent a message to Maggie and Charlie telling them what he found. To increase their odds of a kill, they would need to change up their tactics.

Riley entered into range with his first enemy fighter, locked onto and fired his Gatling gun. Riley tore apart the enemy fighter. "Gatlings are effective at close range. Use at least two missiles per enemy at medium and long range." He also passed this info on to the other squadrons. This told everyone to use Gatlings if you could, and if you had to fire missiles, shoot two per target.

The enemy missiles took out a few fighters from other squadrons so far. Riley could see the red X lingering over the friendly green logos representing destroyed friendly fighters. There were no red X's over any Lucky's fighter yet, and he hoped it stayed that way.

After Riley obliterated the first fighter with his Gatling gun, he rapidly switched targets. His ship swung around him and pivoted violently as it aligned the gun to its next target. This maneuver would have been deadly for Riley had it not been for the fact that his cockpit was independent from his AIMS outer body, rotating only when it needed to in order to balance out any induced g-forces. The cockpit screens showed what he wanted them to show. Currently it was showing him what his gun was shooting at. He zoomed in considerably.

Maggie and James took their own shots, each taking out an enemy fighter while avoiding high-energy beams that seemed to follow them everywhere they turned. They would occasionally get a warning that their energy shields were being bombarded, but those recharged and the heat from them dissipated when they weren't being hit. This allowed them to sustain almost no hull damage to the physical portions of their ships since the first wave of missiles began firing their lasers.

All the AIMS were frantically engaging enemy fighters. There were too many. They were keeping them away from the main battleships as best that they could, but they were getting overwhelmed and running low on ammo. Charlie got on the comms to Ramat. "Trap, you're going to have some incoming. Some of the fighters are leaking through, there are too many of them. We'll keep the leakage to a minimum."

"Copy that, Wisp. Stay safe out there. We can handle the smaller ones. The larger ships are almost in range, be careful of their energy weapons, your shields can't hold up to those shots." Ramat replied.

"We'll do our best but won't be able to completely avoid it. Lucky's one, out." Another problem they discovered was that the orientation of the enemy's ships was not an indication of what they were aiming at. They could point in one direction, but fire in a completely different direction. The larger ships had multiple heavy energy weapons that could fire in any direction of the ship, including backward. They had smaller ones that appeared to be more of a light point defense, similar to the rapid defense systems of the human ships but with energy instead of physical ammunition.

As the smaller fighters got closer to the battle cruisers, they began firing their high-energy lasers at the fleet. Most of them appeared to be targeting the supply ship. This was a strange tactic. Sure, they couldn't repair it after the battle, but they could still fight the battle. The rapid point defense cannons of the battleships made short work of the enemy fighters and sustained minimal damage to their energy shields. It was becoming clear that this enemy had not yet learned that their normal tactics would not work on the human ships. At least they hadn't yet. The human fleet was more than happy to keep on teaching this lesson.

That's when the enemy battleships got within range of the human fighters. With one burst, multiple fighters vanished. Several others lost their energy shields and most of their hull. The enemy battleships continued to fire, relentlessly.

"Nukes, we need to use nukes on the larger ships, everything you got, now!" Charlie said into his squadron net and the larger squadron commander net. "Stay maneuverable and spread out, don't give them a good target." They were already spread out, but they were mostly chasing fighters. With their nuclear-tipped missiles, they broke off from the fighters and went after the larger ships. They were much smaller nukes than the ones they launched earlier. They had used all the larger nukes on the first wave. Several of the fighters targeted the closest battleship and fired their nukes. As they impacted, the light was dazzling before the sensors tamped down the input to something that wouldn't damage the pilots' eyes. But if only a couple made it through, they would need more. Maggie, with Riley as her wingman, took it in a little closer to the big ship. They got much closer to the large ship and began taking energy hits. A new enemy tactic emerged. The spent missiles, no longer able to shoot energy beams, began chasing down and appeared to be trying to ram the AIMS. There were too many of the missiles to avoid getting hit by some. The AIMS automated collision avoidance system kicked in and began maneuvering rapidly. These sharp maneuvers were enough to save the life of the pilots, at least temporarily, but it could also temporarily exceed the maximum g-forces that a pilot could endure and remain conscious. As Riley's visions closed in and faded to black, his system took over.

Riley's body jarred back and forth; he couldn't predict which direction the ship was going to take him next. He could see that Maggie and he were passing through the thickest part of the missiles, rapidly approaching the large enemy ship. His vision was narrowing, his head was aching. He had to hold on a few more seconds; they were almost out of the swarm of missiles. He couldn't do it, though. His vision continued to close off until black. When he came out of his haze, he wasn't sure how long he was out, or where exactly he was. As he slowly regained his senses, he took stock of everything around him. Once he finished checking his ship and himself, he turned his attention outside.

"Face, my ship took over, and I blacked out." Riley called out. He waited. "Face, do you copy?" He thought maybe his radio was out. He checked the system, but it was green. He looked for the link between his ship and hers. Nothing. It wasn't there. "Wisp, do you copy? I can't reach Face on comms. My ship can't locate her." Externally, he was doing his best to stay calm and professional. Internally, he was losing it. He could not have lost her; it was his job to cover her.

"I read you, Rip. I can't reach her either. Join up with Star and keep fighting. We'll search when we can." Charlie replied. Riley could tell that he was concentrating on too many things, but missing Maggie was at the top of their list now.

"Copy, on my way." There was no trace of her and no response on comms. She was gone. They were dodging all sorts of enemy activity, so the chances of getting hit by an energy weapon while he was out were certainly possible. He didn't want to believe it. Riley didn't have the time to think about it now. He still wasn't out of the woods yet. Their attack wasn't completely in vain, though. That ship appeared to be changing course and falling back. There were only four more to go, but the cost of getting that one was high, almost too high for the Lucky's. They couldn't do that again.

CHAPTER 21

Ramat–Space Force Guard Ship Catalyst–Razuud System

The next enemy battleship had moved past the three battleships and the carrier and went straight for the human supply ship. There was a frantic volley of energy and kinetic weapons being exchanged. The enemy ship unloaded a massive energy beam directly onto the human supply ship. The supply ship completely disappeared in a flash. Small segments floated around, but nothing that resembled the former ship. The human fleet had been spreading its firepower out over all the ships, and that one enemy battleship had broken through to the back of the human fleet. The consequences of that were felt immediately.

"Take that ship out now." Ramat ordered Colonel Mantle. Ramat was confused why it hadn't targeted one of their bigger ships instead.

"On it, sir." Colonel Mantle responded as she typed some commands. She redirected some of the fighter squadrons to target that ship. She was also sending firing solutions to the battleships to target the incoming battleships with their larger nuclear missiles and the centerline rail guns. At this range, the larger but slower missiles would have a much better chance at finding a home in the enemy ship.

The next strange thing happened. The enemy ships stopped firing as soon as the supply ship was clearly no longer functional. With no explanation. That didn't, however, stop the humans from continuing to fight back.

Ramat received a message from the communications officer. "Sir, urgent message from the Razuuds."

"Send it over." Ramat responded. It appeared on his screen instantly.

Who is the new commander? The message read.

As Ramat read it, he thought he understood why they went after the supply ship and why they stopped firing. Ramat had read about force structures like this in history books. As soon as the commander was eliminated, they considered the battle done. Humans didn't work that way. So, the aliens were in for a nasty surprise.

If that were true, Ramat had a brief window where his fleet had an advantage. But it wouldn't be long until the aliens figured it out and continued their attack. If they could fire that weapon too many times, there wouldn't be any human ships left to send home.

"Tell them we didn't lose our command ship. Every ship is a command ship." Ramat said. "Mantle, keep targeting the closest ships to the remaining fleet."

That's when another enemy battleship came in range of the carrier and opened up directly on the front hull. It burned through the energy shield and began eating through the front shielding.

Ramat had Tobias sitting in the ship's heart with him in the CC section. Tobias was there to provide his expertise on the ship's systems in the event something broke and it needed fixing. He designed and built most of the systems, so he was the most qualified. Following the most recent barrage, damage assessments poured in. They all felt that last blast, and he knew damage would be major. The diagnostics screen he already had loaded updated with new warning signs of the latest damage. "If they hit that section of the hull again, we'll be fried." Tobias said. "We need to get a different part of the ship in their target path.

"We don't have enough time to spin the ship around before their weapon is recharged!" Colonel Barker said, the ship's captain.

"Do a full reverse now!" Tobias yelled.

"Then that will put our engines in the direct path of the energy weapon, and we'd lose our engines, probably the ship too. And we'd still be facing the same direction." Colonel Barker responded.

"Listen to me and do exactly what I say." Tobias said to Major Larson, the ship's chief engineer. Major Larson gave a quick glance at Colonel Barker to get approval. When Colonel Barker nodded back to follow Tobias' direction, he continued. "Disable the engine rotation limiter. Do a full emergency reverse thrust. Halfway through the rotation transition, re-enable the limiter. This will force the rotation drive to seize and bind with the hull temporarily. The momentum will rotate the ship's hull, rather abruptly. As soon as the damaged area is out of the direct path of the enemy ships, resume forward motion to get the engines out of danger."

"Understood. Stand by." Major Larson said back, already setting up the maneuver on his console.

Ramat understood what was about to happen and decided that warning the crew was probably a good idea. "All hands, prepare for abrupt evasive maneuvers." Everyone was supposed to be strapped down, but since that last hit he knew some would be up assisting the injured and making repairs. They would not fare well with whatever happened next if they were freely floating.

Ramat could see on the primary display the telltale signs of the enemy ship preparing to fire their energy weapons again. Apparently they were charged up enough. "We need to execute that maneuver now. Get on it Major Larson." Ramat said directly to Major Larson and the entire crew in the CC.

Major Larson hit the execute button on his display. When Major Larson executed the command, the ship bent and groaned loudly. The sounds of twisting and screaming metal and exotic composites echoed through the once pristine ship. They were noises nobody had ever heard before, and they were all abruptly rattled and flung in their seats as the rotation gears bound to the already rotating engines and spun them fast. They felt the forward momentum regain. At that moment, the enemy fired its energy weapon again. This time hitting the side of the ship. It quickly drained the energy shield and began eating away at the outer hull shielding.

"They are going to breach, stand by for breach!" Major Larson shouted to those in the command center.

Ramat was looking at the external screens and the overall battlespace, trying to figure out what could be done. His fleet was being overrun. He lost his supply ship. The rest of the fleet, along with his ship, sustained grave damage. Many of his fighters were gone and would be stranded. The Razuuds didn't seem like they were faring much better.

Hope faded in the room. The fear and disappointment of failing was palpable. They were certainly going to be overrun. With no warning, a large flash of light brightened the screen of the main external view display. All the sensor screens went black. The power in the ship went out, and Ramat had the sensation of being pushed away from the fight as his ship moaned and shook.

"What's happening? Status report." Ramat asked. His external comm link wasn't working, but he was still close to everyone in the CC. Nobody responded at first.

"I'm not sure, sir. We're waiting for sensors and power to come back online." The lead sensor operator said.

"No power, main engines, and maneuvering are offline. I'm going to go to the engine room and see if I can help." Tobias said. Ramat wasn't going to stop him. If they were about to get destroyed, it didn't matter where he was sitting. At least he was trying to fix something.

After Tobias exited the CC, everyone was silent for a moment. Ramat felt helpless. There was nothing he could do. He felt like he was waiting for the next blast to hit and finish them off. But it hadn't come yet.

"Sir, the sensors are starting to come back online. Telemetry is starting to flow."

"What can you see?"

They all sat tense in their chairs, waiting for the end. Waiting for the enemy to end it all. Ramat's screen, now on emergency power, showed hints at what was going on outside. It was a strange sight. He expected to see his fleet in disarray and destroyed. But it wasn't. They were mostly where he remembered they were, and they still showed a similar status as they did before his ship went offline. The field of view was nearly clear. That's when he spotted the major difference. The enemy ships that were close by were now gone. They weren't burning back towards where they came from or off in some other direction; they were gone. There were some chunks of ships floating around that gave a clue as to what happened. Ramat zoomed out and could see a debris field expanding out in all directions. Mostly, when a ship got hit, it kept moving in its current direction, with a slight change in course from the impact, until something else stopped it or altered its course. Most of the debris was quickly expanding away from where the fleet was. However, when energy weapons vaporized a ship, it could cause it to disappear. There was a mix of both in this case.

"Sir, the enemy is gone, destroyed!" The communications officer said.

The CC erupted in cheers. Ramat released his breath and relaxed his muscles, something he didn't even realize he was doing. He couldn't help but join in the celebration.

When the noise calmed down a little more, the communications officer continued. "The other ships are reporting that we hit them with our nukes at the same time the Razuuds hit them with their main energy weapons."

Now, two of the three opposing fleets emerged from the fray and were no longer enemies. Their trajectories had them at a standstill with the main fleets that were above the home planet of the Razuuds.

"Comms." Ramat said after a brief pause to let the CC regain their composure. "Ask the Razuud ship what's next. We need to know if we need to be ready to fight or if we have time to recover."

The telemetry coming in from above the planet appeared to indicate that the Tartin fleet was retreating. There were some damaged ships that could not keep up. Most of the enemy fleet had disappeared in a flash, the kind that showed they had transitioned and were heading out of the system to whatever world they came from.

Ramat began calling each of the ships in his fleet to assess their damage from the Captains. Everyone was pretty banged up, but the only major loss was the supply ship. In the background of each ship, he could hear the crew's excitement. He knew that would only last as long as it took each member to see how many fighters and crew members had been lost. They deserved the excitement and relief for now though. There was a long road ahead. The first step was to start recovery operations of the crews and fighters floating off into space. He would let each ship Captain know how best to let their crew rest, recover, and celebrate. He was proud of how everyone performed.

After everything settled down, Ramat came over the all-hands comms. "Everyone, take stock of yourself and your teammates. You all performed exceptionally well. Grieve for those we lost and celebrate those that are still here. We stood our ground against impossible odds and came out on top. You are the reason we live to stand and fight another day. We will be returning home as soon as we are able. Stand by for further orders."

CHAPTER 22

Riley–Advanced Individual Maneuvering Shuttle–Razuud System

"Rip, do you copy? I know you can hear me. She's not out there. You're running out of fuel. Come back, and you can go back out when you get some rest." Charlie called out to Riley.

"I copy, sir. There's just one more section I want to search. Her trajectory could have taken her this way." Riley replied. He was doing whatever he could to postpone going back without some kind of sign of Maggie. He didn't want to accept the fact that she was probably gone forever.

"You already checked there, Rip. I know this is difficult to accept, but you need to come back before you need to be rescued too. Get back to the carrier, and we can take another look at the recordings."

"Yes, sir." Riley knew that the next step was to be ordered back in, but he didn't want to make Charlie do that. It was already hard enough for them. Riley had yet to look at who all the Lucky's lost, or how many from the other squadrons were lost. He knew it was a lot. Firing his thrusters, he turned his AIMS back towards the carrier. He wasn't in a rush, still holding on to the hope he would detect something or get another idea. As he slowly coasted to the ship, no ideas came, no new information made it to his fighter. He went through the motions to land, hardly remembering the events as they happened; he was on autopilot. Making comms calls with the traffic controller, capturing in the bay. The whole time, he was replaying the battle in his head. What went wrong?

The loud bang and sharp clank and jolt of the ship's magnets sticking him to the deck shook him out of his daze. He climbed out of his fighter and greeted the others that were left. Things would never be the same after this.

CHAPTER 23

Mark–Space Force Guard Ship Catalyst–Razuud System

Mark sat in awe in his quarters as he poured over the orders that General Sites received from Rictor. They were remarkably similar to the ones that he had received, telling them not to attack the Razuuds. Had General Sites acted on his own and defied the war council's orders? It was certainly possible. Sites was not one to do anything against what he wanted to do. It was even more likely for him to do it if he thought it would benefit his career, which it certainly would have if he destroyed the enemy along with any evidence that he disobeyed orders. No, it had to be Rictor.

Mark had underestimated Rictor. He knew he was the wrong kind of smart but didn't expect him to go to such great lengths to cover up his tracks. Rictor must have installed some sort of program that erased his original orders. General Sites would not make that kind of leap on his own. Unfortunately, Mark couldn't prove any of that. And so, General Sites would take the fall all by himself. The war council would take his testimony into consideration and likely ban Rictor from participating further in the government, but that would be all. General Sites certainly wasn't in the right for anything he did and would get a fair and lengthy sentence. They may let him keep his retirement, but he would no longer be serving, if that's what anyone wanted to call it for him.

At that moment, Ramat rapped his knuckles on Mark's door. "Hey boss." Mark responded slowly, clearly deep in thought.

"What's on your mind, old friend?" Ramat responded. He didn't have to know Mark all that well to know that something was troubling him.

"Just this whole Sites and Rictor nonsense. I'm having the IT guys go through it, but so far there is no evidence besides what Sites says that connects Rictor to this mess. With what I do have, though, it shouldn't be hard to get him banned from the state building. Even his most loyal followers won't touch him now. I wouldn't be surprised if he goes slinking down to the SHUR." Mark said.

"I thought he despised the SHUR?" Ramat asked. Mark thought Ramat was humoring him with the question as a friend. They both knew the answer to that, but Mark needed a conversation, any conversation, with a friend right about now.

"He does. However, he despises not being able to control and manipulate people even more, and so he will go anywhere that will have him. Given his perceived inside knowledge, the SHUR would surely have them, pardon the pun." Mark said back, beginning to accept the reality of the situation.

"It's out of your hands now, Mark. You've done everything you could. Now you're the first diplomat to interact with an alien species. And you did it peacefully, well, halfway peacefully. Maybe after we helped them put a beat down on the Tartins, that will be enough to convince Earth to create the World Council and get rid of this upper and lower hemisphere crap." Ramat said, trying to boost Mark's spirits by bringing his attention back to the good he has accomplished and setting his eyes back on his goals.

"Oh, you're right, Ramat. Now we need to decide what happens next. Are we going to stay out here longer or head back, maybe even bringing an envoy of theirs with us when we return?

"I want talks to continue as long as we are still making repairs. Earth isn't going to send any representatives until we return, but they are already planning on a trip back." Ramat stated.

Mark knew the people of Earth were going to need as much information about both species as they could get. He wasn't sure yet what exactly he would be at liberty to say to the aliens about humans, but that would get sorted out. The last comm drone from Earth had minimal instructions and said there would not be much guidance going forward until they returned. Mark's first task was simply getting to know them. That continued to be his goal this whole time, up until this point. All their communications had thus far been through who they called Leader Danuibi and General Drobbi. What they could tell, he had a rank that was something like a general in the Earth fleets. Ramat, as the fleet commander, and Mark, as the Ambassador to the Worlds, a title he thought was a little silly, were the only two that had conducted communications yet from the humans. They have only been through radios because the environments that each species survived in were still being analyzed. In fact, that was one of the biggest initial hurdles—allowing each other to send small robots on board each other's ships' to do a quick analysis of the environment, and likely a scan of the ship to find any other secrets they could. The humans certainly did that.

While that information was being processed,

communications continued through the radios. It was an exhausting event. Mark and Ramat never thought that sitting and talking would be so mentally draining. Their focus was intense for those periods of time; after all, they felt that the fate of humanity could quite possibly hang on their every word.

Mark sat in an exhausted gaze, contemplating everything that needed to be done still and over-analyzing all the conversations he already had.

Ramat snapped him out of the tired look he had. "Are you ready to go to the ceremony?"

Mark had to think for a second and switch gears. What ceremony? "Oh yes, I completely lost track of time. You wanted to do this before we departed."

"Yeah, the crew's morale is a little low now. They finally have some downtime to process what happened, all of the losses. They are missing friends that have been bunking with them for so long. I need to take their minds off of that in a way that isn't more training and patrols and cleaning." Ramat said.

"Yes, that should help. I only understand a small part of what they are going through from my time in, seems like forever ago now. I'll be right behind you." Ramat nodded. He turned around and walked out. Mark sat in contemplation another minute, gathering the mental strength to force himself to get out of his room. The last few days had been rough, not to mention the battle and loss of life. He had become acquainted with many that were no longer here. They never found some of them. Maggie came to mind as tears built up around his eyes. When it became too much, he shut his eyes, causing tears to drift away from his face. He took a deep breath and wiped his face. Although it wasn't his job, he had to be strong for the crew. He wanted to be someone that they could turn to and see that everything was going to be alright. With his magnetic boots he was still getting used to, he made his way to the hangar bay.

As he entered the hangar, it was much emptier than it was when they departed. They lost many fighters. Before they left, with all the ships and crew, this place would not have been large enough. But now, it was more than enough room and Mark shuddered at the thought of what once was.

Mark made his way up to his seat at the front. It was an age-old tradition to have distinguished visitors and guests to a ceremony like this to sit in the front to witness and participate in the events. Since he was the only one on this trip, he sat up front, mostly alone for now. The rest of the leadership team, including his old friend Ramat, filed in as the first notes of the ceremonial music played.

The experience was somber for Mark. It had been a while since he had last taken part in a ceremony like this. It was during one of his deployments a long time ago. There was an ambush on their unit, which handled diplomatic outreach to the neighboring towns. There were three people killed from his unit during the attack. One was a close friend. But for those that survived, there was a mix of emotions. Mark was feeling a lot of the same ones now. He remembered being told that it was called survivors' remorse. They all did what they could to survive and make it back home, like anyone else would have. But they, and not their friends, were sitting here getting honored and awards.

No unit stood above the others. No individual performed any more or less gallantly than another. It was exactly what Mark expected from the caliber of troops that volunteered to come on this mission. Mark zoned out, thinking about his own experience, while Ramat gave his remarks to the ship and broadcast to the fleet. The bits and pieces he caught were essentially what he was already thinking himself. There was nothing else he could say. Mark knew that Ramat had been in this situation before and there was nothing that would make it feel better, maybe only remove some of the sting.

Mark caught the end of Ramat's speech, though. "We'll be going home soon, within two weeks when repairs are complete enough." Mark saw Ramat glance over at Tobias, who led that effort. "But before we do, we will honor all of those that we lost." As he said that, the names of those that were killed or lost and presumed killed scrolled across the screens that were hanging in the background. Ramat read them. At first his voice was firm, void of emotion. But that façade rapidly faded, and the emotion rushed in. Finally, on the last name, Ramat couldn't keep the tears back, nobody could. "Captain Maggie Lorrent."

Mark watched his old friend regain his composure and walk off the stage. Mark had more respect for him after that. He had seen too many commanders act as if nothing bothered them. Ramat showed he cared. Mark stood up and greeted his friend with a hug. The leadership party all rose, embraced one another, and walked out of the hangar.

Mark and Ramat walked back to their rooms in silence. Everything that needed to be said already was. As they both made it to Mark's room, Ramat paused at the door. "Will you be ready for talks tomorrow? We should still have a few good days left with them before we have to leave."

Mark knew it was time to get back to business; he had a job to do. This was the sole reason he came along. "I'll be ready. It would be nice to have some guidelines from Earth, but we can wing it."

"That seems to be working so far. They can slap our wrists when we get home." Ramat responded.

"It's unfortunate that our supplies won't last long enough

for a full envoy to make it here." Mark said back, hinting at wanting to stay longer. Deep down, he knew it was best to leave. Even if the Razuuds offered them supplies to stay. The fleet was in no shape to stick around for another fight. The morale of the crew would not last that long.

"Yeah, but we'll be back. Humans, that is. Hopefully, me personally. That probably depends on how we did with this whole mess. I managed to damage a huge chunk of our Earth fleet so they may not be very happy with me. You're doing a great job, though."

"Don't sell yourself short, you were handed a hot mess and still managed for it to not come out smelling like an overused porta potty. We're gonna be alright. Earth is going to be alright. If there is one thing I know, it's that humans don't give up, and they don't go down without a fight." Mark said back, letting him know that this mess was not his, but still did a good job cleaning it up.

"The problem is, I don't think the Tartins give up either. I'm afraid we're going to be in a war with an alien species for a long time." Ramat said.

"True. But we also have new allies. Rest assured – the time is coming when our knowledge of the universe is going to get a whole lot bigger."

EPILOGUE

Maggie–Advanced Individual Maneuvering Shuttle–Location Unknown

Captain Maggie "Face" Lorrent woke up with a start. She immediately regretted trying to get up so quickly. Her restraints grabbed her and stopped her body and head from moving any further. A sharp pain shot through her temples and made her nauseous. She squeezed her eyes tightly, fighting back the urge to throw up, hoping it would make the pain coursing through her head stop. She slowly remembered to breathe. At first, she started taking in deep breaths rapidly, but then they became long and even. Once she got her heart rate settled, at least lower than what it was, she tried to open her eyes.

Her cockpit was pulsating with red blinking lights and pitch black. She tried to see her hands and feet, but it was tough in the low light. She couldn't feel blood anywhere. Her limbs felt tired, but nothing worse. Her heads-up display scrolled. This grabbed her attention away from checking on herself to checking on her ship. Her memory of recent events returned.

She realized where she was and that frightened her. Before panic could set in again, she gently closed her eyes and turned her focus inward. She sucked in a long slow breath through her nose, then exhaled through her mouth.

She knew she didn't have time to do this all day, so as soon as she felt ready, she opened her eyes again. The air had an acrid burning smell, with some smoke visible in the cockpit as more and more lights and screens turned on. 'I was in a battle' she told herself, trying to force herself to recall what happened. She couldn't remember the last thing she saw during the battle. 'Rip and I were heading for a close pass of the warship. Was it an incoming energy bolt, or did I collide with a ship or one of the missiles? Did something happen to Rip?' It was all a blur.

She found her flashlight in her flight suit and pulled it out of the arm pocket. As she flipped the switch on, it slipped out of her hands and fell on her chest. "That's interesting." She thought out loud again. There was gravity, but it was pushing her back in her seat. It wasn't her engines doing that, though. She could see that those were offline. Her cockpit shook. She could see a white-hot dot forming on the inside of her cockpit. She pointed her flashlight in that direction and could tell that was where some of the smoke was coming from. The dot grew into a larger ball. It moved. 'Was that a cutting torch?' The point moved in an arc.

When the realization set in that there was someone outside of her ship trying to get to her, her heart skipped a beat and she couldn't control the rate anymore. This time it was with excitement instead of fear. She screamed out. "Help, I'm in here! Help!" She wasn't sure anyone could hear her outside through the ship and through the noise of whatever was cutting her out, but she didn't care. She tried anyway. "Thank you, thank you, thank you." She said lower, figuring at this point that it didn't matter if they heard her. She was being rescued! Once the light had made a full circle, someone removed a section.

To her surprise, and horror, it was not a human figure that looked through. She unbuckled her restraints, mentally kicking herself for not doing it sooner. Once she was free, she reached behind her seat for her pistol. She knew that there were two species that they were dealing with. She knew what one looked like, but not the other. These looked like the ones that they were supposed to be friends with. But they did not appear to be acting like friends at the moment.

As a long metal-looking stick started making its way towards her with a small arc of electricity going between points, she got the hint that they may not be the friendly ones. She tried calling out, "What are you doing? Do you understand me?" No response came, but what looked like a prod continued to advance. She had to make a snap decision. 'Do I shoot at our new friends and start an intergalactic incident? Do I defend myself against an enemy trying to capture me? Or do I do nothing?' She thought quickly to herself. As the prod got closer and closer, she acted. Raising her pistol, she pulled the trigger as bullets leaped from her gun and through the open hole of her ship.

The prods reeled back when she fired but returned once she stopped, this time with more vigor. There was nowhere for her to go inside her ship. Using her now empty handgun, she swatted the prod to one side and proceeded towards the new exit. She made it halfway out when a new prod appeared from one side and contacted her ribcage. Frozen in place, she watched as her vision faded. She had no control. The image of an alien looming over her was the last thing she saw. An alien she thought were her friends. Fear overtook her as she blacked out.

For a more in depth look and visualizations of the characters, ships, and worlds, visit my website at:

www.archergrantbooks.com

For a glossary of terms, visit the website or jump to the end of the book. Be sure not to spoil the ending!

If you would like additional information about upcoming books, such as Relativity: Returning Home, and The Breaker Series, visit the website and join the mailing list. I'd love to go on this journey with you.

GLOSSARY

Advanced Individual Maneuvering Shuttle or **AIMS** are single-seat fighter spacecraft equipped with smaller versions of the engines and weapons systems as the larger ships. They are highly maneuverable and equipped with a subset of artificial intelligence to aid in piloting.

Space Force Platform or **SFP** are large rotating platforms that offer partial "artificial" spin gravity and long central structures for docking of larger spacecraft for cargo and personnel delivery.

Space Force Guard Ship or **SFG** are most closely related to battleships. They are well armored and well equipped with multiple weapons systems to include centerline rail guns, missile tubes, and close space defense rapid fire machine guns.

Space Force Shuttle or **SFS** are small shuttles used to transport crew and cargo between Earth's surface and into orbit. These are typically not named but are given a numerical identifier.

SFP Kennedy or **The Spin** is the pride and joy of the Norther Hemisphere Nation Space Force. At one point, it was the only space platform that has a strictly military mission.

SFG Minotaur or **The Mino** is one of many guard ships owned by the NHN Space Force but is the first that is dedicated to training new crew.

SFG Catalyst or **The Catalyst** is the flagship guard ship for the NHN Space Force. This ship was in the middle of construction during the attacks on earth. Following the attacks, it's mission and construction was modified to act also as a carrier for several AIMS squadrons instead of the typical single squadron. This ship can bring the fight to anyone, anywhere.

Battleship Ryceen is the flagship of the Razuuds. Its capabilities are unknown but seem to match closely with an SFG class ship.

Razuud is the home planet of the Razuuds and located an unknown amount of light years away from Earth.

Rutaun is the capital city of Razuud and the crown jewel of the above ground cities. The underground cities are even more impressive.

City Rache is a small Razuud city. It was created out of necessity due to overpopulation on the planet but is not a desirable travel or work destination. It also on the opposite side of the planet as Rutaun.

Earth Light Gates are a collection of circular gates or tunnels that are used to accelerate outgoing ships to speeds much over the speed of light and receives incoming ships from light gates in the outer solar system to slow them down to relative speeds. They are located at strategic solar orbits or Lagrange Points within reach of earth.

World Council Delegation Room is what it sounds like. All political happenings are discussed here, but instead of for the world, it is for the NHN.

Southern Hemisphere United Republic or the **SHUR** is the collection of countries and territories, primarily but not exclusively located in the southern hemisphere, that most benefited by the proximity to the newly discovered natural stores of rare earth and exotic materials.

Norther Hemisphere Nation or the **NHN** is the collection of the countries and territories, primarily but not exclusively located in the northern hemisphere, that did not directly benefit from the discoveries of the natural rare earth and exotic materials.

ABOUT THE AUTHOR

I grew up with a deep love for flying, space and space exploration. To nobody's surprise, I also had a hatred for reading and writing. While I pursued my love by consuming anything I could on the topic of flying and space, typically in the form of shows and video games, I eventually discovered science fiction books and was hooked. This love led to a Bachelor of Science degree in Aerospace Engineering, and later a Master of Science in Astronautical Engineering. My education was accompanied by a career in the Air Force where I was a developmental engineer on ground, air, and space projects. Following my time in the Air Force, I worked for several space companies working on advancing the human presence in space. With a mind for the technical as well as science fiction, I decided to finally try my hand at telling stories from my mind that merge the two in a fun, but believable way.

CONTACT ARCHER AT:

Website: Archergrantbooks.com
Email: archeragrant@gmail.com